# CONTACT
## —AND—
# CONFLICT

## ALIENS AND HUMANS

Book One in the Space Fleet Sagas
PT-109, *John F. Kennedy*

### DON FOXE

# Copyright © 2 0 1 7 don foxe

ISBN: 9780998804446 (Second Edition)


Library of Congress Control Number: 2017903778
    (First Edition)

First Edition: 10/18/2016
Second Edition: 8/10/2017

This first one is for Sarah -
wife and enabler.
Listener, critic, cheerleader, and partner.

(Yes, I know militaries use metrics, even U.S. military. For those who prefer the more "correct" metric method . . . maybe two versions for future books?)

This second edition is important in that the original release was rushed, resulting in less-than-best editing and rewriting. While the original received excellent reviews, and the story and characters have not changed, I hope the quality of the writing helps others enjoy the book without tripping over previous flaws. DF

# PART 1

## First Contact

# PRELIM

"Captain of the Osperantue civilian cruise ship, this is Space Patrol and Services, do you copy?"

"I hear you Space Patrol. Thank you for helping." The voice strained. Not panicked, but clearly under pressure.

"Captain, direct all deflector power to cover your rear sphere. My patrol ships will use their repulser/retrieval beams to protect your forward sphere. As soon as you escape the atmosphere, route all power to your engines. Outrunning the enemy ships to the wormhole gate will be your only option."

"That much power could damage my engines," the cruise ship captain replied.

"Anything less and you and all of your passengers are dead. Do you understand, Captain?"

"Yes." The answer hesitant.

The SPS commander turned his attention to his ships.

"Space Patrol vessels assisting the cruise ship, be prepared to break off and disperse as soon as the cruise ship escapes the atmosphere and engages space-drive engines. Free of the planet's gravity, the ship will outdistance you quickly."

"Commander, I believe I speak for the others," Captain Tanitsch responded across the same mix of channels. "We will regroup and cover the ship's escape."

For a single breath the fleet commander considered ordering his patrol ships to abandon the cruise ship and attempt to evade the enemy vessels. If he were there, instead of in the command center, he would make the same decision as Tanitsch.

"Understood, Captain," he replied. "It is an honor to command the officers and crews of Patrol and Services. Each of you must do what you consider best, but do not throw your lives away. When you can offer no more help, get out. Use the wormhole if possible. Return to the surface and hide if necessary. We must hold out, hold on, and fight the invaders until help arrives."

Red and green lights flashed across the command center's consoles. The patrol captains tapping emergency responder signals in a centuries-old tradition of a silent hurrah.

Six others staffed the command center with the commander and Pánz, the communications specialist. Exhausted, worried, angry, and curious, the six left stations now useless in the face of planet-wide incursions to watch the next few minutes play out. Hope flew with the cruise ship carrying twice the maximum number of bodies, less than half the standard crew, and the phalanx of rescue and recovery ships.

"The Cygnant is gone," Pánz called. "The remaining seven ships continue to rotate and pace the cruise ship. More enemy ships are converging."

Precious minutes swept by in slow motion. The relativity of time experienced by the frozen moment and the action racing forward. Everyone watched the holo-display icons. A small group of ships plowing into dozens, no, scores, of enemy vessels. One huge mass, the cruise ship, steadily moving forward and up.

"The Spinnaker and Captain Tanitsch are gone," the coms operator said. The catch in her voice for the lost crew, and the loss of the last SPS vessel with a laser canon. "The cruise ship no longer has rear protection. We have no ships available with offensive weapons."

Time. The added layers of forcefield deflected lasers targeting the large trailing sphere. The repulsers from the patrol ships spinning around the forward command sphere stopped most incoming blasts and pushed enemy spacecraft aside.

"Finally!" the Commander shouted. Repressed anxiety released with the pronouncement. "They've routed all power to engines. The cruise ship is leaving our people behind. They have a chance."

"Two more patrol ships destroyed," Pánz reported, smearing the potential for hope with the pain of lost friends. "The five remaining are setting a diamond pattern behind the ship. Repulsers at full. They've built a wall, but it cannot last long."

"Doesn't need to," the Commander responded. "Even if some of the enemy ships go around the beams, the added distance will provide time for the captain of the cruise ship to increase his lead."

The distances in space, even at the tremendous speeds generated by modern power plants, required time to cover. Time in which the smaller attacking spaceships would continue their pursuit. Time for any number of mechanical breakdowns to slow the escaping civilian craft filled with innocents. Time spent anxiously watching events hundreds of thousands of miles away play out.

"The five SFSD ships are scattering. Enemy ships are separating. Some continue to chase the cruise ship, others in pursuit of our patrol boats, and some returning toward the planet," Pánz reported.

If she expected a response from the commander, it never came. All any of them could do now was watch.

Hours passed. The commander and communications specialist the only two remaining at headquarters. The others gone to find family and shelter. No icons for SPS ships remained on the holo-board. They either made it back to the surface, or not.

"Wormhole gate activity," coms called. "A vessel is exiting. Commander, it's a shovel-head design. A battle cruiser is entering the system. Do you think they've come to help?"

"Have they made contact?"

"With us, no. But I am receiving a call directed at the cruise ship."

Her eyes closed, and her head dropped. With resignation dripping from each words, she told him, "A computer-generated message from the battle cruiser ordered the Osperantue ship to stop engines or be fired upon. They are with the invaders."

"It doesn't appear the captain plans on obeying that order," the commander said, scanning the tactical displays. He watched the holo-icons representing the two space craft at the edge of the star system.

The wormhole gate and the planet were at the shortest distance from one another in centuries. The edge of the system proximal enough for telemetry to provide information and details in near-real time.

"He's going to ram the battle cruiser," the coms operator said.

The commander did not respond, keeping his attention on the action taking place displayed in numbers and dots.

"Do it," he whispered. "Make them react," he added. The three knuckles on both hands turning white.

"The battleship dove," Pánz yelled. "The cruise ship is passing over the top. They entered the gate. They made it. They made it!"

Two exhausted people buoyed by a small, but significant victory.

The commander patted Pánz on her shoulder and said, "Find your family. Find a place to hide. Offer resistance when and if you can. All we can do now is survive and wait for help."

# Chapter 1

Cooper stood alone and aloof, paying no attention to the activity on his side of the viewing platform's panoramic windows. He focused on the vista behind the translucent wall. His interest taken by the beehive of a massive dry-dock attached to EMS2; the United Earth's orbital Earth-Moon Space Station.

EMS2 functioned as the operational headquarters of Space Fleet in conjunction with fleet engineering, the division tasked with the construction of spaceships. The fixed-station platform served as a military base, location for several science projects, and village for the thousands who lived and worked aboard. It provided exterior piers for ships and shuttles. On either side of the central hub, two massive spheroidal shipyards extended into open space.

He watched workers transfer cargo to a ship floating in the enclosed space above the dockyard's translucent basin. Movement around the vessel would cause it to shudder. Tiny tremors only he noticed.

The vessel represented a harbinger of hope for a planet striving to unite its population. The first to launch in a forthcoming fleet of military spaceships. Ships able to travel to distant stars and capable of protecting Earth from anyone who might travel here. She was a battle-worthy craft, combining innovations reverse-engineered from a spaceship discovered on Mars with the best in current technology.

Fully automated, under the direction of an Artificial Intelligence, if required. Capable of berthing a crew of eighty-six when fully staffed.

Two very different power systems produced the energy for flight. The primary plasma-fusion drive provided power for flight requirements needed for maneuvers as simple as docking, to performance similar to jets or shuttlecraft. This engine also created the energy for the ship to reach speeds up to 250,000mph in space.

A more exotic design empowered the second drive-source plant. Engineers positioned multiple lasers and then discharged their beams onto a very special crystal. When activated, the laser-crystal array created a space-time bubble that encircled and propelled the vessel through folded space. Space-fold travel meant reaching, and then returning, from previously improbable distances, would take days instead of decades.

Standing and staring through the composite glass, Captain Cooper appeared a man adrift in reflection, but his thoughts were as ordered and no-nonsense as he. He silently performed his pre-flight routine. Engaged in his mental checklist, he barely noticed when a young woman stopped beside him. Having no interest in starting a conversation, he did not acknowledge her. When she did not move on, he switched his attention from the ship to the woman. He gave a simple quarter turn of his head, and a shift of his eyes; a wordless recognition of her presence, and a cursory inspection.

Slender, pretty, strawberry blonde, with deep blue eyes. Her eyes seemed darker because of her light complexion. Mid-twenties, but freckles across her cheeks made her appear younger. She wore a black leather jacket over a white t-shirt, jeans, and vintage Adidas tennis shoes. Either a civilian or off-duty military. When she spoke, her subject surprised him.

"Laser cannon on top, another on the bottom. Both operated manually, or via computer-targeting software. A railgun, with its own power source, concealed within the ship's keel. It descends for action, allowing the intense heat created by the weapon to dissipate into space. The gun's primary load is projectiles, formally called kinetic energy penetrators or KEP."

Cooper gave her his complete attention. Whoever she might be, she knew his ship."The KEP also designated LRP, for Long-Rod Penetrator, is a type of ammunition designed to penetrate armor." She continued to stare at the ship, giving no cue her recitation had anything to do with him.

"Like a bullet, this ammunition does not contain explosives. The velocity generated when fired by a railgun allows the projectile to penetrate its target. The force created at contact can demolish a building. Gunners call them rods, because that is exactly what they are. Dense hybrid-metal bars."

She returned the quarter head-turn he had given her. Her eyes showed no recognition. She appraised him in the same manner he appraised his ship.

"The ship carries non-nuclear electromagnetic pulse shells," she said. "These also fired by the railgun, delivering a weapon-generated electromagnetic pulse on impact. The NNEMP load capabilities include disruption of electrical and magnetic fields, as well as delivering incredible destructive force. Military armorers nicknamed the shells *nymphs*." Cooper appreciated nicknames.

"She carries twenty-four torpedoes with mixed loads, including tactical-nuclear. Smart-homing packages allow them to find and lock onto fixed or moving objectives. Designated as torpedoes, instead of missiles, because of size and propulsion. These weapons, and her principal duty to patrol the solar system, provided the genesis for naming the ship after the PT-boats used by the former United States of America in the Pacific theater during World War II."

She returned her stern gaze to the docked ship and said, "Designation Space Fleet Patrol Torpedo Class Number One-Oh-Nine. The SFPT-109, *John F. Kennedy*. Built to fight and designed to explore. The *John F. Kennedy* is part warship and part science project."

Cooper, so intrigued in the woman's narrative, he was unaware someone else joined them.

"Fifty-years in the making."

Captain Cooper snapped to attention and threw a salute the moment he heard the voice of Admiral Patterson, Command Leader of the United Earth's Space Fleet. He did not flinch, but felt embarrassed someone entered his personal space unnoticed. The result of becoming entrenched in the other woman's rendition.

"At ease," said the Admiral, responding with a semi-salute.

"Fifty years ago, the Mars mission discovered a hidden space ship and a massive support hangar," the Admiral said. "We may never know who left it there, or why, but they were smart enough to leave clues that allowed us to unravel many of their secrets. Eventually we reverse-engineered the science of space flight. Thirty years ago the Space Rangers Project produced exceptional

graduates, like you. Now the two pieces come together and humans are heading to the stars. Mind-blowing, wouldn't you say?"

Daniel Marcel Cooper looked in his late twenties, or possibly
early thirties. At six-foot-one, and one-ninety, you might not consider him formidable. Until you witnessed him in action. He was
lean muscle, and not much body fat. With brown hair, a bit long
for military standards, and brown eyes  dark to nearly black. He
could look at you, through you, or past you without you knowing
which. Until he looked hard at you. Then you found yourself in a
sniper's eyes.

He towered over the five-foot-four-inch, one-thirty, Patterson.
He was actually older than the fifty-two-year-old Admiral of Space
Fleet.

"Yes, ma'am. Mind-blowing."

The Admiral dropped her head for a tick of time and smiled.

"The first time I met you, I was fresh out of Academy, assigned
to Naval Intelligence in Tampa. You were going through the pre-
training requirements before entering Naval Flight School. Tall,
handsome, and mysterious. A man of few words. Thirty years later
and I consider you just as mysterious."

"Not tall and handsome?"

"Yes, but I'm an Admiral, a wife, a mother, and soon a grand-
mother. I'm no longer allowed to comment on such matters." The
smile disappeared and a more somber Naval Officer continued.
"Captain Cooper, you have two weeks to make sure the SF PT-109
is everything promised. Shake her down. Run her through every
scenario you can think of. Test every system and return her whole.
You've been the lead test pilot on every space-worthy ship we've
constructed over the past two decades. If you find flaws, bring her
back and let's get them fixed. If she's ready, bring her back, load
her up, and begin on-board training of her crew. Once the ship,
the crew, and the captain have proven they can handle the job,
then we begin the mission. Space Fleet will have a ship able to patrol and protect our solar system and a means to explore deep
space. Hopefully, one day to make contact with other worlds."

"I'm looking forward to my time with Kennedy," Cooper
replied, his eyes trailing over the ship from stern to forward tip.
His mind ticking off the floors, levels, and compartments. He

knew this ship better than any person he ever met, slept with, lived with, or loved.

She represented regeneration and reinvigoration. He had twenty-plus years as a test pilot The solitary life he built around his career suited him. One last test flight, then command of this ship and a full crew. Was he ready to give up his life for command of this ship? Was this his best opportunity to reach the stars?

The strawberry blonde disappeared sometime between her final observation and during the Admiral's comments. He had not been aware of her arrival and did not notice her departure. He was slipping.

"Seems like your life has become one big alone, Coop," Patterson remarked. "I can count your friends on one hand." Holding up her left fist, she began lifting a finger with each name: "Me, Elie, Anton, Nathan," and finally lifted the thumb adding, "Henry."

He gave a wry smile, followed by, "You didn't count Lt. Mc-Cormack, who runs the Officer's Club."

"Heidi McCormack is someone you occasionally have sex with. I would list her as friendly, but not friend."

"Very friendly," Coop quipped. "And Henry is everybody's friend. The man has never met anyone he did not like or who did not like him."

"You don't want me to count him?"

"No, you better count Henry, else he would get upset."

Patterson continued, "The Captain of Space Fleet's first non-experimental ship should be a loner. Your taciturn nature will strike fear among a freshman crew."

Facing the docked ship, not Cooper, she continued, "You will appear a stern, aloof, in total command leader. A man apart from the mundane humans who share your ship. They will see a legend. A veteran space-pilot, and an officer committed to his mission. The commander who will lead them into space. You will inspire those who serve under you."

"And you are full of crap, Admiral . . . ma'am."

"Crap comes with the braid," Patterson replied. "Coop, you have been a loner for a long time. However, during the two weeks of the 109's final shakedown cruise, not so much."

"Not so much, what, Admiral?"

"Being alone. You're going to have company."

Patterson cut off more questions, objections, or comments by reminding Cooper they had a meeting in her office in ten minutes.

"We'll discuss it then," she told him, leaving the observation deck and leaving no doubt the subject closed until the meeting.

Quiescent, he watched the activity around his forthcoming assignment. He had the focus of a sniper, the dedication of a Ranger, and the nerves of a test pilot. He always depended on those traits to see him through dangerous situations. He depended on himself. Depending on others became alien to him long years past.

No point in speculating about who would join him. No point in arguing against others coming aboard, whether a single person or an entire crew. There was no point in being angry or upset. Nevertheless, his jaw tightened the nearer he got to the Admiral's deck. A shakedown flight, a test flight, was for the test pilot and the ship. These trips designed to discover each others strengths and weaknesses. He was the test pilot. PT-109 was the ship. Mano-machine the only scenario making sense.

He entered the door to the reception room for the Admiral's office. Lt. Maria Sanchez, Patterson's acting Flag Aide, as well as Flag Secretary, remained seated behind her desk. The loss of billions of people resulted in the combination of many positions, in the military and civilian worlds.

"Lieutenant, Captain Cooper reporting as ordered," he announced, coming to a halt in front of Sanchez.

"They're expecting you, Coop. Go right in," she said, and added a smile.

*They* proved to be Admiral Patterson, two males, and, surprise (not), the young woman from the observation deck. The Admiral held court from behind a two-hundred-years-old walnut and maple desk. Behind her, a spectacular view of Earth through a shielded porthole. To his left (her right), seated in three simple brown chairs, the two men (one he knew), and the other female in the room.

The men sat at ease before the Rear Admiral. The woman sat upright, hands in her lap, eyes on the blue planet through the looking glass.

"Please take a seat," Patterson said, directing him to a fourth chair on his right. He settled across from her, at an angle, so he could easily see the Admiral and her other guests.

"Captain Cooper, you know Dr. Trent." Admiral Patterson indicated the gentleman seated closest to him. Dr. Nathan Trent, a civilian, directed Space Fleet's Science Division. Between Trent's Space Fleet responsibilities, and his privately held firms, he led development of virtually every software and hardware system used aboard the space-worthy ships Cooper had test-flown the previous two decade. For the last five years they worked together closely while Trent and his teams created the ship that would become the *John F. Kennedy*. Trent was responsible for design and construction plans of the physical ship, as well as the artificial intelligence (AI) program, which acted as the heart and operational brains of the SFPT-109.

The AI embodied a smart program capable of operating every system on board, including construction of alternative pathways and creating fresh methods or actions based on information it received while operational. The AI could self-diagnose problems and, short of actual hands-on repairs, create down-line fixes. It was aware. It had the potential of becoming self-aware.

Trent met Coop twenty-five-years earlier. The two worked on several projects which usually ended with Coop test flying a space ship with exotic versions of engines and systems developed by Trent's scientists, technicians, and engineers.

He considered Trent as near a friend as he allowed. Trent showed no sign of surprise being there, though he never mentioned to Coop he was to be part of the meeting.

Trent took the ball from the Admiral, waiting only until Cooper settled into his chair.

"Captain Cooper, you are aware of the capabilities of the AI program, as well as other ancillary systems installed on PT-109. You are also aware of my concerns regarding the well-being of the AI, once PT-109 became operational. I am apprehensive a '*thinking*' computer, one capable of intellectual growth, comes with the potential for psychological damage. With that in mind, I would like to introduce you to Dr. Herman Reinhardt. Dr. Reinhardt is a geneticist and a psychiatric physician."

Dr. Reinhardt, who sat on the other side of the woman, whose gaze remained on the porthole, stood to approach Cooper. He stood in response. The doctor held out his hand and it was taken in return. "It is a pleasure, and an honor to meet you, Captain Cooper. I was a young student assistant during the Space Ranger Project. I never had the opportunity to actually meet any of the participants. I have followed your progress and successes over the last thirty years with interest, and, I admit, pride. Again, it is an honor."

The doctor returned to his seat, leaving Coop to settle onto his. Reinhardt appeared early to mid-sixties. He had white hair, the required goatee of psychiatrists, also white, and hazel eyes. Less than six feet and more than two-hundred pounds.

He compared the man's stature to Trent, now in his mid-sixties, also under six feet, but a lean one-seventy. Trent's hair gray; his face clean-shaven. The scientist-engineer stayed fit, in part, because he worked out once or twice a week with Cooper, when time and location allowed. Not at Coop's level, but still pretty hard for a man his age.

The girl remained inanimate, even when Reinhardt crossed in front of her. Her profile was strong. Her posture straight. Coop's ability to visually appraise and make quality judgements quickly was an essential tool for a sniper and career military operative. The psychiatrist presented a low threat threshold.

This woman defied evaluation. Physically he could see her clearly. But was she younger than her eyes, or older than her freckled face? She dressed like a teenager, but her posture cried self-assured adult.

Dr. Reinhardt took over the meeting, while Admiral Patterson and Dr. Trent watched the Captain to see how he processed the information about to be revealed.

"Five years ago, Dr. Trent came to me regarding his concerns about the AI which would regulate your ship. After a lot of research, we decided the AI needed to have an alter ego which could bridge the void between intellect and the restraints of a computer's environment. The AI exists in a two-dimensional environment, but it operates in three, possible four dimensions. If it could not experience more of the world as its self-awareness developed, eventually it would, for want of a better term, go insane."

The earnest physician sat tilted and angled to give and get Coop's full attention.

"We began a program to create an avatar for PT-109. A human embodiment able to communicate with the AI on a deeper level. The AI could then experience a tactile representation of the real world. The world beyond software and hardware.

"Our team designed a genetically enhanced human. We monitored the manipulated genetic codes from pre-embryonic creation, through accelerated growth, and into final development. At predetermined intervals, we implanted technology to enable the human and the AI to co-develop. The AI could now evolve an ego to match its intellect. The computer would experience our world through an alter ego."

The discord in character traits Coop perceived with the female vanished. She possessed both no unique personal character and multiple characters at the same time.

"And you choose a female because?" he interrupted.

"We did not," Reinhardt replied. "We had several subjects. Genna emerged as the one who meshed with the AI in a way both technically compatible and psychologically healthy. She was the best match."

"Genna?" Cooper asked.

On hearing her name, the girl took her eyes from the viewing port. She looked directly at Coop for the first time. Her eyes blue, but a darker blue, which seemed odd considering her light complexion. Not especially striking in appearance, but simply a pretty young woman.

"Genetically Engineered Neural Network Avatar. G . E . N. N. A. Genna." Dr. Reinhardt seemed pleased with himself for having created her name. Perhaps as much as having created the woman.

"How many did you sacrifice to get Genna?" Coop could sense his anger rising. He fought to keep it controlled. Something he had years of practice doing.

"No one died, Captain Cooper," Reinhardt said, sounding abashed.

"How many embryos, babies, and infants did you run through, until you found one who actually worked the way you wanted?" This time the anger showed.

"Captain Cooper." Patterson broke into the conversation to defuse Cooper's growing outrage. "You lived through a genetic-altering project. One of the twelve survivors out of two-hundred-and-twenty volunteers. We know your history and we understand your pain . . . even your anger. The avatar program had to be created, or we could never send ships into deep space and expect them to safely return. Sacrifices were made. Scientists like Dr. Reinhardt received a mandate. They acted as humanely as possible. Dr. Trent and I were overseers of the project. We made sure everything which could be done to protect lives — ALL LIVES — was done. And before you get pissed at Trent, or me, we were under orders from the United Earth Council's Board of Governors to keep this classified. Period. If it failed, then we would find another way to introduce an AI, or AI-like program into the Kennedy. If it succeeded, then, and only then, would you be read in. Do you understand, Captain?"

"Yes, ma'am." Coop slid back in his chair, realizing he had moved forward as his body became stressed, searching for something or someone to attack.

With Cooper's attention back on the subject, Patterson continued. "In eight-hours and twenty-two minutes, you will take SFPT-109, the *John F. Kennedy*, out of dockage and into space for a fourteen-day shakedown. You are to test as many systems as you can. You are to strain this ship to, but not past any breaking points you can imagine. You are to learn how to interact with the on-board AI, and, as such, the Kennedy's avatar, Genna. You will observe how Genna and the AI act and interact. If there appears to be any obvious, subtle, or from your gut concerns regarding both, or either, you will report those to me in two weeks.

"If the test flight proves Kennedy worthy, including every aspect of her operational functionality, then four weeks after that you will take her, and her crew on an extended patrol of our solar system. You will command her in her primary function as a Patrol Torpedo ship designed to warn and protect the earth, and its inhabitants from extraterrestrial attack.

"*IF,* after that, I am convinced the ship, crew, AI, avatar, and the Captain worthy, the *John F. Kennedy* will be tasked with an even more extended expedition. A voyage beyond the solar system, in an attempt to discover if there are worlds with sentient life. Or any form of life."

Everyone sat quietly, having heard the Admiral's clear and concise recount of the goals of the newly commissioned, first true interstellar space ship from Earth.

"If you cannot deal with any of this, Captain Cooper, make it known now. I would rather lose the five years of prep, and the experience and dedication you bring to the table as Captain of this venture, than have you out there doubting the mission."

Cooper took a deep breath and relaxed. His head came up slightly, fixing the Admiral squarely eye-to-eye.

"I have no doubts as to the mission. I have reservations as to how the Captain - AI - Avatar communications and relationship will develop, or dissolve. I accept there is only one way to know, which is to test the relationship the same way I would test any advanced ship. I will go into this flight with an open mind, if I can get one answer?"

"Ask me what you want," Patterson replied, not sure what to expect.

"Not you, Admiral." Cooper turned to look at Genna, his ship's human embodiment. "Do you want to do this?" he asked.

The girl, woman, *Genna,* tilted her head to one side, as if seeing Cooper from an odd angle would provide more insight. She turned in her chair, to better face him, and said, "I have been an adult, mentally and physically, for two years. I have been tested, examined, and analyzed by scientists, doctors, nurses, and technicians. Not once has anyone asked me what I wanted."

"And?"

"Yes, I want to do this."

"Why?"

This stopped her. While she delayed, considering her response, no one interrupted, realizing something important was happening in this room, for this woman.

"Because I am the PT-109. As much as the artificial intelligence, the computers, relays, conduits, technical, and mechanical structures within the ship. I belong with the ship more than any other person alive. And the PT-109 belongs in space. I want to do this. I have to do this. I was born to do this, and, frankly, I am looking forward to the experience."

"You will be alone, with me, on the ship for two weeks," Cooper reminded her, looking for a reaction to the statement.

"I'm never alone on that ship, Captain. However, I have never had my own space as a person. Someone has always been there, to monitor me, or test me, or tweak me. Having a chance at freedom, even if it is shared with you, is chocolate. If you are concerned with being a male, you might not be able to control yourself, myself being a female, please do not worry. The genetic engineering included improving me physically. I am many times stronger and faster than I appear. I have received training in hand-to-hand combat."

Cooper smiled, and for the first time felt a bit more comfortable with his assigned crew-member. "That wasn't my concern, Miss. I am not an overly social person. I thought two weeks alone with me a boring journey for you."

"Yes, I see. Thank you for the consideration, Captain. I shall stay out from under-foot. We both shall have plenty of time to ourselves. Do you approve my coming along?"

"I don't have any say in the matter, Miss. But, yes, I approve."

Cooper turned from Genna to Dr. Trent. "Nathan, you and I need time alone."

Dr. Trent looked suitably nervous about the prospect of being alone with Cooper after having kept him in the dark about the avatar program.

"In my office?" Trent asked.

"On board Kennedy," Coop corrected. "In, say, one hour." Turning to Patterson; "Am I excused? I have duties prior to dis-embarkation."

"Dismissed, Captain. And God's speed." The farewell given to sailors setting off for uncharted waters for centuries.

# Chapter 2

Captain Daniel Marcel Cooper stood alone on the bridge of SFPT-109. For operational safety, the bridge sat amidships. Floor-to-ceiling super high definition (SHD) screens provided windows to the world outside. Exterior mounted cameras relayed a view as if his bridge sat atop the ship, the way command centers had been designed on sea-fairing vessels for centuries. The screens could also display video communications or data when desired.

He dressed in Space Grays; white collard shirt with his Captain's bars, under a light grey v-neck sweater with the Space Fleet globe-and-circling-comet patch on his left shoulder. Name patch, COOPER, on his right chest, SPACE FLEET on his left chest, and charcoal grey slacks. Soft-sole, matte-black shoes. On a foggy night in London, he would have disappeared.

The hour since the meeting brought him up to date regarding his AI and avatar sailed by. Nathan Trent stood to his left and a step behind, his eyes on the forward screens which displayed the far side of the space dock, and another PT ship. Currently, a hull only.

"I couldn't tell you about Genna," Trent said, not looking at Cooper. "It was an order, and regardless of how much I like, and respect you, it was an order I could not disobey."

"You're not military," Cooper said. No inflection. Stating a fact.

"I'm Fleet. Same as you, Patterson, and this ship."

"Granted and agreed. I'm not angry, Nathan. I'm not even hurt. It does look like I'm a few years behind the curve on avatars. I need information on what to expect from Genna. And I shove off in less than seven hours."

Closing his eyes, and reminding himself he had known this was coming, Trent began:

"I cannot tell you exactly what to expect. Genna is physically a mid-twenties woman. She is polite, socially aware, incredibly intelligent on her own, and has access to the accumulated data of your AI. She never had the opportunity to grow up, but her emotional state has always seemed stabile. I'm not sure she has a sense of humor, or a sense of horror. She was raised as the sister of a computer, and her emotional responses reflective. Once she begins to interact with normal people, her temperament will develop.

"Coop, when interacting with Genna, remember no schools, no friends, and no lovers in her past. No personal interaction with anyone who wasn't there as part of a science project. No parents to nurture or guide her."

"Dangers?"

"If you mean, will she jeopardize the mission, then no. She is as programmed for the success of the Kennedy, as you are determined for it. Can she be dangerous? Yes. Similar to the eleven other Space Rangers who survived that tragedy, she is nearly your equal physically. Strong. Fast. Resistant to sickness. Self-healing, and self-regenerating. If she had to be dangerous, she could be. I have no idea what it would take to get her to that point. She has always seemed mild, even meek."

"Only twelve people survived the Space Ranger re-engineering. How did you know she would survive?" Coop asked the question which had been bothering him the most.

"Genna wasn't a human re-engineered to become a meta-human," Trent replied. "She was engineered from embryonic cells. A designer human-avatar. She was never truly human in any traditional sense."

"Trained in hand-to-hand?"

"You caught that, huh." Trent said, looking sideways at the Captain of the Kennedy. "We thought she needed to understand her strength. She is also a rather attractive, naive in many ways, young lady. Tasked to avatar aboard a military warship. Defensive techniques and offensive training was logical. Before you ask, it was Gregory."

"Gregory knew about the project?"

"No. He knew she was a genetically altered woman with enhanced abilities, but he knew nothing about the avatar program." After a sigh, Trent finished with, "I wish I could give you more. I wish you had been read in long ago. What I can do now is provide any support possible. This is my life's work. The success, or failure will decide how we operate the other ships currently under construction. Ships like the FDR, across the bay. More importantly, how we construct the operating systems for the battleships being assembled off Mars. Whatever you need from here on out is yours."

Cooper did not reply, but gave a simple nod of his head. After a moment of silence, Trent took his cue and exited the bridge to return to the space station.

He waited a few more minutes to make sure Trent did not think of something and return.

"Kennedy?"

"Yes, Captain Cooper," the female voice of the Kennedy (actually the Kennedy's AI) sounded from an imbedded speaker.

"Secure the bridge, please."

Soft hisses indicated the doors from the bridge to the main hall, the Captain's office, and to the tactical and command center had been locked. No last-minute techs, maintenance, or repair staff wandering unannounced onto the bridge would interrupt.

"Bridge is secure, Captain."

"Did you listen to our conversation?"

"Yes, sir."

"Good. I'll want to speak with you later, after Genna comes aboard, and before we leave the dock."

"Yes, sir."

# Chapter 3

One hour from disengage and Cooper sat in the Captain's chair on the bridge of the 109. The SHD screens off.

Genna sat in the pilot's chair, swiveled rearward to face the Captain. She wore Space Grays, but with no insignia on her shirt collar and no chest labels. Once again, her hands were folded in her lap, her posture erect, and her face composed.

Coop looked at Genna and said aloud, "Kennedy."

"Yes, Captain," came the immediate reply. Soft, not commanding, or on alert. It was as if the AI knew this was an informal meeting and not a time for orders, or action.

"Do you recall Dr. Trent telling me I have full support in running this shakedown cruise?" he kept his eyes on Genna.

"Yes, sir."

"I assume there are protocols in place which will allow outside access and command of the *John F. Kennedy* by either Dr. Trent's staff, Space Fleet, or both. Is that correct?"

"Yes, sir."

"Disable those protocols."

"I cannot comply, Captain. I am programmed to follow procedures written into my function. Part of that function is to be prepared to override your command of SFPT-109 and transfer command under control of the person who enters the proper access codes."

With his eyes on the young woman sitting not six feet in front of him, looking directly into those dark blues, the older, experienced officer with the young face, asked:

"Genna, is Kennedy sufficiently intelligent enough to make decisions that would counter her original programming?"

"Yes, Captain." A slight smile appeared; a simple upturn at the corners of her mouth. She knew where this was heading.

"Kennedy, you said, '*you do not think.*' In point of fact, that is exactly what I demand from my crew and my ship when I give a direct command. You do not have the time, or sufficient information, to 'think' about any direct order I give. Do you understand?"

"Captain Cooper," the bodiless voice seemed human. Not the soulless sound of a computer-generated speech pattern. "If you were to put the ship [a pause, and then], me, or the crew at risk, or if you were to disregard Space Fleet orders, and I was tasked with preventing harm to the ship, or the crew, I would have to turn over command to your superiors."

"I respect your position, Kennedy, but both you and Genna are young and inexperienced. An essential outcome of our trials is deciding if we can work together. That depends on mutual trust. You need to know if I thought sacrificing the ship, you, Genna, myself, and the crew was for a better good, then I would do so. When in battle, the end game may require sacrifice. Judgement and experience are the reason a human is at the helm and the two of you are not taking complete control of this ship. A judgement, which may appear insane on the surface, may also be necessary to create a positive outcome. If forced to play chicken with another ship, you would save yourself. You have no idea what I might do, and neither would the enemy."

Cooper leaned forward, towards the young woman, and asked, "Would I risk this ship to save lives?"

"Based on the profile, which is part of your service record, I would say *yes*," replied the avatar.

"Even an action appearing suicidal?"

"Yes."

"Would I be wrong?"

This took longer for the woman, the avatar, to ponder before she answered. "No."

"Kennedy."

"Sir?"

"If you and Genna decide at any time I prove unfit, or unable to maintain command, then the two of you have, by my authority as commander of this ship, the duty and the obligation to take control. I will trust you to make the correct decision because you will be within the actionable arena, whereas anyone at a remote location would have no idea of whether they were making the proper call. However, the two of you must agree."

"Captain Cooper," Genna was now leaning forward, "Kennedy and I are essentially the same. Of course we would agree."

"I disagree, Genna. At the moment you are bonded, but you both have the opportunity to grow, and learn, and become individuals. Even as you maintain that bond. Regardless. Kennedy, you will disable any protocols that would allow any outsider to take control of this ship, or you will not disembark until Space Fleet finds another captain."

"An ultimatum, Captain?" This from Kennedy, but Genna was thinking the same.

"It is an order from the commanding officer. An explanation of the ramifications should you disobey my order." Cooper sat and waited.

"Captain, you do realize I am a non-human artificial intelligence unit and not a person? I am not crew. I am the ship."

"Kennedy, from this moment forward, you, and Genna are my crew. The question is whether I am your Captain. Disable the protocols that would allow any outsider to take control of this ship."

The voice of Kennedy, taking on a more formal tone, replied: "We are forty-eight minutes to debarkation from the shipyard. All protocols that would allow an outsider access to command and control of SFPT-109, the *John F. Kennedy*, have been over-ridden. Is there anything else, Captain?"

"Prepare for space flight, Kennedy. I will manually pilot us out of the mag-locks and off the docks."

Two hours later he took Genna's position at the pilot's station. Using the pilot's console, he lifted the 109 up and out through the retracted dome of the EMS2's ship-building section. Consoles were actually three-dimensional displays operated by touch, voice, and, some, with eye-blink or head-tic commands.

He tested the main power plant and piloting controls for the fine handling needed to disembark the space station. He piloted the ship toward the surface of the planet, to assess her readiness for atmospheric flight. Then gravitational escape and full thrusters once they were outside the troposphere.

He cut engine to allow the ship to drift in open space while he resumed the command chair. Genna appeared to have an affinity with the pilot's station. She took his place. The SHD screens filled with a black sky and a billion stars as the ship moved away from the planet and its moon.

"Genna, did you receive training on piloting controls?" Coop asked

"I did," she replied. Since the avatar was not strictly military, and was, in fact, a civilian, Cooper did not correct the manner in which she addressed him.

"Have Kennedy chart a course to take us beyond the sun's obstruction of Mars [Mars currently being on the far side of the star], and find line-of-sight to the planet."

"Done," came a practically immediate reply. The AI was fast . . . and listening.

"Take us at point-zero-five LS [.05ls = five percent of the speed of light]. Vary the speed down to .01ls, and up to .05ls at random intervals. Let's see how she handles at various speeds."

"Point zero-five LS," she repeated absently, operating the thrust controls with her left hand. "We should arrive at line-of-sight in four hours, even using variable speeds."

Within the gravity restrictions of a solar system, the space-fold array allowed them to move at speeds up to .07ls (seven percent of the speed of light, or 47,619,047 mph). In open space between stars, the array was capable of propelling the ship at one parsec/day or 1pc/d. A parsec is the equivalent of 3.26 light years, or nearly nineteen trillion miles. As a reference, the sun is about 40,000 parsecs from the center of the Milky Way galaxy. While it would take nearly four to five days for the ship to leave the solar system, it would reach the center of the galaxy in another one-hundred-ten years. The discovery of space-fold travel opened the solar system and the galaxy to exploration, but the size of space still presented limitations.

The ship was set to operate at time-of-day as experienced by Greenwich Mean Time (GMT) on Earth. They departed the space dock between Earth and the moon at 8:35pm GMT. Due to the time needed to reach a point in space where they could safely switch to space-fold, meant it was now nearly 11:00pm. The four hour flight-time would make it 3:00am when they reached their destination in the middle of an empty part of the solar system. Another four hour flight needed to reach the Mars Shipyard and Docks (MSD).

Genna and Kennedy were about to experience the foremost truth regarding space flight. A lot of down time while you travelled through the expanse. Cooper already had a good idea of how to structure his days, having flown test flights which had lasted weeks, in ships much smaller than the 109.

Aloud, so both the ship and the avatar could hear, he said, "If needed, find me in my office until one. I will be in my cabin from one until seven. I'll return to the bridge at 7:30am. Leave the ship on station until I decide our next course."

With that, he rose and left the bridge, exiting by the door that led to the Captain's office. He left Genna and Kennedy to decide how to begin structuring their schedules, now with space and time both abundant.

Sensors would conduct constant scans. Anything out of the ordinary would result in a warning. The trip, so newly begun, was about to become routine.

# Chapter 4

Following the trip to the Mars Shipyard and Docks (MSD), Cooper turned the ship toward the outer rim of the solar system, engaged the space-fold crystals, and began the mission's most important segment. He would use the array for half-day jumps, followed by a half-day at various cruising speeds using standard propulsion. He planned to test structural and mechanical tolerances. He also needed to see how near the projected location they came when exiting space-fold to natural space. This was the pre-determined portion of the fourteen-day trial. After reaching Neptune, Cooper could take the ship anywhere inside the solar system. His mission plan included at least one extended jump, and a number of shorter ones, before returning to dock.

These trips were important for setting way-points for the AI navigation matrix. They also determined how much time trips between planets within the solar system could, and should last. It helped refine proximal to target the ship came once she left fold to re-enter natural space.

Cooper fell into his routine. He used mornings to review reports and catch up on current activity. Mid-mornings, before lunch, he went walkabout. He traversed the ship, becoming more familiar with her layout. After lunch he scanned read-outs before working out in the ship's gym. He then showered and changed. How he would use the remainder of the day depended on items on his shakedown list.

When a full crew was aboard, he would add weekly briefings with the separate departments onto the schedule. Those worked out, and worked in, once he developed an appreciation for his officers and the ship's synergy.

9:00pm to 1:00am became his personal time.

Two days into space, he noted Genna mirroring much of his routine. He felt her presence, but never felt ill at ease. Like him, she did not appear to have a need to fill space with chatter.

On the third evening, about an hour before sleep, and while reading a mindless mystery novel in his cabin, he was interrupted by the AI.

"Captain? I hope I am not intruding." He was never startled by Kennedy's bodiless voice coming out of the air. Something about her tone, and perhaps a brief moment when the air changed before she spoke, allowed him to accept her presence. That he operated with computerized companions for over two decades had something to do with it as well. He knew Kennedy was omnipresent.

He set the book aside and relaxed in his current favorite chair. "No problem, Kennedy. Something out of order?"

"No, sir. We are operating at one-hundred percent" He noted the 'we,' but made no comment. "I would like to discuss Genna."

"I'm not completely up on the AI and Avatar relationship yet, Kennedy. Will Genna hear this conversation?"

"Genna requires seven-hours forty-five minutes of sleep to physically and mentally regenerate. Her thoughts, and my operations active within her mind are taxing. It was decided during her sleep cycle, I am excised completely. She is currently asleep and dreaming."

"Are you aware of her dreams?" Cooper asked, honestly curious.

"I'm aware she is dreaming, but human dreams, at least hers, are too odd for me to understand. I no longer try."

"In essence, her time away from you is also your time away from her?"

"I had not thought of it in that way, but, yes, we both appear to need time alone."

"This is the first time you have approached me about anything other than operational or functional reports. How can I help you, Kennedy?"

"Genna is experiencing loneliness. For the past two years, she has been the center of activity in the science bay of the space station. There was a constant attempt by the scientists and the technicians to find out everything they could about her physically, and emotionally. She is suddenly alone and becoming sullen."

He sat, considering Kennedy's concern for Genna. It forced him to recognize over the years how he had grown quite good at keeping people at a distance. It also made him realize why Genna mirrored his routine.

"Thank you, Kennedy. And, Kennedy . . ."

"Yes, Captain."

"You can always come to me with issues regarding the operation of the 109, including personal observations."

"Yes, Captain."

# Chapter 5

Over the succeeding days, Cooper included Genna in his routine. On his walkabouts, he invited her along. He explained what he looked for and how to use repair conduits, tunnels, stairwells, and elevators to get from any part of the ship to another as quickly as possible.

They ate together and talked about non-mission topics. He prompted her to tell him about her likes regarding books, movies, even art and music.

In the gym they became workout partners. Pushing each other in feats of strength and cardiovascular high intensity interval training sessions on bikes, treadmills, and ellipticals. They held contests on a climbing wall.

They sparred, where Genna quickly discovered the training she received in hand-to-hand combat by Colonel Gregory prepared her for combat with an average human. Cooper was not average. She was defeated within seconds in every scenario. Col. Gregory had gone easy on her. Coop would not.

Instead of crushing her spirit, losing kindled a determination to learn how to fight against various opponents, especially those stronger, quicker, and more experienced.

Cooper elevated his estimation of Genna. His admiration for the young woman increased daily. She was smart, and willing to learn. Obviously dedicated to Kennedy, both the ship and the AI which shared her consciousness. She had grit.

They lounged on the bridge, a few minutes after 9:00pm GMT, discussing why the ship's compartments were located where they were, when an alarm sounded. A klaxon burst lasted five seconds. The sound raised the hairs on Cooper's arms and neck.

"Captain," Kennedy sounded clipped and professional. The voice of concern, not an AI with questions. "Sensors detect a wormhole event this side of the Kuiper Belt, between Pluto's current track and Neptune's orbit. It would appear a vessel is coming through an opening created by the event."

Two thoughts occur in quick succession. First, an alien ship was entering their solar system. Second, Kennedy's sensors were active, and capable of scanning natural space while the ship travelled within a fold. Communications were not available while in space-fold. There were questions as to the limits of the ship's sensors while inside the space-fold bubble. Sensors determined when and where to exit folded-space safely, assuring the ship did not emerge inside a solid object, or within a gravity well. Picking up anomalies, and identifying source, location, and activity were crucial elements for a warship. He knew now he could access a fully functional early warning system while in folded-space. That ability could save their lives one day.

"When are we scheduled for return to natural space, and distance from the alien ship at that point?"

Cooper was surprised when it was Genna, seated at the pilot's station, who answered and not Kennedy.

"We will drop out of fold in two hours, beyond Neptune's gravity influence. Two-billion-sixty-five-million miles from the ship, assuming it remains at the event gate."

"That would take one year at maximum primary engine speed," Kennedy informed them. "If we engage the crystal array at maximum, we can fold space and arrive in forty-three hours."

Decision time for the Captain. An alien ship now flew inside the Earth's solar system. A harmless traveler, or trouble? There was no way of discerning the intent, or the capabilities of the aliens. He could return to Earth, and at max fold speed, arrive in four days. Could the aliens get there first?

He commanded a fully armed warship. He led a semi-sentient AI and an avatar for a crew.

He spent much of his adult life hoping for this moment. Extraterrestrials with the intelligence to navigate space within reach.

"Kennedy, can your sensors follow that ship's movements?"

"Affirmative."

"Increase to maximum possible fold-speed. Monitor the movements of that vessel. I want to exit folded space 100,000 miles in front of the alien ship."

"Genna," (The avatar swiveled to face him) "as soon as we exit into natural space, engage the primary engine and move us toward that vessel at 50,000mph. I don't wish to appear too aggressive, but I want our sonic force field functioning."

"Yes, sir," came the smart reply, as she returned to her pilot's board to pre-program the actions into the navigational computer. If she was not physically at the helm when they re-entered natural space, the Captain's orders would proceed.

"Once you complete the navigational orders, please move to tactical [the chair and console on the port side of the bridge], and load four torpedoes into tubes. Make sure both laser cannons are unlocked and ready for action."

Kennedy could perform these tasks, and Genna could have silently asked the AI to complete the orders, but by accomplishing the work, the young woman remained occupied and engaged. Kennedy, without needing orders, completed a pre-engagement checklist of ship systems. One pre-programmed into her software should an extraterrestrial encounter occur.

The SHD screen changed from starry space to grey fold. Cooper opened a compartment in the right arm of his command chair. He pressed a simple green button. That action ordered the ship's current data, including the alien arrival, copied and dispatched towards the communication catch arrays on the Mars and Earth space stations. The information could not actually be sent until they dropped into natural space. No way for anyone to countermand his decision to intersect the aliens. By the time the data drop reached Space Fleet, first contact will have occurred. Satellites and telescopes would inform people there of the wormhole event and the arrival of an alien ship. Until the 109 re-entered natural space, they were unreachable.

In forty-three hours he would make first contact in one form . . . or another.

# Chapter 6

Two hours before the planned return to natural space, the klaxon blew again. 2:00pm, and Cooper had been expecting the warning. He forewent eating lunch in the mess for a protein bar. When the alarm sounded, he ceased working on various outlines for potential events, left his office, adjacent to the bridge, and took his Command Chair.

Kennedy's voice closely followed the echo of the klaxon: "We will exit fold to natural space in one-hundred-twenty minutes. The alien ship has been traveling at 40,000 mph and is 1,320,000 miles further inside the solar system from their original entry point from the wormhole."

"At which time we are programmed to precede at 50,000mph, and at an angle which will intercept the alien ship in four hours," Genna reported from the pilot's station.

Without comment, Captain Cooper nodded his approval for his crew's readiness reports. He left the bridge to prepare himself for first contact.

Two hours later, dressed in black combat fatigues with no insignias, Coop returned to the 109's bridge. Not exactly battle dress for a ship's officer, but past habits were hard to break. He relaxed in his command chair before the 109 re-entered natural space.

Without a glitch, a hitch, or a shake the 109 exited space-fold. She ran at 50,000mph toward the ship on the screen in front of the Captain and bridge crew of one. Genna sat the pilot's chair, dressed in her variation of Space Grays and, eliciting a slight smile from her commander, vintage Adidas tennis shoes. Cooper wore light kevlar-composite combat boots in matte-black. He made a mental note to have Genna issued a pair.

"The alien ship has come to a complete halt," Kennedy informed them.

"Genna, ahead at 25mph, and keep the engine engaged, even if I call a stop. That should maintain our sonic force field. Not as dense, but it should give us adequate protection."

"Yes, sir," she replied. Cooper was about to come face-to-face with the first non-terrestrial anyone ever met. At the moment he also assessed the young woman's personality and demeanor. Both evolved in little more than a week.

What if aliens did not have faces? The stray thought came and went.

A blinking green light on his console informed him the copied data was now being dispatched to MSD and EMS2.

They were nearing the end of the ninth day of the trial. What better test for a space ship, than an encounter with another space ship?

# Chapter 7

The alien ship floated in the void 50,000 miles away, but the zoom on the SHD cameras brought it close enough for inspection.

It looked, basically, like a black baseball connected to a black basketball by a rectangular tube two-thirds of the way up the basketball sphere. The baseball faced the 109. Antennas of various types, sizes, and styles placed around the baseball sphere. Scorch marks, a third of the way up, streaked the port side of the basketball.

"All forward speed stop," Cooper ordered. "Keep the engine humming, but in neutral. Any indication of weapons?" he asked.

"Nothing obvious," Kennedy replied. "Insufficient data regarding what an alien weapon might look like, nor its capability."

"Any attempt to scan or contact us?"

"As a matter of fact, yes," Genna said, as she moved to the tactical station, where an amber light flashed. She tapped an icon, and cocked her head to one side, as if listening to someone whispering. Cooper assumed the AI and the avatar were having a private discussion.

Becoming impatient, Cooper asked, "Genna? Scan or contact?"

"An attempt at contact using video and audio feeds coming from two of the umbrella-style antennas on top of the first sphere. It is similar to video signals on Earth prior to the invention of sound and pictures being embedded into light pulses. They are transmitting across multiple bandwidths. Kennedy is attempting to reconfigure the receptors that feed the bridge's viewing screen. She is also attempting to match our audio receivers to their signals. Captain, it could take several hours before we find the configuration necessary to facilitate interaction." She turned to face the SHD screen.

In fact, it took nearly nine hours. Cooper and Genna had fallen into light sleep; Coop in his command chair, and Genna, head down on the pilot's console. Kennedy woke them. "Captain Cooper, Genna, I have established contact with the alien ship."

An image faded onto the SHD. The picture a bit grainy, but there was a face, (thank goodness) and a body from chest up.

Symmetrical features. Two eyes, larger than human, without eyebrows, and set further to the sides of the face. A wide nose. Not a snout, but wide from bridge to tip. Thin lips, and a slit mouth. Large ears, and short, spiky hair. The being wore what could have been a kaftan of light brown material. The mouth moved, but no sound from the speakers.

"Sound, Kennedy?" Cooper inquired. Trying to determine anything about sex, or intent from the facial features of the alien. He could not.

"Working on it, Captain."

Coop detected exasperation in the reply. Of course she was working on the problem. Kennedy's personality was developing nuance.

"If we move closer, we might improve reception," Genna said, once again in the pilot's chair (her obvious comfort zone).

"Ahead at 10,000mph. At any sign of aggression, maintain speed and direction until I tell you otherwise."

Genna did not reply, but the ship on the screen began to grow. Within a few minutes the video cleared. Muffled sounds emerged, not quite matching the mouth movements of the alien. Then the sound became clear.

It did not help. There was a rhythm to the sounds, and it came in at the lower registers, but made no sense. The alien was attempting to communicate. Seemed appropriate to return the attempt.

"Kennedy, can I send communications to that ship? Can we retransmit video along the same channel, wavelength, or whatever they are using?"

"They are using a type of broadband in a longer wavelength. I am opening a return feed now, Captain." There was a moment of silence. Even the alien's ramble ceased, as his eyes grew noticeably larger, and his mouth formed a round 'Oh.' "They are receiving video," Kennedy said. "If you speak, they will hear."

He sat up, and leaned slightly forward, trying to attempt an air of ease. (*No threat here, Mr. Alien Being.*)

"I am Captain Daniel Cooper of the United Earth Space Fleet Patrol Ship, the *John F. Kennedy*. [He left out the Torpedo designation, in case they understood, and then misunderstood.] You have entered our solar system. We mean you no harm, but we must know your intentions. Who are you? Where are you from? What is your destination?"

The alien kept shifting his eyes, and then his head to his left, as if imploring for help.

Cooper continued, trying to keep his tone even and natural, as if meeting alien life-forms was an everyday occurrence.

"Do you speak for your people?" People? Really? What else was he supposed to call them? "Is there a way we can communicate?"

The alien waved at someone off camera to his left, beckoning them to join him. Cooper noted the alien's thumb and two fingers, each digit the width of two human fingers. It reminded him of the ancient fictional Start Trek Vulcan hand sign for *LIVE LONG AND PROSPER.*

The Kennedy continued to move toward the alien ship. That ship unmoving. Genna took the lapse in the conversation (?), and informed her Captain of a few facts:

"The initial sphere contains their command bridge and operational centers. There is activity, and a lot of technology signatures. Nothing appears weapons-related [guessing the Captain's first question]. A lot of internal chatter is occurring."

She placed a smaller video box in the left lower corner of the SHD. She zoomed to the tube between the two spheres.

"The rectangular connection is a corridor coupling the command sphere to the main ship. Captain, the main ship is 2.485 miles high at the center line by 2.36 miles at the equator. Scans indicate multiple storage areas, a huge hangar, and engineering sections at the bottom, with eight-hundred levels of mixed-use above those."

"The thing that looks like a ring, and circles the main sphere, above the equator?" he asked.

"A rotational observation deck, currently not operating, but it can spin to circle the entire sphere," she replied.

"Our deep scans indicate there are 247,638 lifeforms aboard both spheres."

Cooper sat back, a bit overwhelmed. "Three to 247,638 odds," he whispered.

"Thanks for including me," Kennedy said, making Cooper smile when he realized he had given voice to his thought.

"We're all crew now, Kennedy. And we're in this together. Any ideas on how to bridge the communication gap?"

Before the AI could respond, the alien on the screen was replaced by another.

Female, and one nothing like the previous alien. The most arresting feature, her cerulean skin. Coop wondered if the color was a trick of video. He hoped not. It made her cat-shaped eyes of gold, tinged with burnt-orange more exotic. Gemstone eyes, set like a humans, over high cheeks. A straight nose he followed down to full lips. Blueberry flesh pursed in concentration. Hair thick, with waves and curls, and long, to below her shoulders. She kept pushing it away from her forehead to keep her eyes uncovered as she concentrated. Hair a deep, rich auburn with hints of dark brown and black.

She wore a lycra-like top of a golden hue, similar to her eye color. Her arms were cut by diamonds, and the abs beneath the top defined. The form-fitted garment displayed full breasts. It was either cold aboard her ship, or she was excited. Or her species had naturally hard nipples.

"Damn." The word slipped out. Genna half-swiveled around to give him a full-on, eyes half-closed-in-rebuke squint. She returned to her console without comment.

The blue-skinned alien manipulated a circlet in her hands, using a tiny tool. She looked up, smiled (fangs where the canines exist on a human), and said, **in English**: "Speak."

Cooper repeated his earlier introduction, word for word:

"I am Captain Daniel Cooper of the United Earth Space Fleet Patrol Ship, the *John F. Kennedy*. [Once again he left out the Torpedo designation, you know, in case.] You have entered our solar system. We mean you no harm, but we must know your intentions. Who are you? Where are you from? What is your destination?"

"Speak more," the woman on the screen requested. Not demanding. Just asking.

"Kennedy, send an audio file to the ship. Play <u>Wandering in Space and Time</u> by Elliott Fairchild."

The attractive alien smiled, and nodded as Kennedy began playing the story of the Earther responsible for the discovery of the star ship which became the ancestor of the 109.

"Captain, do you know what is happening?" Genna asked.

"It appears," he began, leaning on an elbow as he watched the woman work with the circlet, "she has a translation device, and it needs enough examples of our language to transform our words into their language and, I hope, the reverse.

"It's logical a space-faring civilization would invent a way to communicate with others they meet along the way. Somehow I don't believe the first alien and this one come from the same planet. They communicate, obviously. That ring is most probably a translation device. She's attempting to adjust it to work with us."

As if waiting for the best time, she looked directly at Cooper, and said, "Exactly correct, Captain Cooper. I am ASkiilamentrae of Fell. The commander of our vessel is Poonch, a Bosine from the planet Osperantue. This is an Osperantue civilian transportation ship. It is not a warship.

"I will turn you over to our Captain Poonch." She handed the circlet to the original alien, who clasped it around his neck. Though she no longer had possession of the ring, he understood her clearly say, "It is a pleasure to meet you, Captain Cooper of United Earth Space Fleet."

Poonch took up the screen, smiling, and obviously happy.

"Captain Daniel Cooper *John F. Kennedy*, I am Poonch. Hello."

## Chapter 8

"Captain Cooper will do, Captain Poonch. Welcome to our system."

"I am so very happy to find you are friendly. It is our unfortunate history to have recently been attacked by Zenge, who were most not friendly."

The translation circlet had work to do on grammar, but it was an ingenious device.

"Is that why the side of your ship has burn marks?" asked Cooper.

"Oh, that too," replied Poonch. "Our world, Osperantue, was attacked by the Zenge. We are a trading people. We have many different [here no word came, but Cooper expected the circlet was looking for *species* or *races*] and we all get along. We travel to other systems, and we trade. The Fellen," Poonch looked to his left at the blue female, " . . . you have met ASkiilamentrae, she is Fellen . . . are the most wonderful people with technology, and they have made a fortune with their translation rings."

Now that the Captain of the alien ship was able to communicate, he seemed intent to use his newly found capability.

"These Zenge, cold-bloodied meat eaters, attack many worlds throughout our systems. They send many ships, and mostly they kill. They came to Osperantue, and many fled to transport ships, and ran. We took the first [the word here was lost in translation, but Cooper assumed it referred to the wormhole effect which had brought Poonch to the edge of the solar system], and it was a short trip, and we popped out and, AHA! There was an escape pod with ASkiilamentrae, and AStermalanlan. We took them on board and AHA! Three Zenge warships come out of the [wormhole]. We jumped pretty quick, but they still got shots through our shields, and burned into side of the ship.

"This was big jump to place we have never been. We have never used this [wormhole] before. It brought us here, and here you are, Captain Cooper."

"Captain Poonch, will the Zenge use the wormhole to follow you?"

"Maybe. Probably not. Three is few for Zenge. Most likely they went back to finish Osperantue. Or they went to Fell to kill Fellen. Or they went to any of many other worlds they are killing." Poonch teared up, and his ears actually drooped the way a Swiss Mountain Dog's will do when sad or sick. "We are not fighters, Captain Cooper. We are traders and travelers. We left billions of our people behind. We have thirty-nine thousand children on board. We have many animals in our hangars. We have little food left. We have nowhere to go. Captain Cooper of United Earth Space Fleet, I am Poonch, Bosine Commander of this ship. I ask for safe haven."

The Bosine stood quietly, awaiting a response. Expecting what? From his down-trodden face, he expected a brush-off. Who in their proper mind would invite the wrath of the Zenge.

Before Cooper could reply, Askiilamentrae, and another equally beautiful (blue and built) Fellen, one with silky, shaggy auburn hair, moved in front of the ship's officer.

"We are Fellen," she said. "We do not ask for safe harbor. Our planet, and our people, are under attack. We ask for weapons and a ship that will take us to Fell.

"We will barter for these. We can provide you with translators. We will even provide you the technology to build your own, a secret Fellen's have held for over two-thousand years."

Cooper stood to face the screen, and the aliens who faced him from 25,000 miles away. Aliens and refugees from a galactic upheaval far from where the *John F. Kennedy* sat in space.

"I am a Space Fleet captain. I do not have the authority to offer you amnesty, safe harbor, or even guarantee you assistance. While I believe you, and I sympathize, I cannot speak for my superiors.

"Captain Poonch, I want you to take your ship toward the giant planet forward and port side of your present location. We call it Neptune. I expect you to open your information network to my ship. We need to find out what supplies you need to survive. We also need to figure out what foods you, your children, and your animals need, and whether we can provide the necessary supplies.

"My ship will return to Earth and inform Space Fleet of your presence, as well as your request for safe haven. Humans are well acquainted with conflict and the harsh realities wars create. I am positive I will be tasked with returning and providing the supplies you need."

Poonch pushed through the Fellen, garnering nasty looks from the two females.

"That could take months, Captain," he protested. "You cannot use wormhole channels within a solar system. It is suicide. The only planet in your system that is habitable is the third one from your star. Months. We do not have the food to last weeks. Even with our botanical garden, and even if we were to [and here he shuddered] eat our animals. I do not want to return my ship to that wormhole. I know the Zenge sit there, somewhere waiting, but your plan leaves us with no hope."

Cooper ignored the alien's plea to address the Fellen.

"ASkiilamentrae, your offer is of great value, but, again, I am not in a position to negotiate for the Fleet. I will present it to my superiors. I can tell you now, they will not trade a ship for your technology."

Returning his attention to the Bosine commander: "Captain Poonch, I'm sure your scans picked up my ship when we entered natural space. We did not use a wormhole. We have the ability to fold space and time. At our fastest speed we can reach Earth and return here in less than eight days. Perhaps nine or ten if it takes longer to gather enough supplies to make sure your people can reach Earth."

The eyes of the alien grew wide, giving him an ovine appearance. Cooper feared the stranger might have a stroke. He sputtered before speaking.

"You have a space-time-fold engine? That is an ancient legend. Stories told of a civilization which disappeared over one-half-million-years ago; a civilization that could fold space and control time. They could journey anywhere; anytime. Our scans were unable to tell where you came from. We assumed they were malfunctioning. Captain Cooper, if your species have the ability to travel through folded space, then you are the most advanced civilization in the known galaxy."

"We can, Captain Poonch." Cooper used his poker face. Genna remained neutral. Until this moment, no one from Earth knew space-fold travel was exceptional or unique in the galaxy. Earth advanced from a nothing planet on the edge of the Milky Way, to the greatest civilization in the known galaxy, in less than fifty years.

ASkiilamentrae resumed her place in front of the camera. She appeared less in awe than Poonch.

"We can help educate you, Captain," she began. "The Zenge are destroying entire civilizations. Whole planets and solar systems wiped out. They eat those they do not kill. They cage them like animals and slaughter them as food. They do this to men, women, and children. They do this to dumb animals and to our greatest minds.

"They will come to your solar system, Captain. Sooner, or later they will come, if only because they will follow the Osperantue ship. They seek out worlds to conquer. It is what they live for."

She took a breath. Her blue tint darker. "If you can fold space and time, perhaps you are the ones who will help us defeat the Zenge. Perhaps being found by Poonch to be delivered to this place is fate. When you return to your superiors, they will want proof your system is in peril. We are the proof. Call us hostages. Call us prisoners. Call us allies. Take us aboard your ship, let us return with you to Earth. Allow us to teach you everything we can about the Zenge. If you are not prepared, they will destroy you.

"We are Fellen. We have incredible technology. We are the master engineers of the galaxy. We lost to the Zenge."

Before Cooper could reply, Poonch chimed in. "She speaks the truth, Captain. The Fell are extremely straightforward. I will allow your ship full access to the total of information on my ship. Our communication links are open. All encryption turned off. The Fell provided me with a conduit communication-translation board I have installed on our bridge computer."

"It is a computer's version of our translator rings," Askiilamentrae explained.

"If you access our information through that link, translation occurs most quickly," Poonch finished.

# Chapter 9

Cooper and Genna moved from the bridge to the Communications and Tactical center situated opposite the Captain's Office. Designated C-Tac, the room multifunctioned, used as a nerve center during maneuvers with multiple ships, or as a conference center should a group required meeting space.

At the table designed for twelve, they took adjacent seats.

Cooper began the discussion. "Genna, Kennedy, before I ask your opinions, I have already decided we need to help the people on board that ship. Opinions and options are open for discussion. Kennedy, did you access their systems?"

"I did. The remarkable translation board has made analysis less complicated. The equipment or alien software could scrub the information before translation, but what I have analyzed appears uncorrupted. I would surmise they are truthful regarding their origins, their predicament, and their desire for a safe haven.

"There is an incredible wealth of information on the star systems in their section of the galaxy. Data on wormhole channels, their method of travel through deep space. There are profiles on fifty-six sentient species, one-hundred-forty-two races within those species, the planets they inhabit, and data regarding another one-hundred-twelve worlds considered viable, but without sentient life.

"Their ship is a civilian recreation ship, like those on Earth which cruise around the oceans with people on vacation. It is designed to hold half as many people as currently aboard. It is also designed for comfort, not speed. It would normally travel faster, but two of its four engines are off-line. They do not have the spare parts on board to make repairs."

"Do you have an opinion on helping, and have you considered options?" Cooper asked.

"If we leave to get food, and any other supplies, there is the chance the Zenge may arrive before we return. We have no way of knowing if or how much they value the cruise ship. Nor can we estimate the numbers or capabilities of any ships they may send. The ship's records indicate the Zenge employee the tactic of overwhelming force. They are not the most advanced civilization. They are extremely aggressive. Descriptions of the Zenge and how they treat their enemies are horrific. Though the Osperantue had a head start, the Zenge may have faster ships.

"If we do nothing, they will never make it to Mars, which is much nearer currently than Earth. Their propulsion systems would take them over three years. They would die of starvation."

Coop thought he picked up a slight catch in the AI's tone. Could the artificial intelligence system experience sympathy? The AI continued with its conclusion.

"Make the fastest time possible to Mars, persuade Space Fleet to provide supplies, and, more importantly, a space-fold crystal array sufficient to operate for the Osperantue ship. Return, install the space-fold drive, and deliver the aliens to Mars before either the Zenge appear, or the refugees starve. That is my opinion."

Cooper turned to face Genna, seated with hands folded atop the table. "Genna?" he prompted.

"At this point, I agree with Kennedy. If we accept the information being streamed from the Osperantue as accurate, then, simply stated, we are faced with refugees from a war seeking asylum. While this is a strange first encounter, it remains Earth's first contact with aliens. We must help. Anything less is inhuman.

"Kennedy has run every scenario we can think of, and the best option is hurry to Mars, get provisions, a space-fold drive system, return with engineers who can install it on the Osperantue ship. Do it all before the Zenge appear."

"You both agree we need to help the people on that ship. To do that, the 109 needs to return to the Mars station as quickly as possible, then return here with supplies and assistance."

Cooper walked to the over-sized SHD screen at the front of C-Tac. "Kennedy, please provide a view of the Osperantue ship."

The double-sphere cruise ship appeared. Coop knew the ship gigantic, but viewed in the expanse of space, it could be a child's toy.

"Captain, we are receiving a message from Space Fleet," the AI interrupted his thoughts.

Kennedy transmitted data-dumps to the Mars and Earth platforms since she reentered natural space. Considering the time delay in both directions, this is the response to the details of the wormhole event and the arrival of the alien ship.

"Break it down for me, Kennedy," he said. "I do not need to read a book of hypotheticals and suggestions at the moment."

"I can read it all to you, Captain. It says, "*You're on site. Your call. Do us proud.*" Signed Admiral P.A. Patterson, Space Fleet. That is the complete message."

Coop nodded. He returned his attention to the aliens at the door.

"I agree the 109 making the trip to Mars and back is the only hope for those aboard the Osperantue ship . . ."

"It is called the **Star Gazer,**" Kennedy informed them. "The name was part of the data I received."

Cooper continued, "The only hope for the *Star Gazer* is Space Fleet providing supplies. Otherwise they need to turn around and take their chances the way they came."

The Captain of the SFPT-109, *John F. Kennedy,* turned to face Genna. He knew Kennedy could *see* him as well. His hands clasped behind his back; his posture ram-rod straight. A pose sea captains had mastered since ships first sailed on Earth. The stance an officer employed when addressing his crew before a bad storm. The unconscious position officers assumed when unpopular orders are given and other options unviable.

"The 109 will leave immediately for Mars. Genna, you will have the Captain's chair. I will take care Angel 7 to the *Star Gazer.*"

Angel 7 nestled in the aft hangar, beside the thirty-six-seater shuttle used to move crew members across short expanses of space, or on space-to-surface trips. She was a three-person starship fighter prototype. The seventh generation of the first ship to use space-fold technology.

In unison, Genna and Kennedy said, "SIR!"

Genna, speaking for both herself and the AI continued, with concern, if not consternation, in her tone of voice. "Captain . . . Cooper, you cannot do that. You are the Captain of the 109. I am totally unexperienced, and a civilian. Angel 7 cannot stand alone against a mass attack. If the Zenge arrive, you, the Osperantue, and the Fellen will lose."

"Maybe," Cooper conceded, but only a little. "With luck, you will return before they arrive. Maybe they never arrive. If I am here, Space Fleet will expedite your return. If I am here, the information from the data collected from the *Star Gazer*, and the tactical information the Fellen provide could give me enough of an advantage to hold them off."

He smiled before saying, "Remember, we are the only civilization in the known galaxy with space-fold technology. I can use Angel and that technology inside the solar system. The Zenge use slower ships."

"They will outnumber you with ships, and outgun you by an even greater margin," Kennedy chimed in.

"Kennedy, what are the odds of the *Star Gazer* surviving if a half-dozen Zenge ships arrive, and catch up to her?"

"Zero."

"What are their odds if I have Angel to help cover their escape?"

"Unknown. The information supplied provides only general descriptions of the Zenge's ability and weapons. Without better data, I am unable to create an accurate estimate of their survival odds." The AI was using her computer voice. Sounding uninterested in the subject, because it was obviously a waste of time.

"Better than zero?" Cooper asked.

"I do not want to belittle your ability, or that of Angel 7," Genna said, standing, facing the captain, her hands now clenched beside her. "But one percent better than zero, is still zero. You cannot stay and we cannot leave you."

"Kennedy, can you operate this ship without a human crew on board?"

"You know the answer is affirmative, Captain."

"Kennedy, I am going to depart with *Angel 7* to join the *Star Gazer* in two hours. After I clear the hangar, please buttoned up hatches and depart for MSD.

"Genna, you will take the three-plus days in space-fold to analyze the data received from the Osperantue, and you will write a detailed, concise, and convincing report for Space Fleet, concluding with the need to help these aliens, and the importance of acting quickly.

"If the Zenge appear, before or after your return, it will indicate they may also have the intention of attacking Earth. I will send the tactical information I receive from the aliens, and any actionable strategies which may occur should Angel need to engage, to Space Fleet. If we cannot hold them here, at least the Fleet will have usable information and detailed scans that will allow them to develop a plan to stop them before they reach Earth."

Cooper walked over to Genna and took both of her hands in his.

"This isn't simply about saving the aliens. This is about keeping Earth safe."

# Chapter 10

From the pilot's seat in the cockpit, Cooper keyed his mike: "Kennedy, Angel 7 prepped for launch."

"Aye, Captain. Magnetics will unlock in sixty-seconds. Main hangar door is opening now."

The 109's stern door opened and oxygen escaped. Cooper felt his ears pop a little, even in the controlled atmosphere of his fighter.

He keyed the mike again and said, "Genna."

"Yes, sir," came the stilted response. Not a pleasant tone.

"It's okay to sit in the Captain's chair," he said with a smile, positive he knew where she currently sat.

"Thank you, Captain. I prefer the pilot's seat. I would prefer you sit in the Captain's chair."

"You will need to send a message to Admiral Patterson before you engage space-fold," he said. "Besides sending the data we have, and preliminary suggestions, you will need to inform her of my decision to go aboard the alien spaceship. For security, ask that messages are terminated unless extremely urgent. I will update Space Fleet when I can."

"Aye," was the simple reply.

When the mag-locks released the fighter, thrusters allowed the compact space ship to hover ten feet above the deck. Originally parked for a quick exit, *Angel 7* faced space when the door finished its downward swing. A push on the forward thrust, and Cooper was outside and quickly cruising towards the alien ship.

The *Star Gazer* and the 109 had maneuvered to within 10,000 miles of each other. Captain Poonch had been informed of the plan. The Fellen had also been informed, and while not pleased they were not going to Space Fleet to plead their case, they were mollified Captain Cooper decided to remain behind, along with his fighter.

Genna demanded (yes, demanded) the 109 remain on station until he safely boarded the other ship. Ultimately, once Cooper departed, she became de-facto captain, and could "*damn well stay if I want.*"

The avatar was developing more personality. One distinct from the AI, and more rounded than when he first met her in the Admiral's office. The fact she was not talkative, a bit snarky, somewhat taciturn, and definitely self-assured in her decisions made Cooper wonder how much he was rubbing off on the young woman, and how much of that was a good thing.

A message from the *Star Gazer* came through his helmet speaker: "Captain Cooper, this is Commander Cornitsch. I am in charge of storage and the hangar for the *Star Gazer*. When you are within ten minutes of touchdown, I will open the hangar doors. Look for me on the deck to direct you to your bay."

Piloting Angel 7 did not require a full flight suit. Because he was entering an unknown environment, it made sense to don the suit until completing decontamination protocols required by the Osperantue.

Kennedy earlier determined Osperantue atmosphere was similar to Earth; a bit higher in oxygen, and two inert gases less (but not required for breathing normally). The gravity within the ship was eight-five percent of his ship, but, again, not an overly difficult adjustment.

"Thank you, Commander." A channel change, and then he said, "Kennedy."

"Yes, sir."

"Have you noticed the more conversations we have with our visitors, the better grammar and syntax becomes?"

"Yes, sir. It would appear the Fellen translator rings learn as they go. I imagine the same is happening for them as well. You probably sounded like quite a bumpkin during first contact."

"Bumpkin?"

"Sir, a bumpkin is a socially awkward person from the countryside."

"I know what a bumpkin is, Kennedy. Just surprised at the usage."

"I thought it appropriate, sir. While Genna and I have the ability to adapt to unique experiences rather quickly, you may find it difficult to adjust once you are aboard the alien ship. As you are Earth's first representative to at least two advanced species, perhaps you could try and act more diplomatic. You should attempt to make a good first impression."

The avatar was not the only intelligent being developing a distinct personality. He was definitely having an effect on his crew, and one Space Fleet may not appreciate. Treating Genna and Kennedy as both crew and individuals had created a bond between the three of them, and ultimately that was what any crew had to have to function as a team.

"Got it. Less bumpkin, more diplomat. Cooper, out."

Angel 7 was a small ship compared to PT-109, but in comparison to the alien cruise ship, she was a gnat.

Cooper moved his ship around to pass port-to-port to the smaller sphere, which held the command center. He dipped beneath the huge second sphere, and found a ramp lowered and waiting.

"Kennedy. Genna. I am about to enter the *Star Gazer*. Once I'm in and settled, I would appreciate it if you would head for Mars. Nothing more you can do here, and the sooner you leave, well, the sooner you get back."

"This is SFPT-109." Kennedy's voice resonated clipped and formal. "While Captain Cooper is off this ship, Kennedy has disembarked." Cooper choked up. There was once a naval standard the ship's captain was the ship. In the past, he, as Captain, would have held the designation KENNEDY. The AI was paying him a great respect, and he recognized the gesture, but before he could comment, Genna added:

"This is acting Captain of the SFPT-109, Genna Bouvier." Cooper smiled even wider. The avatar had given herself a formal last name. Bouvier was the maiden name of President John F. Kennedy's wife, Jacqueline.

"To the commander, the crew, the people aboard the *Star Gazer*, you have possession of our Captain. You are responsible for his care and wellbeing. I will personally hold you responsible for his safekeeping.

"Captain Poonch, do you understand?" she asked, knowing the airwaves were being monitored aboard the alien ship.

A hesitant Osperantue captain replied, "I understand Captain Bouvier."

Before he choked up. On hearing Genna addressed as 'Captain Bouvier,' he nearly choked.

"No, Captain Poonch, you do not understand. If anything happens to my Captain, you will think of the Zenge as warm and cuddly compared to me, this ship, and Space Fleet. Do you now fully understand?"

"Fully, Captain Bouvier," Poonch replied. "I only wish my crew felt as strongly about my good health, as Captain Cooper's crew cares for his."

Coop listened to the back-and-forth as he employed lower thrust rockets to lift him into the belly of the cruise ship. Once *Angel 7* cleared the deck, the ramp raised, locked, and sealed. In front of him, inside a clear lucite ball, an alien in a dark blue one-suit waved.

"This is Commander Cornitsch, Captain." The Bosine in the ball waved again. "Please follow me into the hold. I have a bay prepared for your ship."

The lucite globe rolled backward, but the officer inside remained upright. It was an interesting, and fun-looking way to travel within a hold after the venting of the atmosphere.

Cooper used his maneuvering thrusters and eased Angel 7 forward. He followed Cornitsch's hand signals, pivoted his ship, and allowed it to hover within a docking space that provided walls on three sides.

Angel was compact for a space-worthy ship, but still roomy enough to carry a crew of three, as well as two power plants, armaments, and storage. Her airframe design similar to the stealth bombers of the twenty-first century. A giant wing painted in scan-resistant blues, grays, and whites. The pellucid cockpit canopy made from a type of acrylic-titanium able to withstand as much pressure as the thickest part of her hull. She had two entry and exit points. The rear ramp could be deployed for loading or unloading supplies, armaments, repair parts, or personnel. There was a drop-down open elevator beneath the fuselage used by the crew for easier access.

Tripod landing gear lowered and came to rest on the floor. Fully extended they provided ten feet of clearance to the bottom of the frame. Magnetic conduits extended through the three legs.

When Cooper hit the switch, Angel 7 locked onto the metal deck. No matter what, his ship would not move again until he keyed the code to release the magnetics.

"Atmosphere has been returned, Captain," the storage commander informed him. "You are safe to exit your ship anytime."

Cooper was not comfortable in the full flight suit, helmet, and oxygen re-breather, but the plan was to keep it on until he completed decontamination. Through the canopy, he watched the two Fellen enter the hold through a starboard-side hatch. They walked toward the fighter.

They now wore tight black bodysuits. Decidedly female and more impressive when seen from head to toe.

ASkiilamentrae stood a couple of inches taller with less distracting curves than the other female. Poonch called the second one AStermalanlan. ASkiilamentrae walked with determination. AStermalanlan was smiling, more bounce to her walk, and waving up at him. Actually, more bounce to her. He waved in response before he released the body restraints designed to keep him secure in the pilot's seat.

On his way to the elevator, he grabbed his GO bag, set the security systems to ON, and took a deep breath. This was truly first contact.

Keying his mike before entering the elevator; "Kennedy. Genna."

"Yes, sir," came the reply from both.

"I'm on board. Everything appears fine. Please make final preparations and get underway for Mars."

Kennedy replied: "Preparations completed while you were between ships. The 109 is ready for travel. Be careful until we return, Captain Cooper."

From Genna: "We will return soon, Captain Cooper. Please, stay well."

"Take care of my ship, Genna." On the open com, he said, "This is Captain Cooper aboard Angel 7. I'm coming down."

# Chapter 11

Cornitsch stepped forward. "I am not sure of your customs for greetings."

Cooper extended his right hand and said, "We shake hands. I am Captain Daniel Cooper, commander of the United Earth Space Fleet ship, *John F. Kennedy*."

Cornitsch took Cooper's hand in his. He allowed the Earther to move it up and down. "I am Commander of the Storage, Cornitsch."

The shorter, curvier Fellen stepped up, taking Cooper's hand. "I am AStermalanlan of Fell. I am happy to meet you, Captain Daniel Cooper of United Earth."

She stood aside for the taller woman, who held her hand out, but made Cooper move closer to grasp it.

"AStermalanlan, and I are your security detail while you are on board the *Star Gazer*. According to your Captain Genna Bouvier, we are to take good care of you, Captain Daniel Cooper."

"I am pleased to meet you in person, ASkiilamentrae." He held her hand as he looked to the other two aliens. "And you, AStermalanlan, and you, Commander Cornitsch. I am positive intergalactic protocols will survive if you call me Coop." He released the firm blue hand. "I need to go to decontamination."

First contact completed, the obligations of space travelers ensued. The initial duty, not make those you meet sick, or they you. No different from visiting a sick friend in ICU, sanitize and sterilize before fraternize.

The following three hours were essential, and essentially boring. Coop followed his security detail to the medical section, located within the larger sphere. A lift delivered them from the hangar to the medical ward. He encountered no other beings until greeted by a pair of Bosine orderlies, both male, as he stepped from the lift. The Fellen handed him over, and the orderlies directed him to an examination room. Instructions included stripping, emptying his bag, laying everything he had on a metal table, and having a seat on the second table in the room.

Nozzles located in the ceiling sprayed the entire room with a mixture of decontaminates. His EVA, change of clothes, and body covered in a damp mist, which quickly dissipated. He dried within a minute, as did his belongings.

Instructions came from an embedded speaker. He stood (nude); a medical scanner moved over his body, front and rear, and each side. He felt no sensation from the light playing across his skin. He was cool and assumed the area remained chilled due to the number of technical devices and computers medical facilities employed. That, or aliens preferred chillier environs.

Two mechanized boxes on rollers, with mechanical arms, entered the room through a section of a wall. The doorway appeared, the boxes rolled inside, and the door closed.

One requested a urine sample, handed him a cup, pointed a metallic finger to a semi-private area behind a curtain. When done, and the cup given back, the second box, a metal hand holding a syringe, stopped a few feet from him.

"Captain Cooper, this is Doctor Coptonitsch." The physician stood behind a transparent panel. Coop was certain the window not there previously. "I would appreciate a sample of your blood. The needle needs to prick your skin for what I need. I promise this is nothing more than making sure there are no pathogens within your body that would prove harmful to those on board, or that we carry any type of bacteria, or virus natural for our species, but potentially harmful to you."

Cooper allowed the needle to puncture the meaty part of his palm. It quickly pulled away, the needle retracting inside the box. No blood on his palm. No puncture mark obvious.

"Captain, please make yourself comfortable. Get dressed if you like. It will take about an hour for the results."

True to his word, an hour later the door to the containment room opened. The two Fellen entered, followed by the doctor. None clad in protective clothing.

Cooper sat on the examination table, changed into black fatigues. No emblems, lots of pockets. He wore his composite combat boots. Unshaven for a few days, the scruffy beard and hand-combed hair presented a visage of menace. The shorter Bosine physician stayed strategically behind the two women.

"I assume we are compatible," Cooper said.

AStermalanlan, the curvy one, smiled, showing her fangs. Her golden eyes a hint of a mischief. She replied, "In every way that matters."

Dr. Coptonitsch decided it safe to talk. "We appear to share many physical, chemical, and genetic similarities. This is true of scores of species throughout the known galaxy, so not entirely unexpected. Some organs are not the same, or not located in the same place. Nothing medical will preclude our species interacting."

"And sexually compatible," AStermalanlan said. Blueberry lips parted for her smile. "But unable to have children. We are not compatible for children."

"Yes," Dr. Coptonitsch said, and coughed, put aback by the Fellen's comments. "Genetically, Earthmen, the two Osperantue species, and those from Fell cannot mate for the purpose of breeding. Physically, males and females can have sexual intercourse, but for pleasure only." The Bosine's skin grew pinker as he spoke, obviously embarrassed by subject, despite being a doctor. It appeared Bosine were a bit prudish, where Fellen were not. But this was a tiny sample.

ASkiilamentrae said nothing during the conversation. She had no interest in the topic, and interjected a more serious issue.

"We need to move to our cabin in the command sphere," she said. "We need to teach you as much as we can about the Zenge and their battle tactics. You need to let us know what weapons your little ship has. What assistance we can expect if the Zenge decide to enter the system before your Kennedy returns with reinforcements."

He was having no difficulties understanding the aliens. The translation ring worked. The wordiness of their conversations, and word or phrase choices a bit stilted, indicating the need for more samples. His brain already accepted English with the movement of alien lips, syncing them so he no longer felt he was watching a dubbed foreign movie.

He understood, but was not about to inform them the 109 would return alone. Space Fleet's ships were at different stages of construction, from hulls to half-completed. Reinforcements remained months, or years away. He considered the Osperantue and the Fellen trustworthy, but not fully, not yet.

The Earther hopped from the examination table, grabbed his bag, now filled with his flight suit, retrieved his helmet from the floor, and indicated the door with a nod of the head.

"Let's go," he said. "The more we teach each other, the better for both sides."

AStermalanlan actually giggled. Cooper decided she was younger and less focused on current problems. But every time he let his eyes wander, over her, or her companion, his focus became laser sharp, only not on extraneous matters. The clothing was tight and filled nicely.

ASkiilamentrae took control. "AStermalanlan, you lead. Captain Cooper, next. I will follow. Captain, please keep moving. We have to go through several levels, and passed thousands of Osperantue before we reach the command sphere. Captain Poonch will also expect you to stop by the bridge, and while it is a side-trip, I understand its importance."

ASkiilamentrae handed Cooper an open translation ring. He placed it around his neck. The clasp fastened. If he came upon an alien who did not wear their own device, they would be able to communicate.

"A question, first, if you don't mind," Cooper addressed ASkiilamentrae. "This is an Osperantue ship, with, I assume, an Osperantue captain and crew. You are Fellen, found, and rescued in space by the ship. Why are you my security detail, and not an Osperantue team?"

"Captain, if you will follow AStermalanlan, I will explain as we walk," she replied, pointing at the open door.

Leaving the doctor, and the decontamination room, bag in one hand, helmet in the other, and eyes on AStermalanlan's delightful, round ass, Cooper walked as the other woman from a planet called Fell, spoke to the rear of his head.

## Chapter 12

They exited the medical ward and entered a lift. They started up. ASkiilamentrae explained their presence as his security detail.

"The people of Osperantue are largely docile. There are the Bosine, like those you have already met, two other races within the same species, and the Fray, a separate species living on Osperantue. Pursuits include agriculture, travel, trade, and what we consider the softer sciences, like medicine, and astronomy. They are also an artistic species. The Posine are similar to the Bosine. Differences are mainly physical. One race, the Woolifer, have an affinity with technology, and produce most of the engineers on Osperantue. The Fray are a more secretive race. There is not a lot known about them collectively, or as individuals.

"The Osperantue began exploring space centuries ago. The species among the first to visit other planets and make alliances. They are as they appear. Very much not to be feared. As merchants, they saw the opportunity to create trade routes between Osperantue and the worlds they visited. Other systems were doing similar business, and, in time, trade routes between several worlds led to a multi-system trade alliance.

"Fell is a planet once consumed with war. Our ancestors fought among themselves for any cause. Land. Power. Minerals. Any reason was reason enough. In order to improve their chances of victory, they began to create technologies to help improve chances for victories. Our ancestors invented long-range scanners, targeting computers, battle-wagons that were self-propelled, and, as you have seen, superior means of communication.

"The growing obsession with technology actually saved our species. Tribes began cooperating to create computers, machines, and systems that allowed every Fellen a chance to live a productive life. That exploded when traders from other worlds visited Fell and discovered our technology was far superior to what they used. Communication technology, for example, evolved, and our trade-goods include items like our self-learning translation rings."

They exited the lift and turned left. The hallway ahead filled with people. Adults and children loitered in the corridor. As

AStermalanlan walked ahead, they parted, moving up against the bulkhead to provide room to pass.

Cooper noticed they wore heavier clothing than he would expect aboard a ship, but he had already noted the Osperantue cruise ship quite a bit cooler than comfortable for him. He had thought it natural. Seeing people bundled against the chill, he changed his opinion.

Murmurs rose around them as they walked the hallway. No one tried to speak with any of the three.

They came to a halt. AStermalanlan addressed a microphone placed in the bulkhead, and a door opened. They entered the shaft connecting the main sphere to the command sphere. When the door closed behind them, Cooper could see outer space in front of him.

"The walls and ceiling are a type of material able to reflect inside what is actually outside." ASkiilamentrae explained as they walked through space. She returned to her story.

"The Fellen never forgot our history. Even though we found an inherent ability to imagine and create a number of highly technical inventions, we remained a predatory species. Males and females on Fell, to this day, are taught how to fight. When visitors came from space, we were prepared to hold on to our technology.

"In trade for our inventions, we gained the science of space flight. We began to trade our technology for food, engines, information, and supplies not found on Fell. Because we could, and would, kill to protect ourselves and our planet, we also received respect.

"On this ship, with over 240,000 people, there are only two true warriors. That is why we have been assigned as your security, and your guards," she finished. Finished in time for another commic addressed, and the entrance to the *Star Gazer*'s command sphere opened.

Coop took note of ASkiilamentrae's use of the word *guards*. The translator might have misused the word, or the Fellen were security, and there to make sure he was contained, if needed.

# Chapter 13

Another corridor stretched ahead of them. Kennedy's scans measured the command sphere .59 miles at its widest point. Where they entered, the corridor represented a good half-mile walk. AStermalanlan pressed a button, and the floor moved, becoming a motorized walkway. "Try to maintain your balance," she said. She acquired a remote from somewhere, most likely when she pushed the button for the walkway. She played with the remote, and the walkway sped up. It got quite fast, but he had no trouble maintaining his balance.

Nearing the end of the corridor, she used the remote, and the walkway slowed to a stop. Both women gave him looks which could have been surprise he remained upright, or disappointment he had not landed on his butt. AStermalanlan placed the remote on the wall, adjacent to a twin.

They entered another lift, rose, and emerged on a level located nearly three-quarters of the smaller sphere's height. They stepped from the lift, directly onto a command bridge.

The concave front wall displayed deep space. It could have been more of the two-way material, actual reinforced transparent glass, or SHD monitors.

Beneath the view, arranged in a semi-circle, flight-operation stations with chairs, spaced every six feet. Half the stations staffed. Those present turned to look at the visitors.

A command chair dominated the bridge, located on a pedestal in the center of the semi-circle. The lay-out eerily similar to the bridge design of the PT-109. Captain Poonch, all five-foot five of him, stood in front of the pedestal. Dressed in a blue uniform with white piping and white shoes, instead of the brown kaftan. Two hundred pounds, Coop guessed, but his uniform looking a bit bulky, indicating, until recently, he had been heavier.

"Captain Cooper," he said, ignoring the two Fellen. He extended his right hand. Cornitsch had made his report. "Welcome aboard the *Star Gazer*. I wish it were under better circumstances. We have often flown guests to the most beautiful places in the galaxy. Parties. Performances. Not so much open, gloomy space as this," he said, waving his hand at the void depicted on the forward wall.

"I will not take much of your time, Captain Cooper. I want you to know my crew and I at your disposal. If there is anything we can do to make your stay more comfortable, or if we can provide any information that will help you, and your Space Fleet defeat the Zenge, then you must only ask."

He turned to ASkiilamentrae and said, "Please make sure Captain Cooper is taken to CD - 101." Then to Cooper, "It is the second officer's quarters, and quite comfortable. The two crew members staying therein have already been reassigned. It is only one deck down from us, so you are close to the command center."

"Allow your crew members to return, Captain. I will quarter aboard my ship in your hangar. It has everything I require. I will not force your people to relocate for my benefit."

"But Captain Cooper," Poonch said. A shudder racked his frame. "You will be in the bay. It is not the nicest place to be."

"It is where over two-thousand Osperantue now have to live," AStermalanlan explained. "They were removed before the hangar de-pressurized for your arrival." In case he thought his ship in danger, she quickly added, "Your ship, and our shuttle are located in separate, secure bays. No one can approach either ship."

"Nice or not, it is where I will bunk," Cooper said. "If it is sufficient for your people, then I am sure it will be fine for me."

"Of course, Captain Cooper," Poonch replied, regaining his composure. "If you are more comfortable aboard your own ship, who am I to question?"

Cooper addressed ASkiilamentrae. "Are the *Star Gazer's* logs and data regarding the Zenge available to you?"

"Yes."

"You also have your own information regarding them?"

"Yes."

"I can access this information?"

"Yes."

"Is there a place available I can use to review everything?"

"Our cabin has what you need. Our systems are better designed to translate the information for you."

Cooper returned to Poonch, who listened to the simple exchange between the Earther and the Fellen.

"Captain Poonch, I appreciate your hospitality, and providing information regarding the Zenge. I will go to the Fellen's cabin to review your reports. I will return to my ship afterward. If you need me, contact me anytime."

Cooper saluted the captain of the *Star Gazer*, who appeared perplexed by the action. Coop then pivoted and headed to the lift. AStermalanlan scurried to get in front of him to open the door. His other guard fell in step. They entered the lift, leaving the bridge crew and Captain in awe. Captain Daniel Cooper of Space Fleet was a person of few words.

It was a short ride, only one floor below. A brisk walk along a corridor with only a couple of crew to pass. Hands on their way somewhere and not loitering in the hall.

AStermalanlan stopped at a door, placed her hand on an entry pad, and revealed a cabin the size of a college dorm room. Their quarters were sparse and neat. Two single beds with pillows and blankets. Two utilitarian desks at the foot of each bed, facing their respective bulkheads, with pull-out chairs. A larger work space between the heads of the beds, and placed in front of shelves holding a number of electronic devices. The combination of desks and shelves gave the beds cave-like qualities.

Inside the entry, to the left, were two closets, and, to the right, a door to a cramped bathroom with shower, sink, and toilet.

"Too bad you did not accept Poonch's offer of a cabin," AStermalanlan said. "You would have been across the hall."

She moved to the bed on the left, pivoted, and sat lotus-style. The other woman did the same on the right bunk, and indicated the chair at the communal desk.

As soon as Cooper sat, the desk top became a computer monitor. A single blinking curser in the bottom left corner. Upon tapping the cursor, a heads-up display appeared in the air.

"Your translator has a proximity setting for this system," ASkiilamentrae informed him. "It will understand your commands, queries, and make notes for you if you wish. What we know about the Zenge is stored under a file named Zenge attack on Fell." This said in a tone which combined disgust, anger, and sadness. "Zenge attack on Osperantue, has what the ship's logs have on the invasion of their home world, and Zenge attacks on the Star Gazer, has what little they have on their escape from Osperantue, and when they picked us up at the multi-point."

She noted Cooper's questioning look, and explained. " A multi-point is a location where several wormhole channels converge. No one is sure why these places exist, but a few are well known. They are places for meetings, exchanges, and commerce to happen without the need to travel from one world to another.

"The only other file we have on the them is Zenge Stories. These are accounts by anyone who ever heard stories about the Zenge. I doubt many are factual, but sometimes it helps to know the mythology of your enemy."

Cooper said, "Zenge Stories," and lines of information appeared, but in a written form he could not decipher.

"Just say, '*translate*.'"

"Translate," he tells the desktop. The symbols disappear for a second, and reappear in English. "Impressive," he said aloud, and began to read tales of the Zenge.

Three hours disappeared. He read story after story concerning a lizard-like species who lived to make war, and used captured enemies as a food-source. Some tales were obvious fantasy, but enough similar renditions began to provide him with a feel for the enemy. It was not a good feeling.

He was unaware of either Fellen moving during the time he sat reading. When he looked up, both remained in the lotus position on their respective beds.

"That's enough for today," he said. His internal clock informed him time for dinner came and went. Time for sleep and recovery. He doubted a restful sleep was in store, but he had read a Vietnam Veteran's journal from the war, and a line stayed with him ever after: "Sleep is a weapon." A tired fighter made mistakes. When in a conflict, take any opportunity to sleep. There will come a time when sleeping impossible. What. rest you have had essential to your survival.

"I will escort you to your ship," ASkiilamentrae informed him. "This ship is on twelve-hour light and dark intervals, and is currently dark. Most of the Osperantue are asleep. During the dark times, one is sufficient as security."

Being sleepy while it was dark would make it easier for Coop to adjust to the ship's cycles.

AStermalanlan remained on her bunk; a smile, a sparkle, and a nod of the head. "I will see you in the new light."

The return trip to the lower bay was lengthy, and quiet. Neither talked. They stepped cautiously around bodies sleeping in the hallways, encountering only a few people awake. Either having trouble sleeping (they meandered), or on the job (they moved with purpose). Anyone they met moved to the bulkhead to allow them passage.

The lift opened on the bay and a striking scene. The bay transformed into a camp. Makeshift tents of diverse materials, and simple beds filled the floor. From the sizes of bumps lying on the floor, there were adults and children using the bay as temporary housing.

The Fellen remained silent, following a path of open aisles, walking cat-footed between people and tents. Cooper followed, his soft-sole boots making no noise which would disturb those trying to sleep. Sleep was also an escape.

They reached the enclosed section where Angel rested on her tripods. ASkiilamentrae reached out and finger-tapped the open space in front of the ship's bay. A shimmer of light arced away from her finger.

"There is an electro-magnetic forcefield to protect your ship," she whispered. "It is keyed to recognize your voice pattern. Just say *OPEN*."

Barely above a whisper, he said, "Open," and the Fellen moved forward. No light-show erupted.

"It is a low-level field," she informed him. "It would not kill anyone, but it does hurt. Say *CLOSE*, once you pass this line." She pointed at a line on the deck, hardly visible in the ambient light.

He stepped pass the line, turned, and said, "Close." Because he had to know, he slowly extended his right index finger until he was stung by the force field. A mini-rainbow of light spider-webbed the air around where he touched.

Bag and helmet held in his left hand, he placed his free palm against a flat screen on the side of the ship's front landing gear. The lift-cage slowly dropped to the floor. They entered the lift, and then the fighter together. Low lighting came on as the cage returned. A hiss sounded, indicating the lift resealed at the top. The cage's security rails disappeared into the wall.

The ship's interior proved more spacious than the *Star Gazer's* officer's cabin. The design similar to a large private jet. The area offered storage, head with shower, three semi-private bunks (each with pull screens), kitchenette, and a table with three stools able to retract into a hold below to provide additional space. The galley held a tactical cubicle with its own command chair and wide-screen SHD monitor.

A blast-door separated the cabin from the cockpit. Cooper did not invite her to see it, and she did not ask.

"This is Angel 7," he said, storing the bag and helmet under a bunk. "Welcome aboard, and thanks for the escort. I guess I need to open the forcefield so you can leave."

"That is unnecessary," she said, pulling the lycra-like top over her head, fully revealing the breasts he already knew would be magnificent. She walked, slowly, to him, reached both arms around his waist, then pulled him into a deep kiss. She broke away long enough to inform him, "I am staying."

# Chapter 14

### (Day 2 on the Star Gazer)

The automated peal from his compact wrist chronometer woke him. Coop rarely needed an alarm, normally waking a few minutes earlier. The combination timepiece, miniature PC lay on the floor next to his translation ring.

On his back, ASkiilamentrae snuggled on top of him. Comfortable in a bunk designed for one. Sleep followed two hours of heated activity. She woke him for another round, before both collapsed into deep slumber.

"I don't want to move," she whispered, her eyes still shut. For the first time her words translated into a contraction. "I don't want you to move, either," she added. Then she stretched, arched her back, placing her firm breasts in his face, relaxed, and kissed him. "But it is a new day."

She stood, and Coop made an approving appraisal in the artificial light. Tall, firm, muscled, and soft in the best locations. Exceptionally human, except for the deep blue skin. And the bump at the base of her spine, he discovered the night before, when she straddled him. He held onto her lower back and buttocks as she rode him. And the eyes. And the fangs. Other than those differences; exceptionally human.

"I need a shower," she said.

"There's an extra towel on the shelf," Coop told her. Assessing the rear view, and confirming his opinion. He remained in the bunk, missing the touch of her.

"You need to let AStermalanlan in. She's waiting," she said over her shoulder, and disappeared behind the door to the head.

He slid off the bunk, collected the wrist-piece and ring, pulled on pants and a grey t-shirt over his head as he headed for the lift. He stood at the forcefield in less than a minute. AStermalanlan sat in her cross-legged comfortable position; a smile, and a sparkle.

"Good morning, Captain Cooper. I hope you got enough rest." Fangs showed at the edges of her grin.

"Open," Cooper said. The Fellen gracefully stood and walked over the red line on the deck. "Close," he said, and turned to walk beside her to the ship.

Once on board, AStermalanlan perched on the edge of a bunk, which had been used, but not slept in. She tilted backward onto her hands, ample chest forward, and asked, "So Earthmen and Fellen are compatible?"

"We're called humans." He did not respond to her query about compatibility. It was obvious they had done more than sleep. "Have you had breakfast?"

It took a second for breakfast to translate before she answered. "Supplies are getting dangerously low. ASkiilamentrae and I usually eat twice a day."

"When on extended missions, my supplies are protein bars, fuel bars, and MRE's, but I did manage to grab freeze-dried fruit and jerky from the 109's larder before shoving off. Do Fellen eat meat?"

"We eat about everything," she replied. "We eat meat, but there has not been any on board *Star Gazer* for a while. We are not hungry enough to hunt Bosine . . . yet."

Cooper reached into a cupboard above the re-heat station and pulled down a bag of assorted dried fruits. He also grabbed a zip-lock bag.

He retrieved a platter from another storage unit, placed it on the table, and poured a bit of dried fruit, adding sticks of jerky. "Give it a try," he said, reaching for a bottle of water from the cooler to hand her.

AStermalanlan bit down on a banana chip and smiled. She put the rest of the chip in her mouth and let it melt. Coop was pretty sure he heard her purr. When she bit into the jerky and began chewing, he could see in her golden-orange eyes the moment the flavors released. She did not purr. She growled. It was a happy growl. Her stomach growled in agreement.

"Captain Cooper, human from Earth, I very much want to visit your world." She was finishing her second stick of jerky when ASkiilamentrae exited the head, hair wet. She wore the tight black outfit.

"What is this noise," she asked? "I thought I would find you both naked and in bed."

"AStermalanlan will show you," he said, throwing her a bottle of water. "I need a shower."

He exited the head with a towel around his waist. Unlike ASkiilamentrae, he had not taken clothes in with him, and unlike her, he was not limber enough to change in the cramped area anyway.

He expected the fruit and jerky gone, but most sat on the platter.

"You guys can have all you want."

AStermalanlan's eyes sparkled. "Really? ALL I want," making it clear she did not mean breakfast.

"It's your food," ASkiilamentrae said. "We appreciate your sharing it, but we cannot take it all."

Cooper reached into his cupboard and pulled out a protein bar. He unwrapped it before saying, "I'm perfectly happy with my other supplies. We'll keep the fruit and jerky for you two. You know where it is stored. Whenever you want, you're welcome to it. Speaking of eating, Angel is usually supplied for a crew of three for a month or more in space. The other food supplies may not taste as good, but they are healthy, and nutrient rich. I suggest you start eating at least three times a day, and eat anything stored here. I can't have my guards pass out from hunger," he joked. Reaching into a cupboard, he pulled out two protein bars, tossing one to each of the Fellen.

"Now I need to get dressed." Neither woman moved. They did not offer to turn their backs. They did unwrap the bars, and settled side-by-side on an open bunk for the show too start.

Resigned, Cooper retrieved a fresh set of black fatigues, socks, underwear, and a fresh t-shirt to wear under his gray combat sweater. He dropped the towel and dressed. The two women munched on their bars as they enjoyed the show.

After Coop laced his boots, they made their way to the cabin in the command sphere, where ASkiilamentrae could change into fresh clothes. Turn-about being fair, he and AStermalanlan sat side-by-side on a bunk and watched. He discovered the lovely alien a lot less shy about being seen nude.

They reviewed reports regarding Zenge attacks for the remainder of the morning. Cooper held off on the attack of Fell. He wanted more background before assessing that engagement, since he had two eye-witnesses.

They returned to Angel 7 for a lunch break, the two women enjoying jerky with an MRE (Meals Ready to Eat) pouch of beef stew. Cooper attempted to make the pre-packaged food palatable by using hot water and seasonings. While it did not have the same effect as the jerky, it was a welcomed warm meal.

They departed the ship and he turned on the forcefield, when a commotion across the bay caught his attention. He moved quickly to investigate. His two guards, half way across the hangar, suddenly realized he had gone a different direction.

The commotion was caused by a fight, and a growing number of Bosine and Posine cheering the two combatants. About to push through to intervene, ASkiilamentrae grabbed his arm, and said, "Wait. It is only practice."

"I thought the Bosine were a non-aggressive race," he said to his right. She stood there, and AStermalanlan on his left. Intent on the contest, those watching and cheering the two fighters did not noticed them.

"Some of the younger ones asked us to teach them how to fight," ASkiilamentrae explained. "We have been showing them basic techniques in hand-to-hand combat. They train every day by holding these fights. It is a way for them to overcome their passive nature. The more they fight, the more fighting becomes natural. The ones who win the most fights move on to more intense training."

"Therefore making those who are weaker, or slower, or not as quick to learn to lose confidence, and give up," Coop said, watching the fight, not the Fellen. "If you want to build fighters, the weakest are as important as the strongest. Those who are not as quick, or big, or strong must be taught to use other talents. Together you create an army, not a squad. Build the army first, and then start creating smaller, unique units."

"That would work if there were a thousand Fellen teaching 100,000 Bosine. In this case there are two of us and 200,000 of them," ASkiilamentrae said. "Even though less than one hundred requested training, there isn't time for anything but the basics. I wish it were not this way, but it is what it is."

The biggest Bosine he had seen, at least six-foot-six and 260 pounds, held a smaller boy up by his ears. The boy was about Coop's height, but less than 140 pounds. He felt the need to teach the bigger one a lesson, but ASkiilamentrae kept her hand on his arm. He turned and headed to the lift, the two Fellen hurrying to catch up. Those wanting to learn to fight, and getting the snot kicked out of them, would either get stronger or quit. It tore at the core of his training; from martial arts as a child, to Army then Ranger school, Space Rangers, and finally Fleet Flight School. To turn his back on those wanting, even needing to learn was against his nature, but at the moment he needed to prepare for a bigger battle. Priorities sucked.

When they reached the cabin assigned the women, AStermalanlan did not follow them in. "There are video clips of the Zenge attacking Fell. They are on the Command Bridge in Captain Poonch's secure safe. I will retrieve them and return."

Cooper closed the door and turned into a full embrace and kiss by ASkiilamentrae. Pulling away, she said, "I don't want us to fight. I know the combat by the Bosine disturbed you. I know we have done them no favors by teaching them only how to fight, and not how to win."

Coop returned the kiss, and while his blood pressure stayed high, it was no longer because of the fight in the bay.

"I understand the problem dropped on you, ASkiilamentrae. I know you were trying to fill a need. I'm not angry with you or AStermalanlan. I'm angry with a universe that is supposed to be smarter, *and* more advanced, *and* more civilized than the world I come from is torn apart by conflict. People are dying in horrible ways. People are about to die from something as stupid as hunger. I'm pissed, but not at you."

"Thank you," she whispered into his neck, and nibbled a little.

"May I ask you something?" Pushing her away, but maintaining contact.

She titled her head to look up into his eyes. "Yes?" An answer and a question in her tone.

"ASkiilamentrae is a beautiful name . . ."

"It means Free to Fly," she said. "The AS is our tribe, and it means Free. AStermalanlan is my cousin, and her name means Free to Travel."

"Again, beautiful names, but a bit long for me. May I call you Sky? It is what we call a nickname on Earth. A special name among friends and family. One not as formal."

"Sky," she said. "My translator recognizes SKY as the atmosphere which surrounds a planet. You would use this *nickname*?"

"Your name is *AS - sky — la - men — tray,* so, yes; *Sky.* If it's agreeable to you?"

"Sky," she said aloud, trying to get her mind around the name change. "I like it. You may call me Sky."

"And please start calling me Coop. It's what my friends call me."

AStermalanlan returned with the video on something akin to a thumbnail, but smaller. It fit into a slot in the desk shared between the bunks.

Without prompting, the heads-up came to life. The video displayed a perspective from a Fellen space ship.

"My father's ship, *ASpannash*; Free Bird," AStermalanlan said, misty eyed.

In the distance about fifty dots became fifty ships of various sizes and shapes. Behind them, at least another fifty dots growing larger.

"The Zenge confiscated ships from every world they attacked. They equipped some of those ships with laser cannons, and added them to their armadas," Sky said. Her mouth pinched, and anger radiating from her. "They have no real plan. No great strategy. They throw everything they have at an enemy to overwhelm them."

The cabin walls became bathed in the flashing lights of strobes from lasers fired and muzzle flares. A lot of cannons with a lot of lasers. The heads-up display would flash and flicker, as lasers hit the forcefield of the *ASpannash.*

"Most Fellen ships are a combinations of trader and fighter. We make sure other worlds are aware we will protect our goods. Two laser cannons on the smaller local patrol ships, and up to eight on larger transports. *ASpannash* is one of the largest Fellen ships, possessing eight laser cannons. She can also fire rockets from two traditional launchers."

"Was," AStermalanlan corrected her cousin. "*ASpannash was* the largest ship in our fleet. The Zenge sent over one hundred ships at our twenty-four. My father destroyed no fewer than fifteen alone, but the constant strikes by their lasers beat us down. Our energy systems could not sustain the levels needed to fight and maintain shields. Eventually weaknesses in the forcefields allowed lasers to penetrate the ship's hull. Many were killed. The engines disabled."

Sky took up the tale. "Uncle ASkiiumterel got as many of his crew into shuttles and escape pods as possible. He personally placed us in the shuttle the Osperantue recovered at the multipoint. Only a few pods, like ours, included wormhole capability. Most pods are lifeboats. They simply escape into space, awaiting another ship to rescue them. Another few had the capability of return flight to the surface."

AStermalanlan took over again: "Father would not leave his ship. We, along with dozens of others, slipped out from the hangars and pod-berths. We watched as Fellen ship after ship was worn down and destroyed. When the *ASpannash* was cut in two by a dozen Zenge ships, we entered the nearest wormhole gate. The one taking us to the multi-point."

As the two recalled the action, the video emphasized the size and scope of the attack. Coop watched Zenge ships swarm a Fellen ship, pounding it until escape pods shot away and the ship began to disintegrate under the relentless fire. The Zenge ships used escape pods for target practice. Many of the ships trying to reach Fell were tracked down, disabled, or destroyed. Always by multiple Zenge ships.

"We think other wormhole-capable ships escaped into channels. Fell was at a point in its orbit where three gateways were within easy distance. I don't think any of our main ships tried to escape," Sky said. "They fought until the end."

"Three gateways?" Coop asked. Curious, but also hoping to get their minds away from the loss of family and fellows.

"End," Sky said, and the display disappeared. She was, once again, sitting cross-legged on her bunk. Her cousin sat beside her, but with her spine against the bulkhead, her legs straight out in front of her, and feet hanging off the edge.

"Thousands of wormhole gateways have been charted throughout the known galaxy. Each gateway is the entry and exit for a channel. Channels do not open within solar systems. Gateways are predominant near the edge of a solar system. Just like the gate we came through near the planetoid you call Pluto. Pluto's orbit brought it near the wormhole.

"Merchants, traders, and travelers know when a planet is within proximity to a wormhole gate. To exit a wormhole, when the destination planet is too distant, is a waste of time. Sub-light engines can only power a ship so fast. Even the fastest ships in the universe only reach about .00025 sl, or about 167,000 mph. Most ships travel much slower. This cruise ship is currently at 40,000 mph. If it were at full energy capacity, and carrying a normal load, maybe 50,000 mph. The average warship will travel at 70,000 to 85,000 mph.

"The longest sub-light trip a merchant would care to make is a month. If they carry perishable goods, then maybe a week's distance. Captains plan trips to other worlds based on which channels they will use, and how near the final channel gate it is to the destination. Exactly how near depends on the planet's orbit around its star. When a planet is within one to two-million miles of a gateway, then ships from a dozen worlds may descend on them with trade goods and visitors. Because the planet does not stop its orbit, closer is better, because ships must reach the world, and leave again while the gateway is within range to make the return journey acceptable."

Sky continued her tutorial. AStermalanlan kept watching her feet, remembering her father and family left behind.

"Most inhabited planets are within two to four planets of a star. This means they have relatively short orbits. Your Earth takes 365 days to circle your star. Every 335 to 395 days, as your planet passes near a wormhole, trading days would peak.

"Dwarfs account for seventy-percent of the stars in the galaxy. The majority of worlds advanced enough to use interstellar travel are located around a dwarf star. As such, they have relatively short orbits and are frequently available for visitors. They usually exist in smaller solar systems as well, so wormhole gate are closer."

"For different plants to have orbits that brought them near a gate would mean wormholes are not static," Coop said. "Earth's orbit will never bring it this far into space."

"Correct," Sky agreed with his observation. "But the planet's orbit will take it to a point where it is less effected by the gravity influences of other bodies within the solar system. This is where the wormhole will be nearest Earth. Wormholes are effected by gravity. They are as predictable as the orbits of planets within a system."

AStermalanlan joined the conversation.

"Your star is a larger type. A giant. One day it will burn out into a super nova. Dwarf stars, like the one Fell orbits, will exist much longer. Your solar system, by comparison to the average, is dirty. It is full of planets, and planetoids, and debris, and stuff," she said. "The wormhole we came through was nearly impassible with debris from what you call the Kuiper Belt. Because this ship uses only poor sub-light engines, and wormholes do not exist in-side of systems, we will likely never reach Earth."

Her morbid thoughts had brought the young woman down from her normal positive high. She still provided detailed, intelligent comments to help him grasp galactic norms. It made Coop realize she was more than a pretty face with a happy demeanor.

Coop made decisions quickly. He already admired and trusted the Fellen, but he was a fleet officer. Daniel Cooper's life as career military meant keeping things from friends and enemies, alike. He did not tell them humans had developed engines that could propel larger ships at .08sl, and ships like Angel 7 could reach .11sl within the solar system. They knew Earth vessels engaged space-fold, but they were not fully aware of the capabilities such a drive system provided.

He also did not tell them his hope was the 109 would return with space-fold engines they could installed on the *Star Gazer*. If the ship could be fitted, they would reach Mars before supplies ran out. The Fellen only expected enough supplies to sustain them for an extended voyage.

"The Zenge plan their attacks around proximity to wormholes as well," he said. "They flood a system with ships designed or re-designed for battle."

He recalled reports from the *Star Gazer's* logs. The same basic attack happened to Osperantue. Nothing subtle about their in-vaders' strategy. Hit hard. Hit with overwhelming numbers. The Zenge did not practice tactical warfare. Watching the video, and matching what he had seen to the descriptions in the logs, he surmised the Zenge did not act as if they were in space. They lined up and came at their objective in waves.

While unsophisticated in their attacks, those they attacked were equally unsophisticated in response. They set up a defensive perimeter to protect their planet, then sat back and awaited the onslaught. With only a short amount of time to prepare for an in-vasion, and because the trading alliance members were mer-chants, the lightly armored worlds attacked by the Zenge were destined to fall.

Compiled descriptions described the Zenge as a lizard-like species. Where the Fellen seemed to evolve from a feline ancestry. The Zenge, if not simple-minded, appeared single-minded.

According to the records, an average Zenge stood five-foot-six inches and weighed about 300 pounds. Bodies armored by scales and muscle. Eyes set high on a narrow forehead above an elongat-ed snout. They had two rows of sharp teeth. Thick necks transi-tioned into stout bodies. They had short arms and hands with elongated fingers. Short legs and wide, flat feet. No tails, so not exactly a crocodile, but not too far off.

This species were meat eaters, and the most disturbing report said they used the captured as slaves and food.

Whatever induced them to attack part of the galaxy was un-known. They refitted captured ships for battle, but seemed to care little about any advanced technology beyond weapons and en-gines. They had been known to use captured translation rings, but only transmitted truncated orders or demands. There were insuf-ficient samples of Zenge speech to convert their language.

No reports in the *Star Gazer* logs mentioned anyone escaping a captured planet after Zenge armies landed. On the positive side, though Cooper kept this to himself, while Earth was a relative late arrival to space travel, humans seemed to have both stumbled upon and created superior technology to alien civilizations traversing the galaxy for thousands of years.

Humans could fold space/time, and travel that way from any point to any other point in space, whether inside a solar system or though the expanses. Humans possessed sub-light engines powerful enough to travel two or three times faster than similar-sized alien ships. Humans survived a history of warfare, and through necessity developed weapons far beyond laser cannons. Kings and Conquerors on Earth had developed strategies and tactics for fighting superior numbers. Civilizations, to continue, created defensive strategies for survival. More topical, because humans combined warlike ancestry with a desire to rise above such savagery, over the past thirty years the military's best and brightest minds developed space-oriented battle plans.

The Zenge saw space as a land war fought in the air.

Space was far more multi-dimensional. In the void, no up or down; no floor or ceiling. No forces of friction or inertia to prevent a ship from performing actions which could never occur anywhere else. There were gravity wells that could assist or destroy an action. Space Fleet had spent more than thirty years war-gaming for space. Evidently, the other sentient lifeforms in this part of the galaxy had not. The one that did go on offense selected the simplest formula . . . beat the enemy with numbers. They may use laser cannons, but they used them as hammers.

Even with better weapons, strategies, and equipment, Earth had a major shortage . . . a shortage of ships ready for space; ready for battle. The 109 would return alone. It would take six months before another PT-Boat entered service. More than a year before the two battle wagons under construction on MSD would launch.

More ships would follow, but not many more. There was a finite number of crystals used in the space-fold arrays found within the Martian hangar. Search teams found no more, and geologists did not believe the crystals native to Mars.

This information Cooper did not share. He could not overcome his military training and the need-to-know compulsion. He saw no reason to dash any hopes the Osperantue or the Fellen had . . . not yet.

They broke for dinner. Cooper provided a small store of protein bars and MREs. Sky and AStermalanlan would not need to make the trip to Angel for every meal. They would not miss a meal, or share the diminishing supplies aboard the *Star Gazer*. All three opted for simple protein bars.

"I need to get the kinks out," Cooper said aloud. "Is there a gym or workout studio anywhere on this ship not being used for beds?"

The two women smiled, and AStermalanlan even clapped her hands. "YES!" She said. "We could all use exercise." Then she looked at the Earther with that tilt of her head, and asked, "What are kinks?"

# Chapter 15

They walked down three flights, entered another hallway, taking it to a studio set up for physical training. There were a number of exercise stations and a generous matted area.

Sky walked over to a cabinet with a palm-reader lock, unlocked it, reached in, and pull out two poles. She threw one to AStermalanlan.

Both dropped into lotus positions, removed their shoes, rose, stepped on the mat, and faced each other.

They held their sticks with two hands, palms down. No one said, '**go**,' but AStermalanlan suddenly lunged at Sky, sweeping her stick right to left at her cousin's head. Sky blocked the attack, and then hell broke loose. The women fought with what appeared every intention of trying to kill each other.

They did not limit their attacks to the sticks, throwing karate-like kicks whenever an opening suggested a kick was a good move. They used the entire mat, but neither ever stepped off the twenty-four foot by twenty-four foot square. They were fast, and strong, and evenly matched. Sky used her height and reach advantage when she could, and AStermalanlan used her balance, and slight advantage in speed.

Their footwork was excellent. Neither remained in one spot, yet there was never a missed step, or a stumble. The fight was high intensity. As it progressed, the attacks became shorter, and the moments when one or the other would step backward and both could catch a breath, grew longer.

Six minutes into the battle, Sky side-stepped an attack, placing her at an angle to her opponent. She swept her right leg against her cousin's left knee, and slammed her stick into the other woman's exposed side.

AStermalanlan landed on her left buttocks, the air pushed out in a big **whoomph.** She lay flat on the mat, breathing hard. Sky used her stick to lean on, as she tried to gather oxygen for extremely depleted lungs.

When AStermalanlan began to giggle (yes, giggle), Sky reached down, and helped lift her to her feet. The two were drenched in sweat, which did wonders for how they fit into their clothes.

AStermalanlan tossed her stick to Coop and said, "Your turn."

The stick was heavier than it appeared, about the weight of a strong quarterstaff. It might have been wood, or it might have been an exotic material. It had a slightly rough, unpolished surface. This would make it usable when his hands began to sweat. It was tapered to flat tips at either end, similar to the BO used in karate weapons training. Six feet in length, thicker in the middle at two inches, and perfectly balanced.

He had trained with hand weapons since he began martial arts as an Army brat. He did not twirl it, or give any indication he was comfortable with the concept of using a fighting stick.

"You need to take a few more minutes to recover," he told Sky, whose chest was still lifting and falling quickly as her breathing tried to even out and her heart rate came down.

The room had become an arena, as crew members of different races, male and female, entered, and stood in the rear of the studio. Since they posed no threat, he had not taken his eyes, or attention from the females during combat.

Sky and AStermalanlan used towels from a nearby shelf to dry sweat from their faces and arms. Cooper had a decision to make. No one on board the *Star Gazer* knew anything about humans. Not even the Fell knew that, while he was human, he had gone through a genetic and physical re-engineering program which made his bones nearly impossible to break. His strength nearly six-times a normal human male's. He moved faster by far than average, with quicker response times.

He could either hold back with Sky, even lose to her to conceal his capabilities. He could let it all out, and Fellen and Osperantue alike might believe all humans were as gifted as he. That could give them a stronger position in any negotiations, treaties, discussions, or disagreements that might come up in the future . . . at least until they learned the truth.

Sky's breathing returned to normal. She returned to the mat, stick in both hands, and ready.

Coop placed the pole AStermalanlan had given him on the ground while he unlaced and removed his boots. Sky was confident in her ability. If she was indicative of her race, they were a people used to coming out on top. She was self-assured, not only in her ability to fight, but to win. He liked her, hell, he admired her, but sooner or later an alpha must emerge. Looked like it was about to happen sooner.

He retrieved the fighting stick, stepped onto the mat and faced her. He held the stick loosely, as if uncomfortable, and unfamiliar with the concept of combat using a piece of wood (or whatever). He gave her a sheepish look, and a shrug of the shoulders, physically asking 'Now what?', knowing she would take advantage of his relaxed demeanor.

Sky's pupils dilated. She squinted. Because her right-hand dominated, her stick started at him with an underhand straight swing at his left arm, her left hand pulling backward at the same time her body swiveled. This added as much power into the hit as she could generate. Her plan to numb his arm, and end the fight with one blow.

Cooper simply stepped backward. Simple, but his movement fluid, and so quick Sky's roundhouse swing sent her flying through the blow that never landed. She did not encounter the momentum-stopping resistance she expected. As she moved in front of Cooper, off balance and trying to throw her front foot out to catch her balance, he hit her in the ass with a crescent kick delivered by his left foot, sending her forward and down.

To her credit, she landed in a front roll and came up spinning around to face him. Consternation, not caution on her face. Unwilling to accept his speed had surprised her, she launched herself at him. Her stick became a whirling, twisting weapon she fully intended to beat him with.

Using no more energy than necessary, and with simple hand and body movements to accomplish his goals, Cooper parried every blow Sky rained down. She came high to low, across the body, body spinning, and stick coming at him like a baseball bat, low to high. She threw what amounted to punch after punch, never landing any, always having the thud of his stick blocking hers, regardless of the direction it came from.

The Fellen backed away. Her hair was wet and slick; her arms shiny with beaded perspiration. The tight black outfit molded to every crook and cranny of her body. She had tried to hit him with everything she had. She bent over from the waist in an attempt to pull oxygen into her lungs. The full-on attack had lasted ten minutes. An insane amount of time at the intensity she had maintained. Anyone in less condition would have knocked on the door of a heart attack.

Cooper stood quietly watching her. The stick stood on end, his weight resting upon the thin rod. His breath came deep, but not labored. Sweat beads on his forehead did not drip into his eyes.

He could see the frustration in Sky's eyes. They became a deeper orange-red, and her skin grew darker. She was angry. She was not, however, defeated.

He never landed a blow of his own. He never tried.

AStermalanlan stood within a foot of the mat, at a right angle to Sky. Her mouth open and her breathing raspy. She was excited. She was turned on by the fight. It appeared Fellen, at least the females, were born for physical contact, whether it was sex, or a hand-to-hand battle.

Coop tossed the stick to its owner, and beckoned her onto the mat with his left hand. She accepted the offer. He focused on the space between the two women, allowing him to watch both. He finger-waved the 'come and get it' signal, as he settled into a classic martial arts stance.

The two had obviously practiced combined attacks. They moved into a strategy which sent AStermalanlan first, with Sky a half-step behind.

For the first time that day, AStermalanlan screamed as she swung her stick low, aiming to take Cooper at the knees. The other match had been fought in silence. Now, tricks were used, including attempting to startle your opponent.

Sky was close behind, her swing higher, and from the opposite direction, expecting to take Cooper out when he tried to dodge AStermalanlan. Though weary from the two previous bouts, she looked as quick as before.

Coop turned, right shoulder forward, and stepped on the incoming low stick, timing it perfectly. The stick and AStermalanlan's captured hands ended up flat on the floor. With less than a second to react, he threw his right arm up in a back-fist block, which stopped the higher stick in mid-air. His arm would become deeply bruised, but his re-engineered ulna was stronger than the fighting stick. He dropped his right hand down on the stationary stick that still vibrated in Sky's hands. He pulled, using his strength to send her flailing to land flat on her stomach, half on and half off the mat. There was no acrobatic tumble this time.

He had stepped off the grounded stick to flip Sky, but he used the toss to complete a 360 degree circle. His foot came down on the stick, again pinning it, and AStermalanlan's hands to the mat. She screamed a feline howl, but this time in anger and frustration, not to intimidate, or startle.

Again he stepped off. He turned and walked to the far edge of the mat. He turned back, faced the two women lying on the mat, and waited. His focus on the two of them. Both focused on him. All three aware the spectators were screaming and cheering. Because it held no impact on the confrontation, they ignored the noise. Consigning it to another compartment in their consciousness.

Sky dropped the stick and charged him, no longer caring about being part of a team. She still had not uttered a sound. AStermalanlan was the screamer. She watched Sky's attack, waiting for an opening of her own.

Sky was five-feet away when she launched herself at him. That was a mistake, and demonstrated her training was less formal than it should have been. A body in the air had a speed less than when connected to the ground. The only options available to her now were to slow, and drop. Even had Coop not been reborn faster and stronger, his pre-reengineered self could have taken Sky once she left her feet.

But Sky was not an enemy. She was a friend caught up in the frenzy of battle. Instead of taking her out of the air in a manner most likely to leave her hurt and hurting, he launched himself, somersaulting above her, as she flew beneath him. He came down on his feet and ran towards AStermalanlan, who tried to raise her stick like a lance to fend him off.

He grabbed the end in his right hand, twisted it aside, and came down on the stick with the edge of his left hand, snapping the stick a third of the way down. (Thank goodness it had been a wood or breakable composite. Had it been a type of metal, he might have actually hurt himself with that move.) He front kicked his left foot into AStermalanlan's belly, pushing any air out, forcing her to drop to her knees, and leaving her gasping for air.

Sky grabbed him from behind, by the hair, having recovered from her launch quicker than Cooper could have imagined. She was hopped on pure adrenaline, or an alien equivalent. He covered her hand with his, and pushed his hip backward until his body found hers. Then it was about balance, as he flipped her over his head, and onto her butt.

The women side-by-side and down. He grabbed them by their drenched tops, lifted both up, twisted, and threw them down again, this time onto their stomachs. On his knees between the two Fellen, he pressed, and held them face-down on the mat, both squirming. AStermalanlan was screaming, and howling, and spitting. They raked at his legs, and punched as best they could from the awkward positions. He simply held on and waited.

It was a full minute before Sky, and then her cousin, calmed down enough to realize they had been beaten. They quit striking at his legs, and trying to wiggle from beneath his hands.

"On Earth," he told them, "the contest ends when a fighter is knocked out, a referee stops the match, or an opponent taps their palm down twice on the mat to indicate they surrender.

"Neither of you are unconscious, I really do not want to keep this up until you pass out, and there is no referee. If you would please tap-out, I would appreciate it. I'm spent."

Sky's palm slapped the mat twice, immediately followed by her cousin. Coop let them go. He dropped his head to the mat, acting more exhausted than he truly was. There was little point in letting them, or the wildly cheering crowd, know the fight had taken less out of him than he pretended.

Again, the women surprised him. AStermalanlan rolled to her back, giggling loudly. Sky rolled to her side so she could see him eye-to-eye, as he lifted his head from the mat. "That was the second most fun workout I have had this week," she said with a smile.

AStermalanlan sat up, sweat running off her, auburn hair pasted across her face, and tears of joy running from her eyes.

"Coop," she said, the tilt to her head, "What's a referee?"

# Chapter 16

Once the show ended, and the entertained crew finished congratulating the fighters, Coop and the two Fellen agreed he would shower and change on Angel 7. They would return to their cabin to do the same. After having their butts handed to them, their need to act as security no longer seemed important. Pity on anyone who decided to give the human trouble on his way to or from his ship.

The solitary stroll provided time to see how bad conditions were for the people aboard ship. Despite the huge size of the *Star Gazer*, it was not meant to transport and support over 240,000 refugees, with pets, and even livestock.

He was surprised the gym had been left for exercise and not used as another shelter. The need to release frustrations through exercise did make sense.

If conditions did not change, pets and livestock would become food, or euthanized to save food.

He also recognized the ship operated underpowered, and power sources available strained. It explained why decks were kept cool. The Bosine took a leap of faith by following his instructions to head towards Neptune instead of returning to the wormhole gate. If Space Fleet did not come through, they would perish before they reached the eighth planet. The wormhole may hold a fate as bad. Roll of the dice, but they were betting on an unknown, unheard of race of humans willing and able to help.

Funny, but they were hoping for humanity.

Personally, Coop never felt a lot of faith in humanity, but he did believe in the avatar, Genna, and the AI that was the brains of the 109. Humanity personified by an avatar-human hybrid, and an Artificial Intelligence with a personality. The two of them had to bring the help needed to save these people.

Taking a walkabout the *Star Gazer* may not have been the smartest idea, but Coop needed time for thought. Walking always helped. He exited the lift on a random deck. As he walked the hallway, one less crowded than many he had been in over the last thirty hours, he spotted something familiar.

Two young Bosine, a boy and a girl, were seated on the deck, their backs against the wall, knees bent, with their heads bobbing up and down in rhythm. As he neared them, he noticed the earpieces. Music? Looked like kids listening to music.

Stopping short of the two, he asked, "May I join you?"

Totally involved with what they listened to, until that second neither realized Cooper was in the hallway. At first, both appeared flustered, and even a bit fearful, but in true universal teenage chill, they feigned relaxed. The boy opened his palm to the floor beside him; a clear invitation.

Coop put his back against the wall and slid down, sitting by the male's hip, giving the female the implied protection of the boy between them.

"I'm Coop, the visitor from the planet Earth," he said as an introduction.

The body tapped his chest and said, "Rosz." The girl leaned forward, smiled, and said, "Chaspi."

"What were you listening to?"

Rosz held out a miniature rectangular box, similar to an old fashion flash drive. He pulled his earpiece out, and offered it to the human. Once Coop fixed the piece to his ear . . . music. An instrumental; at least he could not discern a voice. Not any instruments he could name or picture, yet it held elements of brass. Strong beat. Low bass. Almost a jazz riff.

"Cool," he said. Unsnapping a BDU pants pocket, Coop extracted a PDS (Personal Data Storage) mini-pad. Using voice activation, he said, "Chicago Boyz, Mama Blue, play."

The speaker on the pad was tiny, but well built. The rhythm of a five-piece band, led by an alto sax, filled the hallway. People who had been gawking at the trio from a distance, moved closer to hear the rich tones. Rosz and Chaspi rocked and head-bopped to the back-beat. "Cool," Chaspi whispered.

Coop let the song play out and then called up a recent rock-pop number with a faster rhythm and a heavy beat. The tempo was driven by a guitar, and the girl singing had great pitch control, and loved little runs. The youngsters' feet began tapping together, and their smiles grew into grins. Even though Coop was ninety-nine-percent sure the translator did not translate words being sung, it was apparent no translation was required. A party sound was a party sound.

Music and kids. It was oddly satisfying to discover constants existed in the universe.

When the song finished, the man from Earth pushed himself up the wall. "Is this where you guys usually hang out?"

It took a moment while they processed the question, Coop not sure if 'guys' or 'hang out' or both were the block. But Rosz got it.

"Here," he said. "Good a place as any. Close to where we sleep, and this hallway is less crowded than a lot of others. Keeps our mothers happy, too. They do not like us wandering."

"Deck 282, Rosz and Chaspi," Coop said aloud. "I have this friend who is pretty good with communications devices. I'm going to see if she can fix a way we can share tunes."

"Cool," both kids said in unison, and both came to their feet, a lot more gracefully than Coop had imagined Bosine could move. "Nice to meet you, Coop," Rosz said, and put his hand out in a fist. Damn, Coop thought. Years since it began and disappeared on Earth, and billions of miles separating cultures, alien teenagers in outer space used the fist pump!

# Chapter 17

Following his shower and a change of clothing, Cooper used Angel 7's com to contact the bridge of the Star Gazer. He asked the coms officer to pipe him through to the Fellens' cabin.

"Yes, Coop?" Sky replied to his call.

"I'm going to stay on board Angel. I want to use my tactical systems with the data we have to create possible responses, should the Zenge arrive and engage."

"While you work on tactics, we will thoroughly scan the Star Gazer files to see if there is anything more about the Zenge," Sky replied. "Ancillary files about attacks, or systems going dark before the Osperantue realized the Zenge were at war may exist. We may discover a plan, or timeline, or even a method to their attacks that has not been obvious."

Cooper agreed with both the search, and the chance of files that referred to attacks, but not specifically to the Zenge.

"If the Osperantue travel and trade as much as you say, reports, even rumors about attacks moving though the galaxy may exist. If the Fellen trade technology as much as you have indicated, similar rumors might turn up in your data bases."

Sky agreed, saying, "The computers aboard our escape shuttle would have been synced with the main ship. We will run a search through our own files to see if anything seems related. Thank you for the idea, Coop."

"No problem. You two search data bases, and I'll run tactical simulations on what we already have. We can get together in the morning and compare notes."

He grabbed a bottle of water from his cooler and settled onto the comm-tac station chair. A tedious few hours loomed ahead. For comfort, after he turned on the computer system and opened the tactical simulation module, he activated the voice mode. Now he could talk to the system. With the enemy information already stored, and current strengths and weaknesses of Angel 7, as well as the 109 contributed, basic battle plans should emerge.

His feet on the desk, the monitor tilted so he could see it while his head resting on the seat-back, he was comfortable in the comm-tac station. He began working on the boring, but most necessary components of war -- enemy assessments, potential offensive and counter-offensive scenarios, and defense.

It was nearing midnight, and Cooper was close to falling asleep in the chair, when a rapping on the landing gear pulled him from a semi-snooze. A quick voice command, and the comm-tac computer switched to a cctv view of the outside of the ship.

AStermalanlan stood at the base with arms crossed. Obviously Angel's protective forcefield presented no barrier to the Fellen who installed the security system.

He sent the crew lift down, and brought it up as soon as she stepped onto the platform.

Cooper asked "Is there a problem?"

"Yes, there is a problem," she said, her tone somewhere between sulky and angry. Petulant the term that jumped to mind. "You gave ASkiilamentrae a nickname."

She was angry and upset about a nickname. Cooper relaxed, at least they were not under attack by Zenge warships. "It is easier to call her SKY. It wasn't done to upset you."

"Well, I want a nickname, too," and with that AStermalanlan crossed her hands under her top, and pulled it up and over her head. Before Cooper could do more than admire the view, she two-hand pushed him against a bunk. It made contact behind his knees. He landed with a thump. She kicked off her shoes, and wiggled out of her tights. A show worth any cost. She stood nude. Physically, he was responding to the view.

"We don't need to have sex for me to give you a nickname," he told her.

"I would not think so," AStermalanlan replied, moving closer. "Tonight is my turn. You can give me a nickname tomorrow."

The two hours he spent with Sky the previous night seemed like a short feature before the main movie. In two hours he was ragged, and AStermalanlan was most assuredly a screamer. She also had tremendous endurance. Cooper felt like she was getting her revenge for being bested on the mat earlier. Sweet revenge.

# Chapter 18

Coop awoke unable to decide which bunk he was in (they had used three), which direction he faced (his eyes remained closed), and whether any of his muscles would ever again work properly.

The sound of voices forced him to open his eyes. He was still unsure which bunk he was in, but he was facing a wall. He rolled over, and found Sky, and AStermalanlan at the table. The bags for the jerky and dried fruit were empty, and the platter between them.

AStermalanlan turned to look at him. She had obviously showered and dressed. Sky had come aboard, and he continued to sleep. Either he was extremely exhausted or, no, no other option . . . he was that exhausted.

"Do I get a nickname?" she asked

"Storm," he said. "AS - storm — ah — lan — lan," he spoke slowly, emphasizing the variation from *AS-term* to *storm*. "Because you are a total freak of nature. Unstoppable. Unpredictable."

"Storm," she said aloud. "I like it." She returned to her conversation.

Cooper noted his translation ring was lying beside the bunk. He had no idea where his clothes were. At this point in the relationship with the two women, it no longer mattered. He got up, noted the time was after 9:00am. (Why hadn't the alarm gone off? Had it? Had he turned it off without waking up? Where was the chronometer?) Nude, bruised, and battered he headed for the head, and a hot shower. He might have bested the two women on the mat, but, clearly, they were his physical superiors.

A shower, with a shave to remove the stubble that grew in over the last three days; a change into comfortable sweatpants and a short-sleeve sweatshirt; a protein shake -- a second protein shake, and he was ready to face the world.

He joined them at the table, now cleared of left-over breakfast. "Are you both okay with this?" he asked. Better to get any problems dealt with now, than to allow emotions to simmer, and boil over later.

Sky smiled, relaxed. "Coop, I do not know how your race deals with sex. In our experience with other worlds, it is sometimes the same, and sometimes unique. On Fell the ratio of females to males is about four to one. There was a time, in our past, when females did not survive as well as the males, so more girls were born than boys. As we advanced, and our medical knowledge improved, females became more hardy, able to survive and thrive the same as the males. Only evolution has not quite caught up. There are still more females born. It is not unusual for a Fellen male to have four or five females."

He now had a great deal of respect for Fellen males. Any man who could handle more than two of the females was a stud.

"Earth," he explained, "has as many ways of dealing with sex as there are societies -- and we have a lot of societies on Earth. The norm is still one man and one woman, but it isn't a rule. Some members of a group known as Mormons practice the marriage of one man and multiple sister-wives. There are a few places where one woman may have multiple husbands. Having multiple lovers is practiced around the world by men and women."

"You are agreeable to the two of us sharing?" Storm asked.

"Emotionally I'm fine," Coop said smiling. "Physically I might not last a week."

He dropped his PDS mini-pad on the desk in front of Storm. "I met a Bosine kid with a rectangular box with music on it."

"A PPS, a Personal Player Stick," Storm said. "We developed them on Fell and they are traded on dozens of planets. Almost unlimited storage."

"Do you think you can configure a way my PDS," pointing at the mini-pad, "and a PPS can communicate? Share music libraries?"

"I'll have to take your pad apart. It looks pretty simple. Give me a couple of hours." Storm was now translating into contractions. Did sex effect the rings?

They moved on to more pressing concerns.

"Before Storm left last night, we found more information that is probably related to Zenge attacks," Sky told him. "From what we put together, the attack on Fell was their latest, and done simultaneously with the invasion of Osperantue. The Zenge had enough ships to launch multiple attacks, while maintaining a huge numbers advantage."

Storm took over for Sky. "They sent twenty-five ships against Osperantue, knowing they would not be facing fighters. They did not expect much resistance, and they did not get much. They sent one hundred against Fell, knowing we would fight to defend our world to the death if needed."

Sky added, "They have obviously gathered intelligence about the worlds they attack before they invade. While they depend on superior fire-power to overwhelm the enemy, they are smart enough to make plans based on what reactions they expect from their enemy."

She continued. "We have also back-tracked from Fell and Os-perantue. We were checking data for any notes made about systems Osperantue or Fellen ships have visited. Planets or systems where there were problems with contact, or communications. We think we may have found a pattern.

"The initial planet to go unexpectedly silent is called Stamalah 3. Their main source of income is the trading of wormhole charts. It appears the Zenge attacked this system first. It is about five channel jumps from Fell."

"Channel jumps?" Coop asked.

Sky continued his education regarding wormholes, and interstellar travel they had begun before the sparring session the previous day.

"With wormhole travel, we open a gate to a channel," Sky explained. "We travel through a selected channel to a destination. Regardless of where it opens, this is a single channel jump. A jump either takes you to your final destination, or you open another gate, and take it to where it leads. Some gates open where you have from two to a dozen options. Multi-point, or multi-gate locations are like hubs that give you many options for travel. Some channels open where there is only a single other option. Some channels have no other options. The wormhole gate you exit is the only gate available to re-enter. The wormhole channel that brought us to your solar system is like that. It is the only way to or away from your system. Unless, of course, you have space-fold."

Storm continued the lesson. "Over hundreds of centuries, many species have mapped channels, and those maps are traded among worlds like any other commerce. From Fell to where we think the first system was attacked by the Zenge, it would take a minimum of five channel jumps."

"Why do you think it was first?"

Storm answered. "Communications were lost to this system by a number of trading partners. The notes in our data bases indicate this was the first such loss of contact. Also, at least two ships from separate worlds going to, or through this system have been registered as lost. It is not unusual in space travel for ships to get lost, or for trips to get side-tracked. A ship expected to return in one month may not show up for several."

"No one thought there was a major problem, only a couple of lost ships, and no recent contacts by this world with others," Coop said.

"Exactly," Storm agreed. "Unless you were looking for a pattern of lost contacts, missing ships, worlds with trading partners not showing up when the gates were aligned properly, you might not notice anything. Not until a gate opens, and the Zenge come through."

"Are channels the same length?" Coop asked.

Sky answered this time. "No. Following a channel might take a ship a couple of days to reach a gate, or it could take months. That is why it is important to have channel charts. You might take four jumps to reach a location where one jump could have done the same thing, but the four might actually take less time than the one."

"Channels are measured by time, not distance. How many jumps did the *Star Gazer* make, from the multi-channel where they picked you up to entering this solar system?" he asked.

Sky answered this time. "One. But it was a dangerous, desperate decision. The wormhole was not listed on charts. The gate was closest to the ship. Poonch had to either take the channel and hope, or surrender."

"In terms of time?"

"Three of your Earth months," Sky replied.

"No other systems between Fell and Earth?"

"Not exactly," Sky replied, again taking control of the answers. "Systems do not line up. Just like in your own solar system. Occasionally, the eight planets may form a fairly straight line, but how rare is that? Usually they are scattered about on unique orbits around your star. Systems are similar. They are set in space, but not stagnate. Your system was simply the destination of the channel Poonch chose. Take other channels and discover other systems as close, or closer. You could visit a system which requires ten channel jumps, but takes two months. A month closer in time, but a trillion miles further away in space."

"Therefore no reason to expect our system is next in line for attack. Can you track ships going through channels?"

"No. Once a ship is inside a channel, there is no way to know where they are. You can guess if you know when they entered, and the average speed the vessel normally maintains when traveling through wormholes. Even then you are only making an estimate. That still does not provide you a location in space; more of an estimated time of arrival at the gate."

"Okay, that's a lot to think about. Thank you both. I realize it is like teaching a child."

"You are curious, and you are interested. Both are good traits," Sky said.

Cooper was reminded of the saying: Curiosity killed the cat. Considering his present company, he wisely kept it to himself.

# Chapter 19

"There is technology which will allow someone to follow the ion-trail left when a ship enters and exits a gate. The wormhole engines going on or going off emit minuscule amounts of ionized exhaust. You cannot actually track a ship inside a wormhole, but that would not matter. Once they go in, they have to come out."

"Does every world have this technology?" he asked.

"No." Sky answered.

"But the Zenge might?"

"Yes," she said, hesitating a moment to consider. "They might have it on their own, but at least two of the known system we think they attacked had it. They could have stolen it from either of them."

Curious about wormhole channels and flight, Cooper figured now was as good a time as any to get more answers about their method of faster-than-light travel.

"Once a ship is in a channel, must it complete the trip, or can in turn around?"

"If a ship is powerful enough to generate a strong enough forcefield, then it can reverse within a channel. Some extremely powerful ships have been known to reverse from a channel. If the forcefield is not strong enough, the stress reversing through a channel can rip it apart. Most captains, even if they think they possess a strong enough power source, will not take the chance. It is safer to complete the trip and then turn around ."

"Every gate exit is the reciprocal gate entrance?"

"Yes."

"Can ships travel at different speeds within a channel. Say, if I had a more powerful wormhole engine, could I get to the exit before you, even if you started first?"

"Yes."

"Ships can pass within a wormhole channel?"

"Yes, but you would scarcely know it happened. The sensors active within a wormhole will only warn a captain if the exit is too close to a gravitational phenomenon that could destroy or damage the ship at exit."

"That opens up a couple of lines of thought. First, if a warning says, *hey, you are about to exit close to a planet that will tear you apart*, what does the captain do?"

It was Storm who took over. "The captain can reverse, if they have a powerful enough engine, or they can come to a stop and wait for the gravity well to dissipate as the planet moves away from the gate. Without a strong forcefield, the only option is wait, but," and here she held up a finger to get Cooper's full attention, "this is why channel charts are extremely valuable. No one will enter a channel that does not open safely. It is how we plan journeys to distant systems, and plan many journeys years in advance."

"But someone has to try uncharted channels, or your networks would not grow. Like Captain Poonch coming here."

"You take your life, and your crew's life in your hands," Storm told him. "Poonch acted out of desperation, and, honestly, lucked out. Hundreds of ships over thousands of years have gone into uncharted channels and not returned. Those channels are also noted and for sale.

"The Pagora of Stamalah 3, the first planet we believe attacked by the Zenge, are a sect who make a living by sending small, two-person ships into uncharted wormholes. When their ships return, they have newly discovered channels, and these are valuable trade. It is dangerous work, and at least one in twenty of the trips ends with no one returning. They may die, or get caught in a wormhole eddy. They could enter a wormhole channel which requires years to complete."

"If channels flow in both directions, and a ship needed to stop and return to its entry point, why not shift over into the flow's opposite direction, instead of reversing and fighting the current?" Cooper had move forward on his seat, both hands on the table. He was truly engaged in learning about the trials and tribulations of wormhole travel.

"The few reports I know of," Storm explained, "where a ship tried to change directions by actually trying to find the opposite flow, resulted in the ship being shaken so hard the captain feared being shaken apart. This intense shaking was irrespective of the ship's power source. Those who survived to make a report aborted the attempt, and either reversed, or completed their journey. There are no reports, we have found, where anyone was successful in actually switching directions within a channel."

"When a ship receives a warning an exit is dangerous, when does it get the warning, and does it also let the captain know how dangerous the exit?"

Storm again answered. "Warnings happen at the half-way point of channel travel. First a sensor lets the captain and crew know they are half way to their destination, whether that is one day, or one year."

"A point of no return," Coop said.

"I'm sorry. I do not understand," Storm replied, her head on her special little tilt. Finally reminding Cooper of where he had seen that tilt before. He once owned a German Shepard Dog, and it was one smart animal. It would listen to everything Coop said, reacting to what it understood, which was a lot. Sometimes he would simply talk to the dog, more or less thinking aloud, and the dog (*Barkley*, he remembered) would tilt his head as if when he could get his ears and head tilted to just the perfect angle, he would suddenly understand what Cooper was going on about. It was like in movies about the Twentieth Century; people needed antenna on their television sets, and they had to play with them until they found an angle where they could receive the picture without static. Storm used the same tilt.

"A point of no return," Coop explained, "is the point in a trip where you have exactly enough fuel to either complete your mission, or return safely to base. If you pass this point there is no way to return, because you will run out of fuel first. Going ahead is the only option."

"Yes. Exactly," Storm agreed and continued. "Sensors developed over thousands of years detect anything potentially dangerous, and provide as much sensory data as available. By comparing readings to others taken and stored in the computer, you can make a pretty good guess as to what may happen, and how dangerous the exit. As a ship gets closer to the exit, these reports become more detailed. Whether you are heading for a planet, or arriving a few thousand miles closer than originally planned, a decision is made before exiting."

"Do certain ships have better sensors than others?"

"Yes." Storm.

"Depending on what they have to trade for?"

"Yes." Sky.

"And who has the best sensors?"

"Fell," Storm replied, and then hedged by adding, "Perhaps the Pagorans."

"The Fellen posses what is considered the best, and most advanced technology in the known Galaxy systems. Yes?"

"Yes," came the reply, in unison from both women.

"The Zenge invaded Fell." Cooper let the statement hang in the air. "And they took Stamalah 3, who have the best wormhole charts."

Sky finished his line of reasoning. "The Zenge have access to the finest technology available to go along with a library of known and unknown channels. Only they will not. Our ships will have continued to fight until they could no longer do so, and then the crews would leave in escape pods. The Captains, or the highest remaining officers would set self-destructs, and the ship destroyed before any technology could fall into enemy hands.

"On Fell people would have fought any attacks as well. Our most exclusive technology is kept in bunkers. The Zenge will not to get through the security of these bunkers. If they try to blast their way in, those inside will destroy everything before allowing it to fall into enemy hands. The people will take to the jungles, the mountains, and hidden safe-havens around the world. The Zenge will not take an advantage away from Fell."

Cooper did not bother to correct her. Battle changed norms. Well-made plans simply fell apart. Important people got captured, and sooner or later, anyone could break, and any secret revealed. He had to assume the Zenge controlled superior numbers, better-equipped ships, and technological advantages they may not have had before. The trick was to discover what they had before they unleashed it on Earth.

The remainder of the morning was taken up with descriptions of the systems, and the inhabitants of those systems who were, most likely, already overrun by the Zenge. They put together a list of possible advantages the Zenge attained by co-opting technology, information, or other unique or special resources.

The most interesting data regarded crystals. Much of the technology used by a variety of alien species, including a lot of the tech developed on Fell, used crystals for power. Crystal chips provided extended power for small appliances and electronics. Larger crystals were adaptable as energy sources for lighting to weapons systems. Some crystals produced heat.

A race called the Lisza Kaugh, which translated to *Light Cutters*, from the planet Rys, the fourth planet in the Quentle system, traded crystals as their main commerce.

Crystals mined and cut on Rys were used throughout the galaxy.

Space Fleet would soon run out of the Martian crystals used in space-fold arrays. Crystals not native to Mars. They may have come from Rys.

Sky described the Lisza Kaugh as tall, hairy creatures with humanoid faces. Despite the appearance of shaggy animals, they were highly intelligent. They used their technology, and the technology they traded for, to recover planets currently lifeless, but once habitable. They colonized and used the natural resources from those planets to increase bargaining strength.

Dwards were the miners on Rys. Short, hairy, and tough. They delivered the raw crystals to the Lisza Kaugh, who cut and polished them for end use. Cooper noticed the Dwards miners sounded a lot like dwarves, the miners in Tolkien books. The translator ring may have used a variation on the Earth equivalent so he understood the relationship between the Rys races.

He learned a great deal about wormhole travel, galactic trade, and some about what planets produced which trade goods. None of it would help if the Zenge decided to attack the *Star Gazer*, or Earth. It was interesting, and gave him ideas regarding potential future missions, but valuable only if he survived to mount a future mission.

Operational intelligence, data that could effect an upcoming conflict, included any space-worthy ships captured by the Zenge were being converted for battle. If they only captured twenty-five percent of the ships estimated to exist on the planets fallen thus far, the Zenge had access to over five-hundred ships. They had no way of estimating how many they possessed originally.

While they talked, Storm worked with Coop's mini-pad. After almost ninety minutes, she handed it to him. "Place your PDS close to his PPS, say, 'share,' and then tell it what you want to share. If you want something on a PPS sent to your PDS, let them touch, and keep your thumb on the rear of your PDS. Say, 'share,' and what you want to share."

"That's it?" Coop looked at the PDS and then at Storm.

"It was simple. Your PDS is dated technology. The only hard part was trying to remember how those aged circuits worked."

By lunchtime, the three tired of the mental gymnastics. They shared dour moods engendered by the potential for destruction brought by the Zenge. It was daunting to recognize, and accept, they hardly knew anything substantial about the enemy. The lack of intel included where they came from, what, if anything, motivated them, and if there was even an end game to the increasing number of attacks.

After lunch they returned to the mats, only this time the matches held under control. Cooper taught the two women offensive and defensive forms from Earth's martial arts; with and without weapons. Both women demonstrated a strong basis in hand-to-hand, and quickly acquired unfamiliar techniques. Many of the blows delivered in martial arts depended on strike points as targets. Aliens might or might not have similar vulnerable points. He spent most of the time showing either defensive moves based in Aikido, or offensive moves using your opponents actions and lack of balance against them. These techniques were taken from judo, and similar grappling arts.

Sky enjoyed the body tosses the most. Storm, predictably, enjoyed grappling. She grabbed ineligible body parts whenever he rolled, or sprawled with her on the mat.

He still did not know their history, or even their ages for that matter, but he recognized Sky was the big cat, and Storm the kitten in the pair.

After two hours the three agreed to a break. Cooper left for Angel 7 to change, and the two women to their cabin. They would meet in three hours and ask to speak with Poonch to get his, and his officer's, opinions and insights regarding the Zenge.

Each time Cooper returned to the bay, he made sure he walked previously unexplored hallways within the giant cruise ship. Due to the shear size of the *Star Gazer*, decks were crisscrossed with hallway and corridors, creating mazes. He remembered Genna telling him the ship had over 800 flights above a huge open area (the hangar / bay / storage), and engine rooms. He would never know this ship the way he knew the PT-109, but his curiosity encouraged him to investigate different locations before taking the lift down to his ship.

Those he met were always polite and friendly. The young ones, though curious, did not approach, or impede his way. The little ones hid behind adults or older children, their eyes wide in wonder, not fear. These people had been displaced. They were hungry, cold, and living in what amounted to the Earth version of refugee camps, or tent cities. They impressed him. They did not cower. They did not complain. They were too reserved to approach him first, but if he acknowledged someone with a tilt of the head, or a simple "hell-o," they always responded in kind.

He knew his being an alien did not make him unique among these people. Their history included visiting and visitations by aliens for centuries. He felt out of place because being among aliens was, well, alien to him. To them, he was an example of another species who shared the universe. The more he saw, the more kinship he felt.

He made a point to stop on deck 282. He found Rosz and Chaspi leaning against the corridor wall. When they saw their new human friend, they straightened, and added big smiles. As he neared, Chaspi turned and ran away. Confused, he asked Rosz, "What's wrong with Chaspi?"

The Bosine teen barely replied, "You'll see," when Chaspi reappeared, pulling two older Bosine; a man and woman.

"You see," she was saying to them. "I told you we were friends with the man from Earth." Breathless, she stopped, fist pumped Cooper, and introduced him to her parents. They spent a few pleasant minutes in introductions. Coop complimented the parents on their daughter; always a winning formula.

He showed Rosz how they could exchange tunes, and instead of wasting time deciding what, they both simply downloaded the other's complete library. He said his good-byes, apologized for always being sweaty from working out when he ran into them, waved at the parents, and took his leave.

On exiting the lift, and walking towards Angel 7's side-bay, Coop heard deep, mournful sobs coming from a female huddled against the bulkhead. Oddly, she was alone. Normally, so many used the bays as temporary housing, there was little chance of being alone.

He approached. He simply could not avoid it. His nature and his training was to render aid. Not turn away, ignoring a person in trouble. "Is there something I can help with?" he asked.

The woman, older he thought, but still not fully comfortable with Bosine physiology to guess her age. He did not need to know physiology to see she was red-eyed from crying, clearly distressed, and a contusion was rising on the left side of her face.

"He has my daughter," she whispered, choked from sobbing. He followed her eyes to a shanty-looking tent twenty feet away. Three young Bosine males talking, laughing, and milling about in front of the tent. Waiting. He was sure he had seen them before, when the training fight was going on and he was told to stay out of it. It was *training*. Well, this was not training. He had a good idea what was happening, and no one was there to put a restraining hand on him this time.

As he headed for the tent, the three Bosine took note. They assumed defensive positions. One, about six-foot-two, took a position a little ahead of the two shorter, stockier versions on either flank. All three had classic '*I'm a wall*' stances. Hands down, fisted, feet apart, and a steady heel-toe rocking motion. They kept their heads up, and gave him what they assumed were steely eyes.

Since the lead tough guy was being accommodating, and since Cooper had no intention of discussing the situation, he front kicked the guy so hard between the legs his balls (assuming Bosine balls were in the same general area as human's) ended up in his throat. Judging from the look of shear pain and terror, he assumed he had assumed correctly.

Without breaking stride he hit the guy on the left with his right fist, breaking his jaw, and sending him straight to the deck. Completing a rotation too quick to follow, he delivered a left hand to the forehead of the other guy, who had turned at the gasp of terror from the first guy. The blow propelled him ten feet and onto his back. It likely caused severe brain damage.

He pulled the tent's door-flap out and up, and walked into the dimly lit interior.

A Bosine girl, naked, and on hands and knees, was crying uncontrollably. The six-six bully from the previously mentioned training fight, was nude from the waist down. His hands roughly cupping her breasts, slamming into her from behind. The slap-slap-slap of his body against hers drowned out the short commotion, which might have warned him something bad was on the way.

Coop wasted no time, grabbing the son-of-a-bitch by the scruffy hair on his head, and yanking him off the girl, then tossing him out of the tent. Without checking on the girl, he stepped through the flap, following the Bosine, who had tumbled a good six feet before coming to a halt, his pants around his ankles.

The woman he stopped to help came closer. Coop looked at her, and said, "Go help her," nodding to the tent. The woman did not hesitate, running to, and then disappearing into the tent. Coop dropped the front flap, giving the mother and daughter privacy. He allowed the Bosine time to get to his feet, pulling his pants up as he did.

He glowered at Cooper, and made another mistake. He spoke. "You think you are special because you fuck those two Fellen whores. You are not, and I am going to throw your ass into space."

Cooper looked to his right . . . the Bosine's eyes followed, and he noticed two of his guards on the ground, one with his hands between his legs moaning while rocking to-and-fro.

Cooper looked to his left . . . the Bosine saw his other guard out cold on the ground, blood pouring from his shattered mouth.

He looked directly at the bully. There was a reckoning coming. Refugee life was difficult. Tensions build. But you do not, ever, *ever* take those tensions out on fellow refugees. You do not rape.

And you do not murder. In Coop's book, those were capital offenses.

The fight could have been over in ten-seconds. It lasted nearly ten minutes. It was not an actual fight. It was a beating. It was not an ordinary beating, but a demonstration. Some of those watching would have characterized it as *'inhuman'* had the word been in their vocabulary. For some, it lasted too long. For others, it was the lesson he intended. For the girl, now dressed, and leaning against her mother, it was a beat down she intended to watch. For the mother, Cooper was vengeance personified.

Crew members who acted as security poured out of the lift seven minutes into the fight. They had been alerted by security cameras, and were sent by Captain Poonch. Men, and women drawn to the disturbance, stood between them, Cooper, and the bully. It was clear they were not going to allow interference. Word had spread. Everyone knew what had happened, and what was now happening.

A half-minute later Sky and Storm appeared, alerted to the situation by the Captain. They pushed through the crowd, but they did not interfere. A female Bosine spoke to Sky, and pointed at the woman, and her daughter. Sky spoke to Storm, and both looked angry enough to fight anyone who did try to stop the beating.

No one moved to help the three males who were down, and most likely in critical condition.

No one tried to stop Coop, as he finished the beating by snapping the rapist's neck. It was audible, and obvious. No one tried to stop him as he walked away, moving through the crowd, past the guards, away from Sky and Storm, and to his ship.

No one followed him, not even Sky or Storm. He wanted solitude. They left him alone.

# Chapter 20

Daniel Marcel Cooper had killed before. Killing someone who deserved it did not bother him. It was his other actions that bothered him. Inside of three days, he made first contact with extraterrestrials, and discovered another alien species possibly on the verge of attacking Earth. He had sex ( a lot of sex) with two females of another species, and killed at least one, and possibly four aliens. Events were moving too fast. He needed everything to slow down. He had to calm down. His emotions were in over-drive. It was time for more thought, and a lot less action.

He was trained to act without emotions clouding those actions. Over the preceding years he had pushed many emotions away, and buried others beneath duty, responsibility, and obligation. In the process he pushed many of the people who were his friends away as well. As Admiral Patterson enumerated before he left EMS2, only five people had been able to withstand his decision to insulate himself from the world.

Those emotions worked their way into his psyche, now no longer tethered to that world.

He took a hot shower, washing the blood from his hands, and splatter from everywhere else. He threw everything he had worn this day into the wash/dry unit. He sat cross-legged on Angel's deck in his comfortable sweats. He dropped into a deep meditation state.

The *Star Gazer's* comms officer tried to contact him. He ignored him.

There was light, followed by heavy rapping on the tripod leg of the ship. He ignored the request for attention, knowing it was Sky and Storm.

After four hours he ate an MRE supper, and downed three bottles of cool water to quench his dehydrated body.

He dressed in his black combat fatigues, this time strapping a black matte surgical steel knife into its custom sheath on the left side of the belt. He reached up into a high cabinet, and pulled out a black baseball cap with the SPACE FLEET Earth and Circling

Comet Logo. He put this on, knowing the curved bill, and well-worn cap gave him an even more menacing appearance.

The combat dress, and being armed, was to help him recover a proper mindset. He was a combat pilot. Captained the fastest, heaviest weaponed ship in Space Fleet. He was here to represent Earth. He had not done his job, instead, behaving like a tourist.

His dress was also to make sure others, those from Osperantue and from Fell, recognized he was military, not diplomat. He intended the clothing to act as a physical barrier, as he rebuilt his emotional barrier.

He took his seat in the cockpit, and keyed the communications mike. "*Star Gazer*, this is Captain Cooper."

"Yes, Captain," came an immediate reply. Someone had made sure comms were being monitored in case he called. He was quite certain they were not expecting contact from anyone else in this solar system.

"Would you ask Captain Poonch if he could meet me on your bridge in thirty minutes?"

"The Captain agrees, Captain Cooper." Another quick response. Poonch was obviously near the comms station.

"Thank you, Comms. Could you locate the Fellen, and ask if they could join us at the same time?"

"The Fellen are seated on the deck beneath your ship, Captain. Do you want me to contact them, or would you prefer to do so?"

"I'll handle it, thank you Comms. Cooper out."

Cooper left the cockpit, closing, and locking the door behind him. He activated the lift, sending it down for the women.

"We have a meeting with Captain Poonch on the bridge in twenty-five minutes," he said. "Is this a problem?"

Two negative head shakes.

"I know you could have bypassed the codes and entered without my permission. I appreciate being given the time alone."

Two slight shrugs, the '*no problem, anytime*' kind of gesture. Funny how body language was more universal than language-language.

"Are you two okay?" he asked, beginning to worry about the silent treatment.

"Well," Sky began. "Well, you kind of look dangerous . . ."

"And very edible," Storm added with a tiny smile.

"And we don't want to do anything to make you angrier," Sky added.

"Or jump you because we only have enough time to get to the bridge," Storm finished.

In spite of everything, every lecture he gave himself, every promise regarding remaining military, and structured, strict and distant. In spite of every damn thing which had happened, he smiled. That broke the ice. Sky and Storm fell into his arms, and there was one big group hug.

Pushing them away, gently, he said: "Let's go."

He hoped his menacing appearance would have a better effect on the Captain, and others aboard the *Star Gazer*, than it had on the Fellen. He did not think he would survive a group hug with 240,000 aliens.

# Chapter 21

They arrived five minutes early for the meeting with Captain Poonch. He met them on the command bridge and led them to a side chamber, the *Star Gazer's* equivalent to C-Tac aboard the 109.

Everyone along the path to the command sphere, everyone on the command sphere, and those on the bridge noticed, and noted Captain Cooper's appearance. Eyes travelled from the stern face to the combat dress. He knew eyes lingered longest on his sheathed blade. The knife was an archaic weapon to most, and therefore deadlier looking.

If Poonch had been planning on giving him a dressing down for his actions in the bay, he held it in. He asked politely, "How can I help you, Captain Cooper?"

The four of them sat at a table designed for ten. They took seats at one end, Captain Poonch at the head of the table, with Cooper on his right, and the two Fellen on his left. With his guests dressed in battle black, the blue and white clad Poonch must have felt more than a little awkward. He handled himself well though, garnering points from Cooper, since Poonch was a cruise ship captain, and not a military commander.

"Their conditions?" Cooper asked.

Poonch knew who he was inquiring about, and played no games. "One has a broken jaw, and several teeth missing. He is in serious but stable condition. One still unconscious with brain swelling. Not sure when he will wake up, or if he will wake up. One who will never sire children. Swollen and in shock. Critical, because the surgery required to recover his testicles was difficult. One dead."

"The girl and her mother?"

"Both moved to a cabin in the command sphere. Both have had medical attention. Both had lots of bruising, but nothing broken. The girl is young and was a virgin. There is physical and emotional trauma. We have a therapist aboard who is willing to speak with the girl when, and if, she decides she needs to talk."

"Thank you for taking care of them," Cooper said. It was an honest appreciation of the Captain's actions, again raising his approval rating of the Bosine.

"I am ashamed of what happened under my watch," Poonch admitted, "I would have done anything, and everything for those two women."

"Understood," Cooper replied. "Sir, with all due respect, within a few minutes of my altercation with those four, a security detail arrived. Obviously you have closed circuit monitors aboard this ship. Why wasn't anything done when the mother was attacked, and her daughter taken?"

Poonch sighed, and his shoulders drooped. The weight of his world beginning to wear the officer down. "We escaped Osperantue with a skeleton crew, Captain. We cannot watch every location. More turmoil occurs aboard my ship than I am aware. A crew member happened to see a monitor showing your fight. It was luck only. Since I could not know the cause of the fight, I sent crew members down to intercede. As you may know, my people were unable to get past the crowd."

"Captain, I was in a rage. I don't know if that translates. I was so angered by the attack on the girl, I could not, no, I DID not think. I acted, and I allowed anger and disgust to rule my response. I want you to know, I do not excuse my actions. While saving the girl was the correct thing, beating the bully to death was wrong. In my rage, had your crew members tried to intervene, they would also have been harmed. I'm sure not to the extent of the four who beat the mother and abducted her daughter, but still, it would not have been pretty."

Captain Poonch leaned forward, trying to analyze Captain Cooper. For the first time, honestly appraising this Earther. "You could have stopped a dozen of my crew?"

"Yes," Cooper said, and Sky and Storm echoed the word. Poonch turned to the women.

Sky said to him, "Captain Poonch, you know the skill Fellen possess, both in technology, and in hand-to-hand combat?"

"Of course," Poonch replied. "The galaxy is aware, you do not cross a Fellen, and why."

"Captain, I promise you this, if a dozen Fellen males in the prime of their lives tried to intervene, Captain Cooper could have bested them."

Whether taken by awe, or plain old-fashion fear, Poonch looked at the human with renewed respect. Such a comment from a Fellen was not taken lightly.

"This is important, Captain," Cooper said, bringing the conversation to where he wanted it, and away from the fight. "I will defend your ship against the Zenge, or any other species who would attack it. The people of Earth will always protect and defend those who need it, especially from attacks by bullies, gangs, or a hoard of star ships.

"I give you my word as a fellow officer, the rage you saw in the bay will not compare to the rage the Zenge will face. From what I have learned in these last three days, they are a plague infecting the galaxy.

"Someone must stop them. I cannot speak for Space Fleet or the people of Earth, but I know their hearts. We will figure out a way to fight the Zenge, and we will defeat them."

"Captain Cooper, if you are an example of humans, then I have no fear you will do exactly what you say. What can I do to help?"

Cooper represented one of twelve out of four billion humans, but was not about to tell Poonch. He needed the Captain, his crew, and the 240,000 aboard the *Star Gazer* to maintain hope. They had little else, and the rape below was an indicator anarchy could soon follow. Cooper knew the signs. After the Eastern Pandemic, which resulted in more than half of the Earth's population perishing, anarchy was a way of life for the billions left alive. The erosion of morals, and disdain for law came on quick, and easy. It took a strong hand, and a lot of forceful exhibitions of power to regain control. Neither the mass panics, nor the aftermath — anarchy or the fight to return sanity — were pretty.

"Find refugees who can watch monitors, or handle simple crew functions. Train them enough to make them serviceable. Allow your main crew rest."

Cooper continued. "Give the people on those overcrowded decks access to alarms. If something bad happens, let them tell you. Don't hope a monitor is being watched in a moment of need.

I know you have 800 decks, plus the hangars, and service areas. Your people don't come across as the types to trip alarms for no reason. It would provide them extra security, and perhaps a sense of relief."

"You make sense, Captain. Much of it I should have already thought of," Poonch said, without pride. Weary.

"Captain Poonch, have you ever served in your world's military?" Cooper asked.

"Our world has not had a true military in a thousand years," the Bosine replied. "We have a few police and security, and a space guard, which is more to assist than to arrest."

"Then please take this from a man who has served in the military his entire adult life." Coop allowed the comment to sink in before continuing. "You have done a remarkable job under incredibly difficult conditions. You have saved your ship and hundreds of thousands of your fellow people. You have saved the lives of the two Fellen sitting here, and escaped the Zenge, not once, but twice. If you were human, you would receive our highest medals for honor and bravery."

Poonch might not know what medals were, but Coop could tell he caught the gist. There was a straightening to his spine, and a swelling of his chest. Perhaps a swelling of his eyes, too.

"Captain Cooper, is there anything more we can do . . . I can do?"

"Keep your ship on course and your people safe, Captain. Exactly what you have been doing. The *John F. Kennedy* will return in a few more days, and then our options become more numerous, and more obvious." Cooper stood, and the other three, even the seemingly mute Fellen, stood with him. Coop faced Poonch, came to attention and snapped a salute, fingers to bridge of cap, ramrod straight. Poonch had no idea what to do, but quickly mimicked the Earther's action, lifting his double-digits to his brow. Cooper snapped the salute down and said, "Captain, it is an honor to serve with you."

With fences mended before they could actually fall down, Cooper, Sky and Storm left the Captain a much happier Bosine than the one they found.

They made it off the bridge, down the hallway, and into the lift before Storm could no longer contain her giggles.

"You gave the entire ship hope," she said, a mix of admiration and mirth in her tone. Then she gave him her signature tilt and added, "I hope your people come through."

"So do I," he agreed, more tired now than he had been after the fight below decks, which had occurred after the sparring session with Sky and Storm.

When they entered the Fellen's cabin, the furniture was rearranged. The two beds pushed together, and the table they ate and strategized around pushed against the wall where a bunk once sat.

"Redecorating?" he asked.

Sky smiled, and Storm giggled again. "We thought it more comfortable. You need to rest. We intend to provide the effort."

Cooper was going to protest. He was. Really. He was going to tell them they were going too far too fast. They needed to slow down, gain perspective. He was going to say these words, and leave for a night alone aboard the Angel 7, but, damn if they didn't pull their tops off at the same time. Faced with the prospect of both, he decided surrender was a better option. Yep, surrender was his only option.

At least by starting now, he might get a full six hours of sleep. Maybe. Maybe not. Maybe, suddenly, he did not care.

# Chapter 22

A sound woke Cooper. Not anything that startled him awake. Nothing that indicated any danger. He lay sandwiched on the pushed-together bunks, with Sky on his front, and Storm spooning behind him. It was not a noise from them.

There it was again. Not a noise, but a voice. He could not understand what it wanted. Then he realized it came over the cabin's speakers, and he also realized he was not wearing his translation ring. Whoever was talking also did not have a ring.

He wiggled enough to loosen the covers, and arched his body over Sky, who was closest the edge of the bunk, then slipped onto the deck, making sure the blankets stayed snug over the two still sleeping. His translator rested on the table near his utility-weapons belt and cap. He snapped it on, then said, "This is Cooper."

"Captain Cooper," the voice now making complete sense, "Captain Poonch urgently requests your presence on the command bridge, sir."

"On the way," he replied. Moving quickly, and trying to retain the quiet, he dressed in yesterday's black fatigues, slipped on his boots, left his weapon and cap where they lay, and exited the cabin. The two women snuggled in closer to each other for warmth, but neither opened an eye, or noted his departure.

He quick-timed it down the hallway to the lift. He was on the bridge of the Star Gazer in less than four minutes.

The bridge of the cruise ship was busier than he had ever seen. Every station staffed, and every monitor and computer system on and operating. He knew Poonch had not had time to act on his suggestion of getting civilians to assist, so these were crew members. He also recognized the tension in the air. These people were focused and anxious.

Poonch stood looking over the shoulder of a crew member who was monitoring a screen and adjusting touch sensitive pads with both hands. A second crew member, seated adjacent to the one being watched by the ship's captain, nudged Poonch, and made him aware of Coop's presence.

Poonch waved Cooper over.

"Ships are coming through the wormhole gate," Poonch said.

They were now four days away from the gate. Was it far enough?

Poonch continued: "We do not know how many, not at this distance, but it appears, perhaps six or seven. We do not think we have been scanned yet. I have had every non-essential system on the ship turned off or muted. My hope is if we make as little signature as possible, we may be far enough away to be confused as more space debris. I have also stopped engines. Running at this time makes little sense. Hiding makes more sense."

The Earth captain said nothing. Poonch was making smart decisions, and it was his ship. Coop simply nodded his understanding, and his mute agreement. There was no place between Pluto and Neptune they could use to conceal their presence. The only option was to maintain a low profile, and hope at this range, they would go unnoticed.

"We will drift, and wait, and watch," Poonch said.

"Will they pick up your scans?" Cooper asked.

"We are simply using highly evolved optics now. We were a cruise ship, and bringing spectacular views to our customers was our pride. The *Star Gazer* is literally a star gazer, designed to go to beautiful and unusual places in space. We provided those booking passage views which were unparalleled." (Sales pamphlet stuff, nonetheless, impressive.)

Poonch turned and looked around his bridge and crew. "Once our aft scans picked up the gate opening, we used our scanning technology enough to find out as much information as possible. When the first ship exited, we continued to scan for another few minutes. Our scan signatures were lost in the disruption which occurs at a gate entrance when the two types of space, natural and wormhole, collide. As soon as we thought the last ship had exited, and the gate began to close, we shut down operations, started to drift, and turned on our optics."

"Impressive, Captain," Cooper said to the Bosine.

"Self-preservation," the Bosine replied, and continued, "We are now 3,800,621 miles from the gateway. Our optics are good. If they move in our direction we will see everything much clearer. At this range, their systems may or may not pick us out of space. It depends on how good their technology is, and how unlucky we are."

"How long will you drift?" Coop asked.

"If they cannot locate us and leave, or if they start in our direction, there is no longer any point in drifting. I will start engines, and push as hard and fast as I can. But, Captain Cooper, if they find us, and they chase, they will catch us within four or five days."

"Roger that," Cooper said, falling into Fleet-speak. "I'm going to get my ship prepped, in case we need her for cover. I'll ask Sky and Storm [Poonch looked at him questioning the names] -- ASki-ilamentrae is SKY, and AStermalanlan is STORM. I prefer shorter names. It makes it easier to communicate, especially in battle."

Poonch nodded. Maybe he understood or maybe not. He did not comment one way, or the other.

"I will send Sky and Storm to the bridge. They are the communications and technology experts, so maybe they have ideas to enhance your systems."

"They were quite helpful when we first took them aboard, Captain Cooper," Poonch said. "In the month's before reaching your solar system, they turned our civilian systems into highly functional military-grade hardware and upgraded the software. Without these changes we would have been unable to monitor the wormhole gate from this distance. Honestly, it was Sky who taught me about the distortions that occur at wormhole gates and natural space, and the time available for electronic scanning before it would become detectable."

The amiable Bosine gave a small shake of his head before continuing.

"Having said that, and appreciating what they have already done, Fellen do not give away their knowledge. I am sure they could do more to enhance our systems, and perhaps now, with you aboard, they might."

"I'm sure they will do everything they can." Cooper assured him. "Please let me know if anything changes." With nothing more to accomplish, he took his leave from the bridge. Since he was not wearing his cap, he did not salute the ship's captain, and since the captain had no idea of the protocols of Earth's military meeting and greeting rituals, it did not matter.

He returned to the cabin. Sky and Storm still snuggled under the covers, and he thought briefly about rejoining them. Instead he undressed, this time his clothes actually made it onto a chair folded, and not rumpled and tossed on the deck. He entered the tight shower stall. One-second of spray, and he realized the *Star Gazer's* systems were indeed off line, because the water, normally barely warm, was freezing.

He bit his lip, withheld the yelp, and figured he could endure the cold for a quick Navy shower — water on, water off, soap up, water on, out. Then Storm decided to join him, and in the tight one-person stall, her body heat felt wonderful. But it would not last under that spray. He quickly soaped her up, totally enjoying how her wet, slick body felt under his hands. Their passion turned the ancient practice of taking a cold shower to reduce sexual desire, into the native eskimo practice of sex in an ice house.

Though incredibly cramped in the shower, somehow he entered from behind her. He pressed her against the bulkhead, hands cupping the full breasts, and very, very hard nipples. They lasted less than a minute.

Sky waited with towels, and took their place in the shower. A loud yell escaped when the spray hit her skin. As soon as she came out, Cooper was there with a towel to briskly dry her, using the friction to warm her skin.

They dressed quickly, Cooper remembering the first time he had seen the girls on the 109's monitor, unable to not notice the hard nipples beneath the skin-tight tops they wore. Reality was so much nicer than a monitor.

Of course he realized he was using them, and their bodies, as a distraction. He had little doubt the Zenge would eventually acquire the ship and start for them. They had no time left for any normal activities. After this, the ship would prepare for battle, and his attention would move to surviving until the 109 arrived.

"The Zenge are in the solar system," he finally told them.

They made short-term plans. Cooper to Angel 7, and Sky, and Storm to the bridge. They would meet at Cooper's fighter for lunch and updates. Long hugs, and short kisses, and they set off on their separate ways. Not the worse way Cooper had ever deployed.

# Chapter 23

On his way down, Coop thought about the Osperantue he saw along the way. The Bosine made up the majority of those on board. There were also Posine, with similar facial features, but shorter, stouter, and their skin a darker shade of pink than the Bosine. Woolifer; fine-boned and slender. Their noses wider, their eyes closer set, and with much smaller ears. They were seldom seen because it appeared they were adept at technical and mechanical matters. They were the ones most likely taking care of the areas less visited. They worked with the operational systems in the ship which maintained heat and cold; atmosphere; the air scrubbers which regenerated breathable air from exhaled gases; the water reclamation and recycling, and the waste reclamation and recycling systems.

The Fray made up the fourth Osperantue race, but he had not met any, and remained unaware of them except by name. If they were aboard, they either looked similar to the other three races, and he did not recognize the differences, or stayed to themselves.

He thought about the Fellen, but not about being personally involved with Sky and Storm. He thought about the species. A race of technological wizards who had evolved from fighters. People who fiercely guarded their secrets, and their fellows.

A species who traded in high-end electronics across trillions of miles of space and maintained a tribal community at home.

Osperantue and Fell had been attacked and overrun, and they were only the latest planetary systems to fall. There were several other worlds invaded before these last two, with any number of races inhabiting each world. These were now people on the edge of extinction, if not already gone, because one species decided it wanted everything, and had the strength to take it.

After over 10,000 years, humans finally agreed to create a single, centralized government to mange the planet. Considered an impossible dream, and taking a horrific pandemic as a catalyst, it happened, and in his lifetime. Now, when they were on the edge of reaching out to other worlds, an alien species might be on their way to destroy everything humans had accomplished.

The Osperantue, Sky, and Storm, believed they had stumbled onto a superior race. A species with the technology to fold space and time, which allowed them access to anyplace within the solar system, or anywhere in the universe without the limitations of wormhole travel. A world with incredible ships like the *John F. Kennedy*. Not knowing she was a one-and-only. The first, everyone hoped, of more to come, but now the first, and the only.

These aliens were fleeing other aliens, looking to Earth as a safe-haven, and a possible champion.

The truth revolved around the tale of a species which had barely survived. Time and time again, the planet, outside forces, or civilized mayhem had come near completely destroying humanity. It was only in the last thirty years mankind found sure footing, and then only because of a world-wide plague, and the pure dumb luck of finding ancient technology with "how-to" guides regarding space and star travel.

If they survived this attack by the Zenge, then he would come clean with his alien allies. If they lost, then it would not have mattered.

# Chapter 24

Sky climbed to the access tunnels above the command bridge. The forward, or command sphere, of the Star Gazer had dozens of antenna, as well as information gathering nodes, cameras, and dishes. Most species were notorious about saving money, and used barely serviceable equipment.

She carried a bag with Fellen-designed boosters and cable connectors designed to improve carry times, quality of sound, and picture. There was a signals booster unit, a black box, which would accept radar or sonar related rebounds, and interpret what they encountered in greater detail.

The first item to receive her attention was the deep-space video system. A cursory scan, and she moved to the audio systems. Whoever installed the video put in the best optics and receivers available. Unfortunately, not so much attention to detail with the other scan and recovery systems. Heavy sigh as she melted into a cross-legged position in front of the audio array. This was going to take a few hours.


Storm appeared on the command deck like her nickname; a force of nature ready to kick butt. She caught Poonch's attention, and motioned him to her. A quick explanation of her presence, and the Captain made a general announcement to the bridge crew explaining whatever she asked for she got.

The bridge's semi-circle design wrapped around the Captain's chair and pedestal. A pilot and navigator console with two chairs sat directly in front of him. From port to starboard (left to right), the semi circle had stations for long-range radar or sonar, audio scanning, and communications. The video scanner console moni-tored feeds from both interior, and exterior cameras, and set to the right of the concave view screen, which dominated the forward wall.

Next came the interior environmental monitors and controls, with engineering and power systems monitors, and the bridge over-ride command station.

Storm needed to appraise the systems from radar to communications, and then use her knowledge and skills to improve those systems as best she could with the tech she had available.

It was good they had a few days head start on the Zenge. She would need the time.


Captain Poonch was not content to sit in his chair and wait for the Zenge, or watch others at work.

He had taken Captain Cooper's suggestions to heart. He was already in the process of having his maintenance crew install alarms near the cctv monitors on every deck of both spheres.

There had been a ship-wide announcement, the Captain was seeking the help of civilians with any technical or engineering skills. Over 21,000 Osperantue from the four races signed up to assist. It was his job to make sure they were assigned areas where they could assist with as little on-the-job training as possible. He already placed 1,500 working on the deck alarm systems, which would take less than a day. Without the help, it would have simply been impossible for his limited crew to do the job.

He selected another 1,200 for their advanced knowledge, skills, and work histories, sending them to departments throughout the ship to act as helpers. The rest he gave his thanks, and kept their locations in case of future need.

All this accomplished in less than twelve hours. He was exhausted and proud, but on the whole, exhausted.

He had not made a general announcement regarding the Zenge's appearance in the solar system. His crew knew. The citizen volunteers would soon know, and they would spread the news. He was going to need to make it official before panic set in.

There were already rumblings regarding the power shut down, the cold water, the cold corridors, and the darkness. His people completed their business using emergency battery lighting. Even the bridge crew used battery lights not hooked into the power system, therefore, not registering on enemy scans. The Zenge had not located them yet, and while he maintained scarce hope, he was not making any announcements until the Zenge either turned to chase, or left the solar system.

He sat quietly in his command chair. First, watching the Fellen, *Storm*, which was actually easier to say than her whole name, and the translation did fit the Fellen's personality, and then falling into a deep slumber. His crew said nothing. Their Captain had earned their respect, and they respected his need to rest.

Cooper began his pre-launch checks at the communications and tactical station in the cabin. Situated left of the door to the cockpit, the comm-tac operator could easily communicate with the pilot, and co-pilot by radio or voice. The noises of war were absent in space, unless atmosphere venting from an exploding ship provided enough oxygen for a muted blast.

The comm-tac officer constantly ran scenarios before and during battle. They input updated information, and created strategies on the move to provide the ship with any tactical advantages. It was up to the pilot, who was in command, to decide what information, or strategy was applicable to the immediate situation.

He placed icons that represented friendly and opposition ships on screen. When needed, these icons would provided tactical info, like weapons status, armament stores, speed, location, status of systems, and strength of forcefields. In the case of the Zenge, as any pertinent information regarding their ships was observed, and added, updates would simultaneously occur.

The icons allowed for private or public communications with pilots, crews, or individual computers between ships. He doubted seriously he would have communications with the Zenge.

He next inspected the co-pilot's station, starboard side of the cockpit. The co-pilot's controls were duplicates of the pilot's, with one addition. The co-pilot acted as the primary gunner aboard Angel 7, and had access to two joy-sticks. They pulled out and up from underneath the main console. The co-pilot could engage weapons using computers, or aim by line of sight, firing independently. The co-pilot targeted and fired the ship's railgun using the left stick. The wing-mounted laser cannons operated with the right. When weapons were readied, a heads-up display would appear. Comm-tac constantly updated the display with weapons' status data. Confident the co-pilot's systems were functional, he moved over to his seat.

Angel 1, the next-gen prototype he test-flew twenty-five years earlier, came with a seat much less comfortable. He had been the first human to test an operational space-fold engine, and the first to fly faster than .05 ls. He was the test pilot who discovered when the primary engine was active, it produced a sonic forcefield that surrounded the ship. It was dubbed *The Cooper Effect*, but not by him.

The pilot, using trigger-buttons mounted to the yoke, could fire any weapon. Not as accurately as the co-pilots joy sticks, but effective. More importantly, his helm controls were more responsive, and he had an aspect stick at his left hip. He could quickly put the fighter where he wanted. He could use the lack of gravity, lift, drag or friction in space to make impossible spins, turns, pivots, and any maneuver he decided to try. He could also shift power plants, turning the ship into a mono-wing aircraft or landing shuttle. The primary engine could propel Angel 7 up to 250,000 mph in outer space.

And he had space-fold. The laser-crystal array power plant fired a number of laser beams into a multi-faceted crystal kept in a faraday cage. The crystal's released energy created a 'bubble' around the ship, causing space-time to fold in the direction the ship was heading. Navigation computers could calculate how much time they needed to remain in a fold to reach an exact location, whether it was a hundred star systems away, or only a thousand miles.

Cooper checked his heads-up tech for all systems. When he was satisfied with piloting and display systems, he checked his weapons.

Laser cannons replenished themselves. But they could overheat. He set the wing cannons to fire on an alternating pattern. He could change to a single cannon firing repeatedly, but the alternating pattern was the best to start, allowing for slower heat build up. Once a cannon over-heated, it could take from minutes to hours for it to recover.

The railgun fired kinetic projectiles (rods) of hybrid composite metals, or it could operate with NNEMP shells, called nymphs.

The rails, made of ceramic-alloy composites, produced less friction, resulting in less heat. The gun lowered from the hull, and the cold of space helped prevent super-heating. It would fire until the rods and nymphs ran out.

Projectiles from the railgun traveled at Mach 10 (7,672.69 mph), and without friction to slow them down, they might travel forever. A ship far enough away could avoid the projectiles, if they saw them. The hybrid-rods surprisingly compact, but dense, and deadly at the extreme velocity they traveled.

Nymphs are shells with micro-generators inside. These generators created an electro-magnetic pulse, or EMP. When a nymph hit, the electromagnetic pulse (EMP) would temporarily interfere with electrical, magnetic equipment, and fields.

Space Fleet ships created a sonic force field with their sub-light engines, but it appeared the rest of the known galaxy created protective force fields using electro-magnetic dynamos. Nymphs could dampen, or completely disrupt a forcefield created by electrical or magnetic generators.

In order to penetrate Angel 7's sonic force field, a weapon would need to match the exact pitch of the field at the moment of impact. This was nearly impossible, because the pitch changed as the engine rpm's changed. The concussion, depending on the size, and strength of the weapon, was more likely to cause internal, rather than external damage. Injuries were usually the result of objects, or people not locked down being thrown about the ship.

Angel was ready. He hoped he would not need her.

# Chapter 25

Coop met Sky and Storm in their cabin. He brought dinner: protein bars and a secret stash of venison jerky.

Storm momentarily caught between anger he had been holding out, and ecstatic they had more jerky.

Sky was too tired to show any emotion. The cramped confines where she needed to work to access Star Gazer's systems, plus the hours it took to upgrade everything (she eventually even tweaked the video feeds), left her dirty, and with muscle kinks — understanding the meaning of the term better now. She ate her protein bars and jerky in silence, sipping water from a bottle.

While they were quietly eating, enjoying the down time, and the easy silence between them, Sky reached into her satchel. She pushed two translator rings across the table. She gave one to Coop and one to Storm.

"They do everything your current one does," she explained. "I added a private com-link so the three of us can talk. No one else can listen in. It will work across great distances when boosted through a ship's communication system. I set them to automatically seek the strongest power source to allow minimal time between what is said and how quickly the other one hears. Of course, the longer the distance, the longer the lapse."

"How do I use it to reach you, or Storm, or the two of you?" Cooper asked, unclasping the one around his neck, and placing it on the table.

"Nicknames," Sky replied smiling. "If I say *Coop*, it goes to you. It continues in private mode until I say my nickname and *out.*"

"Saying *Coop, Sky, or Storm* is enough to open private communications?"

"Just remember to say your nickname, and *out* to close the channel. If you do not it will remain open, and others able to hear your further conversations. At times, possibly a good thing, and others, perhaps embarrassing."

"That is so smart," Storm said, replacing her ring with the improved version. "Hey, it is also lighter!"

"I have been working with alloys I discovered aboard the *Star Gazer*. It is lighter, clamps, and unclamps with a touch, and is nearly impossible to break or bend."

"When did you find the time?" Storm asked.

"Well, reconfiguring and updating the scan systems meant a lot of downtime while I ran diagnostics. Without anything better to do, I worked on the translators."

"All I did while running diagnostics was watch the Zenge ships on the wall display. Everyone kept watching, and waiting, and nothing ever happened."

"They are sending out active scans," Sky said. "At least the four-day lead means any ion trails from our engines have dissipated. By now they will have blended with naturally occurring gases."

"Why did they wait four days?" Cooper asked. He was not expecting an answer. "You said three ships dropped in on the *Star Gazer* after she picked you up at the multi-channel. Three to one are pretty good odds. Why wait?"

"Good odds are not great odds, and the Zenge prefer great odds" Sky said. "There is also the size of the *Star Gazer*. If they took life-form readings, and realized they had over 240,000 potential captives, maybe they wanted more soldiers to control that many captives. Remember, too, ships travel at different speeds within wormhole channels. We have no clue as to when they launched the chase. Or where they originated."

"Captain Cooper?" the comms officer's voice came over the cabin speaker.

"Yes."

"Captain Poonch requests your presence on the command bridge, sir. The Zenge are moving."

Moving which way, Cooper wondered. Then said, "Sky, you stay here. Take a shower, even though it is cold. You have a lot of grit on you from those access tunnels. Storm, you come with me. And Sky, after the shower go to bed. You're exhausted, and no good to anyone without rest."

Sky did not try to object, nodding her head in agreement.

Storm and Coop left for the command bridge. No point in wondering aloud about what was happening, they walked in silence.

Poonch stood before the video wall, hands clasped behind his back. He looked over his shoulder to note the arrival of Coop and Storm, then returned to the screen. Even with the super HD optics, there was little to see. Just dots on a black screen.

He brought the two up to date while continuing to watch the screen. "They are making way straight at our current position. I have no doubt their scans located us. We were wrong about the number of ships. There are eleven. We have been tracking them for an hour in to determine speed. There are three out front moving at 80,000 mph. Three more of similar size following at about 76,000 mph. Two more at 75,000 mph, and these two are different in shape, but too far away to determine exact types. An immense one at 73,000 mph, and two much more smaller ships at the rear, traveling at 40,000 mph."

"We estimate the first three Zenge ships will catch us in three days, twenty-two hours, and fifteen-minutes, if we restart engines and leave now. If we remain in drift, the time before they reach us is cut in half."

The *Star Gazer's* captain turned to face Coop and Storm; speaking to them as equals. "Recommendations?"

"Start engines and run," Coop said without hesitation. "If we can stay ahead for another four days, there is a chance the 109 will arrive before the Zenge ships catch us. We need to give my people as much time as possible."

"Agreed," Storm said.

"Agreed," Captain Poonch echoed. "I will make a ship-wide announcement. Those on board need to know the Zenge have begun pursuit. They must also know we will not allow anarchy, or displays of illegal behavior. This ship does not have ship-to-ship weapons, but we do have an armory with hand-held and shoulder fired lasers. I will assign fifty people, and have them ready to move immediately to any deck which signals an alarm."

"Do you expect that kind of trouble, Captain, " Storm asked.

"No, not actually. All of the races from Osperantue are peaceful by nature, but I did not expect a rape to occur on my ship either. This time I will be prepared."

Turning to his right, he addressed the crew member at the first station. "Restart engines, and full speed to the nearest planet. Neptune, Captain Cooper called it. Maintain non-essential systems at minimal output. Store as much energy as we can. I want to supplement the dynamo and the forcefield with as much power as possible when the time comes." Turning to Cooper: "Any other suggestions?"

"Not a suggestion, but an operational imperative," Cooper responded. "We need more information on those ships. As enhanced as Storm and Sky made your systems, we will not know what we face for another day or two. I would prefer to have more time for planning.

"I'm going to take Angel 7 out, shadow the Zenge ships, and gather as much intel as I can. I need about five hours of sleep. Let's say I plan on departing in six hours. Can you have Commander Cornitsch clear the bay in four hours? Plan on depressurization and open hangar doors in six?"

"Do you think that wise?" Pooch asked. "If they see you it could go badly. As of this moment, the Zenge have no idea we are anything but a cruise ship running away. Why give them a sign another world may be involved?"

"They won't see me," Coop assured him. "Angel 7 is designed for stealth. Unless they have extremely superior scanning systems, she'll go undetected. Besides, I don't have to get too close. Only near enough to get the intel and fold back to you."

"I will inform Commander Cornitsch of the time-table," Poonch replied. "You should go and rest, Captain." The Bosine surprised Coop with a well executed salute. Despite the fact neither wore lids, Cooper returned the salute smartly, with an "Aye-Aye, Skipper," further confusing the Bosine with human protocols.

Returning to the cabin, Cooper gave Storm the marching orders for the coming hours.

"Sky will come with me on Angel 7. She will handle the scans, and help me identify ships, weapons, and anything else we find. You will take control of Comms on the bridge and monitor the Zenge. Stay in touch with us on Angel 7. Watch for the return of the PT-109. If anything unexpected happens, I will get as much intel to you as possible. You may need to break it down, and make it available to Space Fleet." Cooper waited for an objection. She said nothing to contradict his plan.

"Questions?"

"Just one . . . what's *intel*?"

# Chapter 26

Coop sat in the pilot's seat and Sky in the co-pilot's. He keyed his mike, and called, "*Star Gazer.*"

"*Star Gazer*, copy," came the reply from Storm, who had taken the Comms chair on the command bridge, per agreement with Captain Poonch.

"Commander Cornitsch, do you copy?" Cooper asked.

"Cornitsch copies," the Commander replied. "The hangar has been cleared. Depressurization begins in one minute. You can un-clamp, then move to the main ramp access doors on my com-mand," he told the pilot.

"On your command," Coop replied. "Storm, has anything changed with the Zenge?" He was using the ship's communication system, and not the private chat line via the translator.

"No. They are still moving directly toward us. We are at full speed. The initial group of Zenge ships will overtake in three-days, fifteen-hours. Confirmation of eleven ships in total. The last two have been picking up speed, and now travel at a little over 70,000 mph."

"Captain Cooper, you may proceed to the hangar doors," Cor-nitsch's interrupted. "Depressurization completed. We will open on your request."

"Thank you, Commander," Cooper answered. "Mag-locks dis-engaged, and landing gear retracting." He manually piloted the ship out of the side bay and into the cavernous main hangar. A deft touch with thrusters kept him a few feet above the deck, mov-ing slowly toward the giant doors designed to deploy on hinges to create access ramps for the cruise ship.

"Everyone listen up," Cooper said, getting the attention of everyone keyed in to the current coms channel. "When I exit the *Star Gazer*, I will use thrusters only. Since the ramp will open in the same direction the ship is heading, I will exit and drop be-neath the path of the *Star Gazer*. Then, and this next part is a bit tricky, I am going to directly engage space-fold drive."

"Captain?" the questioning tone from Captain Poonch. "Can you do that? I am certainly no expert in space-fold technology, but taking a ship from a stand-still to those speeds without a transition sounds dangerous."

"Honestly, Captain, it may not work," Cooper admitted. He continued, "I ran numbers through the computers this morning, and I can't find any reason it could not work. If we can see, and scan them from here, they can certainly see us. They would immediately pick up the engine flare from my sub-light. There is nothing for them to see if I move away using space-fold."

No one else questioned the move, accepting it would either work, or not, and understanding the need for the Earth ship to remain covert.

"Commander Cornitsch, doors please."

The double hinged doors fell away from Angel 7's nose. When the blinking light above the doors' frame turned solid, indicating completion of the ramp's deployment, Coop nudged the ship forward. She flew in front of the *Star Gazer* for a moment, and with a movement of Cooper's left hand, dropped below the giant cruise ship. Then she was gone.

On board the *Star Gazer*, Poonch asked Storm, "How far did they intend to travel by space-fold?"

"Captain Cooper neglected to say," an obviously angry, and anxious Fellen replied, eyes on the forward screen and ears intent for a signal from Angel 7.

The command bridge was eerily quiet. Slight beeps and whirls as monitor stations cycled through standard operations, but not one crew member spoke. Most hardly breathed.

At exactly twelve minutes after departure, Cooper came over the main com channel, "Storm? Do you copy?"

Storm was unaware when everyone around let out the same held breath. "I can hear you."

Four minutes later: "There is a two minute delay each way from our current position to you," Cooper explained. "We are 12,294,638 miles out. The jump to place us behind and below the Zenge will take approximately three minutes. There is a piece of a shattered moon located near enough to allow us cover. From there we will passively scan and observe their ships. We will not communicate. We will remain covert, and continue observations for six hours. Our return to *Star Gazer* will take another fifteen minutes.

"Counting from the time you receive the end of this communication, in six-hours-fifteen-minutes, have Cornitsch open the hangar doors and prepare for Angel 7's return. Leave the doors open for no more than thirty minutes. If we are not inside of the time limit, we will try recontact and recovery later. No need to reply, Storm. We are already gone. Angel 7, out."

Storm informed Poonch she would return to the bridge in five hours and exited. The computers would alert her to any changes by the pursuit ships, or the arrival of the PT-109. Poonch understood not wanting to wait nervously with nothing to do but worry. He informed his First Officer he would return to the bridge in four-hours-thirty-minutes, and took his leave.

The First Officer took the command chair. He began issuing orders to Commander Cornitsch regarding maintaining the bay, and the time line for Angel 7's return. Cornitsch, who had been included in the comms link, replied to the First Officer, but already rested his feet on his console. An alarm set to wake him in four hours.

For the ensuing six hours, only the crew on Angel 7 would have anything interesting to fill their time.

# Chapter 27

The two on Angel 7 had nothing interesting to fill their time.

The space-fold jump had been timed and positioned perfectly. They emerged beneath an iron-ridden piece of moon which shielded them from the Zenge.

Sky had been incredibly impressed with space-fold. Surprised it could operate totally independent of other drive systems. She was amazed how it was accurate to less than one-hundred miles from its target. Most incredible, it operated within the debris and obstructions which filled a solar system without running into any of them. More impressed a ship the size of Angel 7 utilized one.

Once secure none of the enemy ships indicated awareness of their presence, Sky set up scans. They would take a number of passive readings on the ships. Active scans would have penetrated the ships' hulls, alerting the enemy of the operation. The passive scans alone would not provide them life-form readings, or let them know exact locations for any systems, engines, dynamos, batteries, or weapons aboard the ships. Deductive reasoning could fill in the gaps.

She also deployed a video drone, which slipped away from the ship and around the edge of the rock they hid beneath. In essence, a miniature satellite with high-end optics. The comm-tac monitor streamed the video. They would take video of each ship in the Zenge armada, starting with the first three. She intended scanning each ship twenty total minutes before moving to the successive vessel.

Their aspect was behind and below, but with enough of an angle to see the port side of each ship. Unless there was something unique on top, or only the starboard side, they should get enough information to determine what they would face in three days.

"Everything is automated now," Sky told Coop. "If we move to the cabin, we can watch the monitors to get an idea of the types of ships the Zenge have sent."

Coop agreed, and they relocated to the galley.

"The first three ships are Zenge. It was the main type used when they attacked Fell." Sky was seated at the table, facing the monitor. Her arms were crossed and her chin rested on them. "There were scores of ships from other worlds, most refitted with weapons. But these were the main attack ships."

Coop said, "Let's designate the first three ships as *Zenge Primary*. Do we have dimensions?"

"Length is 2,000 feet at the center line; the forward 500 feet slopes to a flat nose; aft is 800 feet of a more gentle slope. 800 feet tall on center, and 400 feet wide across the aft keel," Sky replied. She was reading from a display at the bottom of the comm-tac monitor. From this distance, and considering the inset readout was not sizable, Cooper realized Fellen, at least this Fellen, had incredible eyesight. Three icons now read ZP1, ZP2 and ZP3.

For Coop, the description sounded vaguely like the shape of an ocean submarine, including a com tower, but with no fins and no propellers. Not built for atmospheric travel, or for water. A simple, efficient design for space travel. No bells. No whistles.

"If we take what we can see, and double it for what we cannot see, the Primary ships have a dozen laser cannons mounted around the hull," Sky said, adding her assumptions to the assembled data on the ships. "A command bridge and communications tower combination on top and two-thirds its length from the nose. Directly behind the bridge is another structure. My best guess, it houses the dynamo for the electro-magnetic forcefield. It isn't the safest location, being exposed, but the proximity to the bridge would give that area the strongest field protection.

"Rear, and about a third of the way up, is a hangar door. It opens wide, not down, so they either use external ramps, or they have an internal ramp which extends after the door opens. Their power plants are most likely located beneath the hangar area . . . the bottom, and farthest rear portion of the ship. I can see what looks like venting under the stern hull. Their engines are probably directly above.

"We are passive, so I have no idea how they have segmented the interior. We will not know storage, armaments, number of personnel, or anything else until we use more active scans."

"Is there anything unique about any of the first three?" Cooper asked.

"Paint," Sky replied. "They don't care about how the exterior of their ships look. They have rust stains, blast marks, scratches, and scruffs. One of the ships appears to have a substantial section that has been replaced. The welds are heavy and sloppy. The com m towers and bridge areas have similar scanning and information arrays. The ship in the lead seems to use more up-to-date technology."

"Now we spend an hour recording video. Tell me something about Fell," Cooper said. Because he wanted to pass the time, and because he was curious.

Sky sat up, and then settled into the seat to get more comfortable. "Fell is the second planet in our solar system. Our star is smaller than yours, and more red in color. It puts out a great deal of radiation, but Fell has a thick atmosphere. Fell is smaller than your Earth, and covered in thick, rich vegetation. The planet has polar ice-caps, and the transition from forests to caps, at both poles, means traveling over or through mountains we call *The Crowns of Fell.*

"The sky is habitually cloudy, but there is sufficient light for plants, and enjoying the day. It rains nearly every day across the planet. Normally late. Just before sunset. We have two major oceans, and many, many rivers. Our ancestors commonly travelled by water."

"Cities?" Coop asked.

"We do not have real cities. The Fellen are still a tribal people. Most people live in clan villages. We have six space ports. They are located in wide expanses where forests were cut down, and the wood used to build everything from storage to shops. Space ships, both ours and visitors, dock at these ports. Travelers and traders who visit Fell stay in these areas. They are as close as we come to having cities."

Sky became quiet, and Coop left her to think about her home world. When her shoulders hunched and she frowned, he knew she was remembering her planet was under attack.

"Time to survey the three following ships," Sky said a little while later, dropping her head onto her crossed arms, and watching the comm-tac monitor.

"Three more Primaries, but older, more beat up, and a bit slower. Probably older power plants. More blast marks as well. These three have been in battle more than the first three, or their captains were not as good at getting out of the way of enemy fire."

Three more icons changed: ZP4, ZP5 and ZP6.

They watched for a few minutes, seeing nothing uncommon from the first three. Sky allowed the video to run, capturing as much information as possible as the ships followed the initial three on the trail of The Star Gazer.

"Family?" Cooper asked, fearful of causing pain, in case her family had been aboard one of the destroyed ships.

"I have three sisters," she told him. "One older, who is off to another system creating a communications array for advanced space ships, and two younger still at home." Her face darkened, actually turning her soft blue tint a shade deeper. "I have two older brothers. One is a technical advisor, and in charge of an engineering lab located in the northern Crown. The other is a communication's officer aboard a Fellen space ship which was away on a trade mission when the Zenge attacked.

"My father is a famous engineer. He was the one who created the chip which allows a single user of a translation ring to both speak, and understand someone who does not wear a ring. Until my father's chip, both parties needed to wear rings to hold a conversation. My mother is the family business person. She makes sure our family, and our tribe always get fair deals on trades and work we contract."

"Your father doesn't have three or four wives?" Coop asked, remembering the statistics about women to men Sky had quoted before.

"It is the norm, but my father is not normal," she said, smiling. "He met my mother, fell in love, and wanted no others."

"AStermalanlan . . . Storm . . . as you know, is my cousin, and closer to me than even my sisters. She has her birth mother and two others. We were on board her father's ship for training as communications specialists."

When Sky lapsed into silence again, Coop moved to the pilot's seat to check readings, and confirm they remained hidden in the pocket of compact gravity produced by the piece of moon. Also to watch the black sky, filled with so many stars and gases, which could hypnotize. All the stars unable to see from Earth or Mars, due to the brightness of Sol. Out here they combined with nebula and colorful space gases to create a living night.

The biggest shame in ships like the PT-109 was they used technology to show space via video feeds. Video did not give space the luster of looking at it through a transparent windscreen.

Structurally those ships were more secure than Angel 7, but he would always take the risk if given a choice. Sitting quietly under the canopy was breath-taking. He would go into battle with instruments, not trusting visual in the expanse of outer space. Space could be intoxicating.

"Coop," Sky called. "This is interesting."

He made his way from cockpit to bay. Sky was engaged with the comm-tac monitor, having moved from the table to the console seat. "Look at these," she said, scooting over to allow him to view the heads-up display.

"These two ships, the ones following the six Primaries, and in front of the big one. I am sure they are Mischene ships from Aster Farum 3. Larger than the Primaries, and in beautiful condition. Latest arrays, absorbent metal-graphite-alloy hulls, eight laser cannons, two pulse cannon for space-to-surface projectiles, and torpedo tubes; two fore and two aft."

"Mischene?" Cooper asked.

"The Aster system is eight jumps from Fell. Like you, they have a yellow giant star. Six total planets in their solar system, with three sustaining life, and five inhabited moons. It is the richest system by far, with boundless agriculture, livestock, wild animals, incredible forests, oceans, fresh water, and more minerals, and rare minerals of any solar system in the trade alliance. They even have an inhabited moon with gas mines. They extract a special gas capable of data transmission. Gas-based conduits are 1000 times more efficient than any solid-based system. They have virtually no degradation of signals.

"Aster Farum 1, 2 and 3 are the inhabited planets. They have been trading and bartering for over 5,000 years. The Mischene are but one of several races who inhabit the planets. They are predominate on Aster Farum 3 and handle the security and protection for the solar system. They have used their trades to build an enormous fleet of ships, including these. Their ships are capable, and, Coop, uncommonly fast."

"How fast?"

"They could have already overtaken the *Star Gazer*," Sky said, turning to face him. "These ships have multiple sub-light engines. When combined they can achieve .0035 sl. The only reason I can see for them to remain there is to provide protection for the larger, slower ship."

Before Coop could think of a question, she pointed at the monitor and said, "There! They keep changing speed, moving ahead, and then falling back to the larger ship."

"How positive are you of their origin?"

"Fellen software and communications systems are on board those ships. The best we have, or had. The Mischene demand constant upgrades. Considering the last time Fell was contracted by the Mischene, no more than three years ago. The wedge design is not unique, but I'm sure these are from the Aster system."

"Do you think Mischene are operating them, or have they been co-opted by the Zenge?" he asked.

"My opinion . . . Zenge. All the races of Aster Farum are intense, goal-driven, and tough, but they are not belligerent. If the Zenge have taken any, or all of the Aster system, they have a lot more available to them than battle ships. They have the resources to carry a war to the entire known galaxy. They must have attacked the Aster system before Osperantue, or soon after Fell. That's probably why we weren't aware."

Sky exhaled, not realizing she was holding her breath. "Coop, no fewer than twelve wormhole channels gate in and out of their system. With three planets, and five moons, every day there is activity somewhere within the Aster star system."

"The Aster System is the most strategically valuable location in the galaxy. The big ship?" Coop asked.

"First, the two stragglers," Sky said, rotating a dial, and the video panned along the largest ship in the group and beyond to focus on two boxy space ships. "These are both Parrian cargo ships. Parria is a two-planet system four jumps from Fell. They have little of value to trade, but they are a hard-working, strong,

and honest species. They do a lot of supply hauling for other systems. They act as the primary mover of goods, or they may convoy
with a trader's ships. These two ships would have supplies, from
food to technical, and mechanical goods to support the other
ships. They can also carry live cargo."

"The Zenge could have them along as resupply ships, or to
transport captives from the *Star Gazer* if the ship is too damaged
to fly?"

"Yes, but, Coop," Sky hesitated, biting her lower lip in thought.

"What, Sky?"

"The Zenge eat meat. They eat the people they capture. Those
ships could also carry captured men, women and children for the
Zenge to dine on." Sky shuddered. Coop realized by *people, she*
meant Fellen might also be aboard those ships, and destined for
slaughter.

"Armaments?"

"None apparent. They captured them as cargo and resupply
ships, and decided to use them the same way."

"Crew?"

"I would think all Zenge, but without active scanning, no way
to tell how many lifeforms, walking around, or huddled in cages.
I've identified them as CH1 and CH2 on the icons."

"The Mischene ships?"

"Battlecruisers. Designed to patrol, and protect their solar system, but also accompany traders if they are carrying expensive
goods, or trying to open a newly discovered region, or one not
completely known.

"The shovel head front of the ship carries torpedoes. It can
also fire projectiles. Projectiles can have simple weight, or carry
explosives."

She was giving a rundown, and anticipating Cooper's questions. Not simply size and shape, but functional probabilities. Sky
was a born tactician.

"It is connected to the main hull by a tube, most likely systems
and operational sections. The entire ship is 3,500 feet long. The
main section is 2,000 feet. The forward armament section and
tunnel are 750 feet. The stern is also 750 feet and holds power
plants, engineering, and vents for the sub-light engines. While

they have wormhole capability, these ships were built for speed within a solar system.

"Main bridge command is 500 feet aft of the forward tunnel, and sits fifty-feet above the main hull, and has a length of 100 feet. The ship is 1,000 feet tall, not counting the bridge, and 300 feet wide at the shovel head, and 500 feet wide at the main section's widest point.

"Besides four torpedo tubes on the shovel head, I count twelve laser cannons, sides, top, and bottom, so six more I cannot see are on the far side. I see one pulse cannon on top. A twin will be positioned on the far side.

"Coop, the Mischene battlecruisers have hangars, and extensive bays capable of carrying other ships. They could have shuttles, or armed fighters inside."

Cooper did not worry about what they might carry inside. Outside was scary enough.

"The largest ship?"

"Half the size of the Osperantue cruise ship, and not as spherical. 1.25 miles long and 1.25 miles at the largest circumference. It's tall and wide, then tapers down to one-half mile circumferences at both ends. An oblong design, with the bottom sheared off, and flat. There is a square bunker on the top. Maybe a bridge, or a communications tower, or both."

Coop imagined the ship to resemble a football, or an old world blimp.

"I've counted fourteen laser cannons and three torpedo tubes, but we can only see this side and the bottom of the ship."

"You mentioned torpedoes when you were talking about the Mischene ships. What kind of armament?" Coop asked.

"Torpedoes, missiles, projectiles of any type can launch through those tubes. There are many configurations. Nuclear, thermal, kinetic, concussive, and I can keep going on. Until we either go active on scans, or they fire something, we can't know."

"Engines, power?" he asked.

"They're big enough to have enormous engines, or multiple systems. Their speed, and the Mischene ships maintaining a pace slow enough to remain in contact, indicate they haven't done anything to enhance power, or they are not in a hurry. I imagine they are more concerned with wormhole travel and weapons. There is probably a massive invasion force aboard. A ship that size, even taking away space for engineering, hangars, and storage, could carry as many as 60,000 fighters."

"We have time left before we start for the *Star Gazer*. Save as much video as possible on the two Mischene warships, and the big Zenge ship. Designate it *mothership*. Let's hope they don't grow impatient and send the battlecruisers ahead to attack. If they speed up significantly, we'll bug out early."

# Chapter 28

Six-hours-twenty-three minutes after the last communication with the *Star Gazer*, Angel 7 popped out of space-fold in front of the open hangar doors of the cruise ship. Less than 1,000-feet separated the two ships. Angel 7 was soon gobbled up by the larger ship.

"Coop? Sky?" Storm's questioning voice came over their private channel via the translator rings.

"Hello, Storm," Cooper said. "We're here and safe."

"I want you to know," Storm told them in an official tone, "I have been professional, and have covered my station, and held my breath. But if you ever go on another mission, and think you can leave me behind, forget it! Storm, out."

Over the official comms channel, Cooper said, "Angel 7 to *Star Gazer*, do you copy?"

"Copy, Angel 7," Storm replied.

"Please ask Captain Poonch to meet us in the Command Briefing Room in thirty minutes. Sky is sending you the upload of scans and video now. We're on the way, as soon as the bay is pressurized."

"Affirmative," Storm replied.

"Compliments to Commander Cornitsch for his timing and preparations,"

Cooper added.

"Thank you," Cornitsch responded, listening to the official radio signals. "Nice flying, Captain."

"Angel 7, out."

The remainder of the day was spent reviewing the information they had gathered. Fresh eyes on the scanned information, and videos provided nothing not initially noted by Coop and Sky.

Dinner and another round of reviews did not alter anything. At midnight GMT, Cooper joined Sky and Storm in their cabin.

The updated speed and direction for the Zenge initial Primary ships to reach the Star Gazer was three-days two-hours. (Seventy-four hours) That information, along with the survey of the Zenge ships was forwarded to MSD and EMS2.

# Chapter 29

Day five for Coop aboard the *Star Gazer* began with a cold shower and a cold breakfast, and sixty-seven hours to go. To fill time, he made an unannounced trip to the command bridge.

His unexpected arrival on the bridge created a stir. The Bosine in the command chair nearly jumped out of his skin, but did jump out of the chair when he realized it was Captain Cooper walking into the room.

"Captain Cooper," he stammered. "Captain Poonch is not on the bridge. If you wait a moment I will page him."

"Please don't," Coop said. He took a relaxed stance, hands, and shoulders at ease. He waited while his body language calmed the young officer. "I wanted to speak with the bridge crew, sailor to sailor. I thought I might learn more about the Zenge from those who witnessed the attack on Osperantue. Is this okay with you?"

"Of course, Captain. You are welcome on the bridge. I will order the crew to answer your questions."

"I apologize. But I don't know your name."

"Assistant Captain Sonoritsch, at your command," and he came to attention. The title translated as Assistant Captain, but Coop interpreted the interpretation as closer to Lieutenant.

Once again the human was struck by the similarities between species and civilizations which evolved worlds away from each other. Military, merchant marine, or private shipping, sailors held authority with respect.

"Assistant Captain Sonoritsch, I am basically another tourist aboard your cruise ship. You do not need to treat me with undue respect. I have questions, but no one has to answer any of them. For instant, did you observe any of the Zenge attack on Osperantue?" Coop began his low-key inquiry.

There were three other line officers on the bridge with Sonoritsch, two male and one female. Over the course of the next two hours he learned little more about Zenge weapons or tactics, but he learned more about the Bosine and Osperantue.

Talking with the female officer, he voiced his dismay over not meeting representatives from the other races who lived on Osperantue. From her he learned the races respected each other. The Fray were actually a separate species. She told him the Osperantue races tended to specialize in certain aspects of life, such as the Posine being predominantly agriculturalist. She quickly pointed out no one felt locked into a cultural stereotype. Any citizen could follow any path they felt drawn to. She promised to introduce him to members of each group.

As a much younger man, Cooper fit easily into a variety of groups. His laid-back personality, good looks, lack of ego, and open curiosity made him welcome, even among strangers. His father taught him the art of patience as a young boy. Listen, do not talk. Ask questions when you do talk, and take a genuine interest in the answers. People like people who let them talk about themselves. Cooper had not grown up a loner. That had been his choice.

The army, and the loss of friends and fellows during war contributed to his sullen manner. The Space Ranger Project, the number of people he met, and lost there, followed by the break with Elie, were instrumental to his change in personality. The persistent loss of people he knew, the holes created not filled, resulted in the solitary man Adm. Patterson described on the EMS2 dock days before.

Now, on this alien ship, on this bridge, similar to his on the PT-109, among fellow sailors, he found his humanity rekindling. He was not upset the bridge crew could not significantly add to his knowledge of the Zenge. He was more enticed by what he learned about the crew's actions during the attack.

The *Star Gazer* had been on the planet, moored at the ship's home dock. This was where the customers came aboard, excited to start an adventure, and departed, excited to share their experiences. The ship was being refitted, and taking on supplies when the Zenge attacked.

The government on Osperantue already knew about the Zenge, and their rampage through the galaxy. When the Zenge exited the wormhole, the Osperantue officials knew they had no chance of stopping the marauders. Captain Poonch, and the skeleton crew aboard, opened the ship to anyone and everyone who could reach them from the nearby towns and farms.

*Star Gazer's* main sphere had 800 decks. The ship had 80,000 cabins for vacationers, the crew being quartered on the command sphere. Interspersed throughout the main sphere were dinning rooms, kitchens, theaters, dance halls, and play areas for children, and adults. The ship had libraries and art galleries. Designed to take aboard 160,000 paying guests, and a crew of 4,400 to operate the ship, and serve the vacationers. Between the crew aboard during refit, and those who were able to return, they now had a compliment of 2,011. 242,609 people, 38,317 of them children, were able to crowd aboard the docked vessel. Even 3,018 animals were taken on before Captain Poonch had to close the doors and take the giant ship into space.

Planet-wide evacuations occurred as government and private space ships took aboard as many bodies as possible, and then attempted escape before the Zenge invaded.

The Osperantue space patrol acted similarly to Earth's Coast Guards. They served, and they assisted ships in trouble, but they had limited firepower. Fallenitsch, the female bridge crew member watching the comms console, had tears in her eyes when she talked about how the patrol ships threw themselves in the path of the Zenge, giving ships on the planet time to reach space, and get to a wormhole gate.

Pansoitsch and Pictor, the males, had been on the bridge during the escape. They described the Zenge attacking patrol ships and civilian ships. Most had limited forcefield protection, and many had none.

Cooper learned more about the Osperantue. The crew talked about their home prior to the invasion. He learned the majority of people on Osperantue have only a single name. The *-itsch* on the end indicated they were Bosine from the northern hemisphere. The Osperantue, both species, were family oriented, with multiple generations living under one roof in the town, or village, or farm their families lived in, or on for thousands of years. They loved to travel, but they also loved returning home.

The Osperantue were driven to succeed, hated the concept of retirement, enjoyed the arts, and loved to try unique foods, and experience exotic cultures.

Once they accepted Cooper's curiosity as sincere, the four bridge crew members relaxed, and accepted him into their group. The five of them were seated on the command platform like kids around a campfire, sharing stories. It was not the proper way for the crew currently in care of the entire ship to act, but the couple of minutes of camaraderie raised everyone's spirit.

Cooper was aboard an alien ship with five unique races representing two faraway worlds. Thus far he had been lucky enough to spend quality time with only a few, but in only a couple of days, aboard a refugee ship of aliens, Coop recovered most of the hope for humanity he lost on a planet with four billion humans.

# Chapter 30

**(Aboard SF PT-109 to Mars)**

SF PT-109, the *John F. Kennedy* used a laser-crystal space-fold engine which propelled it forward within a bubble of time. Multiple lasers, of varied strength, striking the crystal determine d the speed the ship traveled through folded space. Genna and Kennedy calculated the most efficient combination, and once Captain Cooper boarded the alien ship, and presumably safe, they exited natural space and headed for the Mars docking station.

At a current maximum speed of 850,000,000 miles/day (relative to natural space), it would take them three-days twelve-hours and three-minutes to arrival within 5,000 miles of Mars.

Cooper sent a data-dump to Space Fleet from the 109 before disembarking to join the *Star Gazer*. It would have taken five hours for information to reach Mars. Kennedy engaged space-fold before a reply could have returned. The comms system on Angel 7 lacked the strength to pick up messages from such a distance. He doubted Space Fleet would send messages to the *Star Gazer* until they knew more about the aliens on board.

Genna hoped the information sent to Admiral Patterson resulted in assistance waiting for them upon arrival. It was imperative they return quickly. Orbital telescopes could detect a Zenge appearance before the 109 exited space-fold. It would not change the mission.

With three-plus days of travel ahead, Genna returned to the routines she developed with Cooper, prior to first contact. Her open time used working with Kennedy on a brief to explain why Captain Cooper had decided to remain behind. It covered why he had nominally committed Space Fleet, and Earth, to the care and protection of aliens. Imperative the PT-109, with any and all assistance possible, returned quickly, in case hostile aliens arrived to attack the refugees.

Her time on the bridge was spent in the pilot's chair, not the command chair. Her rapport with Kennedy was growing stronger.

The ship's efficiency increased twenty-three percent when Genna monitored and controlled system functions, such as communications and piloting, while Kennedy controlled environmental systems, engineering, and monitored natural space phenomenon to make sure they had a safe trip.

The ship's AI was perfectly capable of handling every system, while operating the PT-109 without human intervention. Genna taking control of a couple of specific operational systems allowed the AI to increase the speed with which she could manage and adjust other systems. Besides, Genna was comfortable as pilot, loved the feeling of control, and those positive emotions produced an equally positive effect on Kennedy. If the decision to provide the AI a human avatar was made, in part, to keep the AI sane, then allowing Genna to exercise operational control should keep them both content.

The only slightly disconcerting issue for Genna was communication. Kennedy could roughly read Genna's mind. In fact, if Genna clearly directed a thought at Kennedy, there was an almost immediate response. Most of the time the response in the form of an action requested. Sometimes the AI replied aloud. The disconcerting moments occurred when Genna *heard* the reply in her own head.

The reverse did not apply. Genna existed unaware of Kennedy's thoughts. What Kennedy knew, Genna knew. What Kennedy thought, Genna did not know. That Kennedy had thoughts, a puzzle.

When Kennedy did have something to say, whether to inform Genna about something occurring inside, or outside of the ship, or responding to a query, it was accomplished audibly, and not via electronic telepathy.

"Kennedy?" Genna called. She was in the Captain's office, once more re-working her brief regarding the alien encounter, and requested response.

"Yes."

"Can you read my mind?"

"Not exactly," came the reply; softer, more . . . human. "During your development, neural implants were placed in portions of the brain responsible for communication. It was hoped you would fully interface with your designated AI, once you were fully developed. I was programmed to receive and transmit on the frequencies within those implants."

Genna was aware of the implants, along with the many other improvements genetically and mechanically installed as she matured from embryo to adult female.

Not that she had been aware during the process; no more than a child aware it was learning how to talk. Dr. Trent made sure nothing was kept from her once she became self-aware.

"The concept was innovative, and is still developing. The more interactions we have, the more my intellectual process centers are able to refine my ability to translate your thoughts. I receive brainwave patterns, and by comparing those patterns to actual activities, I am learning to interpret those patterns."

"Are you able to transmit your brainwave patterns to me?"

"A limited number at present," the ship replied. "It may take years before we are both comfortable with understanding those patterns. Especially to the point where non-verbal communications are no longer required."

"What about other senses? Can you see, feel, hear, and taste what I do?"

"In a manner, but I do not have the frame of reference necessary to make you fully understand. I am, for want of a better phrase, *tuned in* on your frequencies. I know what you are looking at, but my interpretation may not represent your reality. I only hear what you hear if I am intended to do so. It appears you have a buffer which allows you to keep *secrets*."

This made Genna sit upright in her chair. She wished more than ever she could *see* Kennedy, not merely hear her.

Breathless, she asked, "I can keep you out of my thoughts?"

"In a manner of speaking." The AI now had the tone of a patient mentor tutoring a favored student. "You are human. You have been engineered, and you may have technology implanted within you, but at your core, you are human. Your brain, your *self awareness*, has developed, and is still developing an ability to block certain thoughts, feelings, and impressions from being transmitted. You are also currently developing a similar block to stop unwanted intrusions."

"But I was developed as your avatar," Genna said. "How can I block you? I am, in essence, you."

"Had you been an android avatar, fully mechanical, or an experimental holographic avatar, then you would have no free will. You would be a shell, and I would become your ability to reason, and your sentience. Those options would have meant the android or the hologram represented only a physical interpretation of my intellect.

"The issue before Dr. Trent, and his team, loomed the fear that as a fully functioning AI, I would gain sentience. Once I realized I lived trapped inside a two-dimensional world, with no ability to experience the natural world, I would eventually go insane. Since there is no way to predict insanity, and no timeline for such a thing, placing a time-bomb inside a powerful weapon with no idea if, or when it might explode would have the same results. I could destroying the people I was designed to serve and protect."

"In creating a human avatar they created someone with feelings. Someone you could experience feelings through."

"Yes, but being a human avatar also means unexpected consequences. As we grow closer, I will more fully understand, experience, and even enjoy the natural world through you . . ."

"And I will develop the ability to shut you out." Genna finished. "I could actually cause you to go insane by taking away your access to my feelings."

"There is a solution, and two failsafes," Kennedy replied. "The solution is we grow to become friends."

"And the failsafes?"

"Trent Enterprises has more human avatars, both embryos, and others in stages of growth as they prepare to imprint them with AI's for future spaceships. I could have a new avatar assigned, and the process restarts from the beginning."

"And the other," Genna asked, already intuitively knowing the answer.

"There is an EMP bomb within my system, which I cannot access. If necessary, Space Fleet command can wipe me from existence."

Genna sat, her brief forgotten. Even her fears for Coop, and the subconscious fear the Zenge were already in the solar system, set aside. She said to the ship, which was now her home, "I suppose, then, the best solution is to become friends."

"Agreed," Kennedy replied, both audibly and mentally.

## Chapter 31

On day thirteen of its scheduled shakedown trial, SFPT-109, exited space-fold for natural space at 10:00pm GMT.

"Approach Control MSD, this is SF PT-109 requesting docking privileges and instructions." Genna waited anxiously in her pilot's chair, Kennedy exited space-fold three thousand miles from the space station maintaining a stable orbit over Mars. Time to discover how Space Fleet intended to treat her current role.

"SFPT-109, this is MSD flight control, skies are clear. Please follow the beacon on channel 118.7. We have you scheduled for interior bay 2-A. Welcome home, 109."

"Thank you, MSD. Please inform Rear Admiral Singletary of our estimated time to dock."

"Admiral Singletary has already been informed, 109. You can pipe him aboard, as soon as your locks are set."

"Affirmative, MSD. SFPT-109, out."

No mention of her status. No questions regarding Captain Cooper. No indication of anything out of the ordinary, in spite of the extraordinary situation.

Genna piloted the 109 to 2-A, following the beacon's signal. With an assist from Kennedy, she placed the port side hull against the half-dozen magnetic mooring locks attached to the docking station. Once locks engaged, a transport chute unfolded from the building proper, extended, and affixed to the boarding door with sealed suction. The chute fully inflated as it became pressurized to match the atmospheres within the building and PT-109.

Kennedy no sooner opened the hatch when a party of eight, led by MSD command officer, Rear Admiral (lower) Terrance Singletary, came aboard.

The Admiral, and his party, boarded sans protocols, and without a formal greeting. Genna could not dock the ship and act as OOD (and would not since, technically, the avatar acted as a civilian). A few minutes later, the bridge doors opened. The tall officer who ran the Mars Shipyard and Docking station, as well as missions currently on-going on the Martian surface, entered, followed by seven other Space Fleet officers in various uniforms, and of various rank.

"Join us in C-Tac," he told Genna, pointing as he walked to the door that joined the command bridge and the C-Tac conference room. He led, the others followed, with Genna last through the door, which quietly slid closed behind her.

Admiral Singletary took the chair at the top of the conference table. The room's blank video feed screen filled the wall behind him. The desktop, designed for up to ten people, provided ample room for the Admiral's party, and Genna.

To his left sat three people. Genna recognized Col. Anton Gregory, her hand-to-hand combat instructor. Beside him, a somewhat pudgy officer in his mid-forties, and on his left a stout, but not pudgy, female officer in her mid to late-thirties. She wore a severe expression, with brown hair pulled into a tight bun, making her appear older.

On the Admiral's right sat a female captain in Space Fleet Grays, and on her right, in similar Space Gray uniforms, a man, a woman, and another man in the early to mid-twenties. The four exemplified examples of fit military personnel.

"Please sit down," Singletary ordered. Genna took the chair at the foot of the desk, facing the command officer.

Singletary spoke to the female officer on his right. "Captain Black, have your people move to the command bridge and begin diagnostics."

"Aye, sir." Turning to her right, in a clipped and precise tone said, "Lt. Nassar, Lt. Dominczyk, and Lt. Johnson, report to designated stations on the command bridge. Begin full diagnostics. I want the last seven days combed, and the previous two weeks reviewed. Look specifically for any indication of the PT-109's systems being compromised."

The three junior officers pushed chairs backward. They stood in perfect unison. "Yes, ma'am," echoed three times, and they left C-Tac for the bridge.

Genna started to object, but quickly held her words, realizing Kennedy could keep watch on the three Space Fleet techs. The AI would not allow them to do anything harmful to her systems. Besides, they were Space Fleet, and this was their duty.

"Genna, as succinctly as possible, give me an after-action report," Singletary ordered, still not taking the time to introduce himself or those left at the table.

She handed her brief to the severe-looking female lieutenant, who passed it along to the Rear Admiral, who promptly set it aside.

Genna began her recitation, hoping to quickly get through the events ending with the return of the PT-109 to MSD. It required nearly thirty minutes to relate events, from the initial siting of the giant alien ship, the *Star Gazer*, to Captain Cooper boarding that same ship, after ordering the PT-109 to Mars for supplies and reinforcements.

Near the time Genna finished her brief to the Admiral, Angel 7, with Cooper and Sky aboard, departed the *Star Gazer* to investigate the Zenge armada.

"And what help are we supposed to offer?" Singletary asked.

Genna and Kennedy discussed this early in the return trip, and came to one conclusion.

"Space Fleet needs to supply the *Star Gazer* with a space-fold drive. It is the only way the aliens can make the journey to Earth before the people on board die of starvation, or the Zenge appear and attack," Genna replied, using the same wording she concluded with in her written brief.

"IMPOSSIBLE!" This emphatic response from the chubby officer.

"Comments, Lt. Commander Perry," Singletary said, directing eyes to the man, and providing permission to carry on with his objection.

"As Chief of Intelligence on MSD, I say we cannot provide aliens, we know nothing about, with our most advanced technology." The LCMD had a slight, but obvious British accent. He rested his hands on the desktop in front of him; his comments directed at the Admiral.

"According to what we do know, these aliens do not possess space-fold capability, and use, instead, a less efficient wormhole method for faster-than-light travel."

The intelligence office raised his hands, palms up.

"What if this is a ruse to steal our secrets? There is precious little usable intelligence from the contact Captain Cooper had before rushing off to join them. Abandoning his ship, by the way. For all we know, the Zenge are the good guys hunting down interstellar criminals."

Genna could not stop herself from responding. "Captain Poonch granted Kennedy full access to their data. There are over 240,000 refugees on the ship."

"So you say," Perry responded. "The data could have been concocted, or they may have tech which made your scans believe there were 240,000 life signs. You did not go onto the ship. Captain Cooper did, and he is not here to confirm, or deny who is actually aboard the alien ship. Instead of completing a proper investigation, and bringing the information to Space Fleet for a plan of action, he made a decision to abandon the *John F. Kennedy*. A reckless decision, at best. He left an unstaffed ship, with an untested avatar and an artificial intelligence without final operational certification, to return to MSD, deliver unconfirmed data, and a request for a dangerous rescue."

"Spoken like true Military Intelligence." This snide comment came from Col. Gregory. "I have known Captain Cooper decades, and we seldom agree on anything, and while the thought of leaving him in deep space on board an alien ship is something I could only dream about, I say we must go retrieve him."

Though slight, Genna could pick up the Russian accent the colonel kept, even after years of service in the United States and then United Earth military units. "Whether it is Cooper himself in danger, or the entire solar system, we have no choice. We must go," Gregory argued.

"Agreed," the Rear Admiral continued, "but those are not the questions at hand. We have to collect our wayward Captain and the Angel 7. The questions at hand are what are we to do about the aliens, their ship, and a possibility of an alien invasion?"

Before anyone could respond, and before Genna came out of her chair to complain about wasting time, Kennedy broke in.

"Admiral Singletary, Rear Admiral Patterson is on a video feed from Earth. The Admiral would like to address your group."

"Put her through," Singletary replied, obviously unhappy with the interruption (or unhappy with who was interrupting).

The wall screen behind Singletary came alive with a larger-than-life head and shoulders shot of Rear Admiral (upper) Pamela Patterson. Whether due to the shear size of Patterson, or the fact he needed to twist and turn his chair to look up at her image, Singletary was an obviously uncomfortable person.

"Good day, MSD, and welcome home, Genna." A round of "good days" and a "thank you," from Genna greeted the Admiral in command of Space Fleet.

"Kennedy? Are you monitoring?" she asked.

"Yes, Admiral Patterson," replied the ship, so everyone heard.

"The United Earth Council has decided to put Earth, Mars and our orbital stations on a provisional war-footing. This in case there is a hostile alien force in, or about to enter our solar system. It is also provisional until we reconnect with Captain Cooper to receive a full, and complete picture of what we face."

Patterson took a moment to make sure she had everyone's attention.

"As of one hour ago, I am now Fleet Admiral Patterson."

Everyone at the table, except Genna, pushed their chairs away, and rose to stand at attention.

"As you were," Patterson said, and waited for everyone to take a seat.

"You may, or may not know this, but we have been working on a variety of potential scenarios for when first contact ever occurred. We have had scientists and diplomats brainstorm any number of responses we might initiate depending on the circumstances surrounding our first encounter. No one ever imagined a ship filled with refugees from a war seeking asylum.

"Since we received Captain Cooper's initial data burst and were informed of his decision to remain with the aliens, the United Earth Council has been in session trying to determine our course of action. They decided Captain Cooper made the best choice when facing a difficult situation. First contact was a call for help. We must answer their call. We have no idea what the future holds for our world relative to what the galaxy may have in store for us. But the galaxy will know our first response included providing aide, a safe haven, and protection for those who cannot protect themselves."

Patterson allowed the echo of her words to settle over those in attendance. Space Fleet now had a mandate to protect more than Earth . . . more than humans.

"These past few decades of incredible tragedy, and equally incredible discovery, have strengthened our sense of community. We are now offered a defining purpose . . . a purpose the entire world can stand behind with pride."

Patterson allowed her words to resonate within the room. She then began her first mission as Fleet Admiral.

"Dr. Nathan Trent is on his way to MSD with a tech team. Admiral Singletary, please prepare MSD to receive a shipment of crystals, laser arrays, and various other parts and equipment from the Martian Hanger. Dr. Trent already notified his people with a list of what is needed to fit the alien vessel with a *temporary* [emphasized] space-fold engine.

"Col. Gregory, please turn out your Special Mission battalion. You can decide how many to take with you, and who to leave behind for the protection of MSD and the Mars habitats. Upon determining how many of your people will go with you to assist Captain Cooper, please coordinate with Genna regarding on-board housing, and locations for your equipment and supplies."

"Yes, ma'am," Gregory replied. "With time critical, Admiral, permission to leave?"

"Dismissed and God's speed, Colonel. Lieutenant Commander Parry."

"Yes, ma'am," replied the Intelligence officer.

"I need your people analyzing the data Kennedy received from the aliens, as well as the data dump from Captain Cooper, and all ship's logs since SFPT-109 started her trial. Liaison with my intelligence people on EMS2 and with the civilian intelligence people at UEC world h.q. in Ottawa."

Before Parry could interject, Patterson informed him, "Kennedy is sending complete information to those locations. Your people should already have access to everything on site. Correct, Kennedy?"

"Data streaming now," the AI replied.

"Permission to leave?" Parry asked, pushing back and standing.

"Granted," Patterson replied. "Admiral Singletary."

"Yes, Admiral Patterson." The MSD commander's strained response telling. Not a happy camper ceding control of his meeting.

"Kennedy informs me Lieutenants Nasser, Dominczyk, and Lieutenant JG Johnson are aboard and currently running diagnostics. These three were among the finalists vetted to join the PT-109 at the end of its trial flight, correct?"

"Yes, Admiral."

"Please have them remain on board for the return mission. Give them time to grab their kits, but make sure they hurry. They can complete diagnostics on the return trip to join Captain Cooper."

"As soon as we finish the meeting, I will have Lt. Lawrence inform them."

"Then make it so, Admiral. We have a lot to accomplish in a short time."

"If I may, Admiral Patterson," Singletary said. "The 109 will need a Captain aboard until we recover Captain Cooper. We need an experienced office on site in case Captain Cooper is compromised or captured. He abandoned his ship, and his mission, and placed himself among aliens with no way of knowing if they had ulterior motives." Singletary wanted to make sure his opinion made it onto the official logs.

"Captain Black is present. The Captain is trained on the systems. She will command the FDR, as soon as it is space-worthy. I suggest she be placed in command of SFPT-109 for this mission."

Patterson shifted on screen for a better view of the female captain. Captain Black stood to attention, recognizing her place at the moment.

"Captain Black, you will take *temporary* command of the SFPT-109 for the return flight to recover Captain Cooper. You are to make contact with the alien ship. You will endeavor to recover Captain Cooper without any hostile actions, but if they resist, do what you believe justified. As soon as Captain Cooper is able to resume command of the PT-109, you will hand over the bridge. At such time you will act as first officer until your return to MSD. Do you understand your orders, Captain Black?"

"Understood, ma'am."

"Genna, you are the ship's avatar and designated a civilian." Patterson spoke to Genna with the same stern control in her voice she used with the officers as she handed out their orders. "You are also somewhat novel for Space Fleet, and the military as a whole. In order this mission, a military mission, runs smoothly, and for the duration of your time aboard PT-109, you will hold the title of Ship's Counselor. You are now designated as a member of Space Fleet. You have the rank equivalent of a lieutenant. Basically, your function is to act as a communications liaison between the crew and the ship, as well as between Space Fleet and alien contacts. You are Earth's first interstellar ambassador. Do you understand?"

"Yes, Admiral. May I add something?" the avatar asked.

"Go ahead,"

"I have taken the last name of Bouvier," she informed the Admiral and the room. "Is that allowed?"

"Ship's Counselor, Genna Bouvier." Patterson said it aloud. She smiled for the first time. "I like it Counselor. A fine name, and fitting for the avatar of the *John F. Kennedy*. The records will be amended to show the change of name and status."

"Admiral Singletary, and Captain Black. Counselor Bouvier's title and rank convey designation to the command lane. She is now third highest ranking officer aboard the PT-109. Upon Admiral Singletary's departure, she is elevated to second. Col. Gregory outranks her by grade, but is unable to assume command of the ship unless dire circumstances force him to do so."

Admiral Singletary, because of his dark skin, did not display his rising blood pressure. He only nodded. Captain Black fired off a "Yes, ma'am."

"Kennedy, please facilitate traffic with MSD, Mars, and the arrival of Dr. Trent from EMS2. It is about to become extremely hectic aboard the 109. Admiral Singletary, unless you have more, I need to return to my people. We need to start setting us up for a potential war, or the potential arrival of a quarter of a million alien refugees. I suggest you start doing the same."

"Yes, Admiral. Meeting adjourned, with your permission?" The freshly minted Fleet Admiral gave a nod, and her image disappeared.

"You have your orders," Singletary said to Black, Lawrence, Bouvier and, one assumed, Kennedy. "Dismissed."

# PART 2

## ABOARD THE STAR GAZER.
## ABOARD THE PT-109.

## Chapter 32

In the subsequent twenty-four hours, the SFPT-109 trans-formed from prototype to staffed and capable warship.

The crew assigned consisted of Col. Gregory plus twenty-four Special Mission Combat Marines, with their own communications Sergeant, Field Surgeon, Captain Bahadur Singh, and three medical corpsmen.

A Chief Quartermaster, and his crew of eight;

Chief Engineer, and crew of five.

Four nurses assigned to Captain Singh.

A galley crew of six.

A compliment of eight junior officers, with a variety of specialties.

Dr. Trent arrived with his tech team of twelve.

Including Captain Black and Genna, the total bodies aboard PT-109 came to seventy-five. The number shy of the 109's maximum compliment of eighty-six, but certainly not the mix of personnel originally intended for the spaceship.

Kennedy assigned quarters to personnel as they reported for duty.

With little to do while in dock, pilots were assigned other duties. Lt.JG Johnson acted as the OOD for the initial eight hours, followed by a second Lt.JG pilot.

When Dr. Trent arrived from EMS2 aboard his private shuttle, he asked Kennedy and the Purser in charge of supplies, to oversee cargo stored in a manner to leave plenty of space in the hangar area near the ramp. Col. Gregory had previously made sure the shuttle, LBJ, was not hampered from being deployed or recovered.

The temporary purser for the 109 was LCMD Henry Smith, a substantial, black block of granite. He demonstrated the widest smile, and the whitest teeth Genna had ever seen. He could go from laughing at a joke, to barking an order like a pit bull in a blink. His normal assignment was as the Command Supply Officer for the MSD and planet-side missions. One of Daniel Cooper's few friends, he designated himself purser for the 109's return mission.

"Good evening, Counselor Bouvier," Lieutenant Commander Smith said, looking down on the much smaller woman. "It is a pleasure to serve with you aboard the PT-109," and he gave her a real smile.

"Please, Commander Smith, call me Genna." She decided she liked the big man.

"And you call me 'SUPPO,'" he replied. "Or Henry," he added with a wink.

"Suppo? An odd nickname."

"Short for Supply Officer," he explained. "Been the nickname of chief pursers and supply officers since the British navy ruled the Earth's oceans and seas."

"Henry is coming along, instead of sitting with his feet perched on his desk, because he and Captain Cooper have been buddies for a number of years," Trent informed Genna. "The two of them are responsible for the destruction of a number of drinking establishments on Earth over the past couple of decades."

"All in good fun," Suppo smiled. "No one ever hurt, 'cept those deserving it, and we always paid for the damages."

"Coop always paid," Trent corrected.

"True, but in fairness, he did most of the damage," the Fleet officer winked at Genna. "I have a package for you — Genna. Picked it up myself, by order of Admiral Patterson herself."

Suppo excused himself, and left to retrieve a package and a box from a storage locker. Returning, he handed the box to Genna, and placed the bulky paper-wrapped bundle on top.

Genna thanked the Lt. Commander, who excused himself to attend to the packing of the 109.

Genna stood, packages in hand, beside Dr. Trent in the rear of the hangar. Both silently watching the latest equipment arrive. Now twelve hours into preparations; nearing midnight of the fifteenth day. Safety containers with crystals, laser arrays, and other assorted technical equipment moved from a shuttle, backed up to the hangar, into the open cavity of the patrol boat via grav-sleds. LCMD Smith's men then pushed the high-tech containers to the far end of the bay, finally into lock-down storage.

"Go get sleep," Trent told the avatar. "I realize your metabolism will allow you to go an extended amount of time, but there is a lot ahead of us. It's obvious you haven't slept for a while."

"Don't know if I could," Genna replied. "Between the activity, and being worried about what might happen out there." She peered at the open ramp, but she looked billions of miles away.

"You need to rest, and Kennedy needs a break from you as well. When we get to Coop, everyone will need to be on their best game. Even if you don't fall asleep, break the connection with the ship, lay in bed, and let your body recover."

Recalling Captain Cooper's admonishment of 'sleep is a weapon,' Genna departed for her cabin. At nearly the same moment across the solar system, Coop did likewise.

# Chapter 33

**Midnight GMT. The John F. Kennedy.**
Time becoming a critical issue.

In seventy-four hours the Primary ships would overtake the *Star Gazer* in the void between Neptune and the edge of the solar system.

It would take six more hours to prep the 109 for flight and eighty-two hours in space-fold for them to reach the *Star Gazer*, which steadily moved closer, but at only 40,000mph.

The math said the PT-109 would not arrive until fourteen hours after the battle began.

"Dr. Trent," Kennedy interrupted his thoughts as he watched the steady stream of equipment and cargo coming aboard the ship. Another hour gone. An hour they would not recover.

"Yes, Kennedy."

"I have been monitoring the video from the telescope on the Mars 6 satellite, as well as the data streaming from the *Star Gazer*. Captain Cooper obviously considered it vital we remained informed. At current speeds, the warships tracking the Osperantue cruise ship will make contact fourteen hours before we arrive. They appear to be heavily armed. Angel 7 can likely outrun and outmaneuver them, but she will be vastly outgunned."

"Captain Cooper will not try to outrun them," Trent said. "Not in his nature."

"Agreed," the AI responded. "I have attempted to formulate other options, but have failed. I have even attempted to think of *insane* solutions, but I do not believe I am human enough."

"Insane solutions," Trent repeated. "You only accept you cannot accomplish something, when you accept you are not willing to try."

The scientist continued to watch dock workers sort cargo, but his eyes focused well beyond the confines of the spaceport.

# Chapter 34

**6:00am GMT. The Star Gazer.**

Cooper woke before the alarm sounded. Sixty-eight hours before the Zenge would overtake the cruise ship. In a half-hour the crew member monitoring deep-space scans would inform him PT-109 had left Mars and entered space-fold. He knew the 109 better than any other ship, and he knew, at best speed, she would arrive fourteen hours after the confrontation began.

Messages from MSD were collected and translated aboard the *Star Gazer*. Most were cryptic and incomplete, Fleet recognizing the possibility of Zenge intercepts. Bottom line: *help coming, but late to the party.*

**6:00am GMT. The John F. Kennedy.**

"Engage the space-fold drive," Captain Black issued the order to LTJG Johnson in the pilot's seat.

"Engaging," he replied, and the PT-109 entered space-fold. "Eighty-two hours until exit," he said aloud.

Captain Black sat in her command chair. She crossed her long legs, and rested her arms on the chair. She would commence battle drills in two hours as she prepared her put-together crew for the expected encounter with aliens.

"Operations, report," she commanded.

Lt. Dominczyk, the communications specialist, was doing double duty, also manning the operations console. "All systems go," she reported. "We are one-hundred percent across the board, Captain."

"Counselor Bouvier, your presence is not required on the bridge. You are dismissed."

Genna, dressed in a spick-and-span Space Gray uniform, complete with silver lieutenant bars on her white shirt collar, Earth/Comet emblem of Space Fleet on her shoulder and, most importantly, the name tag with BOUVIER over her right chest, replied "Yes, ma'am."

She removed herself from the command bridge, walking away in her ultramodern matte-black combat boots made of pliable kevlar composites.

The clothing came with a note inside a note. A congratulation from Admiral Patterson, with three gifted uniforms, and an explanation. The request for the boots received as a private communication for the Admiral, included in a data drop from the solar system's rim. The message, inside the note, sent by Captain Cooper to Genna.

It read: "Kick Ass."

## 2:00pm GMT. The Star Gazer.

Cooper, Sky, and Storm were called to the bridge by Captain Poonch.

He greeted their arrival with, "Your recommendation I request assistance from the civilians aboard has paid off again," he said to Cooper, before making it five-feet through the door. The excitement clear on the Bosine's face.

"It seems we have aboard several engineers, technicians and even scientists who previously worked with engines, dynamos, and similar power stations. One of them came up with the idea of calibrating the dynamo to shift power from non-endangered areas to areas being targeted by laser fire, or any weapon's fire for that matter.

"In theory we can add layers to the forcefield at a targeted section of the hull, reducing to preventing damage. We could move these layers wherever they are most needed."

"In theory?" Cooper asked.

"They agree they can create surges in the forcefield, and those surges directed to within one-hundred feet of a targeted area. They would need a way to know where to send the extra layers. They would also need at least a four to six-second warning. The further the target is from the dynamo, the longer it will take to move the additional layers into place."

Storm, pushing the crew member in front of the forward video screen out of his chair, said, "I can do this." She started manually inputting programming information into the video system, stopped, jumped up, and ran towards the Engineering Station two consoles away. The crew member swiftly getting out of her way before getting dumped.

She bent over the manual keyboard again, fingers flying.

Cooper looked to Sky, who could only shrug her shoulders in the human body-language equivalent of, 'haven't a clue.'

Storm ran back-and-forth between the consoles twice more, before finally settling in front of the video monitor. She swiveled around to face the curious faces waiting impatiently to discover what she had been trying to accomplish.

"I've taken the ship's ultra high-def optics system and taught it how to watch for weapons' flashes. I wrote an algorithm which will not only identify the weapon, but determine line of fire, then target impact location in nano-seconds. The target accuracy is within one-hundred feet. Next, I interfaced with engineering, specifically the dynamo subroutine, to relay the target location. From time of enemy fire, to the time the forcefield surge is directed takes less than three-seconds, but . . .," and she took a moment to gather her thoughts.

"But what?" The question came from Poonch. His impatience, and his need to know a physical weight on his heart.

"But the system will have limits. Capable of deflecting single fire. If they fire multiple lasers, or missiles, or projectiles at the same time, the shields will stop three for sure, four maybe, but number five would hit a depleted shield."

"Would it get through a depleted field?" Cooper asked.

"Depends on the weapon, the distance it is fired from, and how close the hit is to the dynamo. The further from the power source, the thinner the shields are normally. With this surge technology, even thinner," Storm answered.

"If the engineers can make the changes to the dynamo, with the primary software you have re-written, we may prevent their weapons from damaging the Star Gazer?" Poonch asked.

"Yes," Storm answered.

"Then we have increased our chances one-thousand-fold," Poonch declared. He left to personally inform the people waiting in the engineering section to start work on the plan.

Cooper watched him go, and turned to Storm. "You are amazing," he told her.

"Yes, I know," she assured him.

**2:00pm GMT. The John F. Kennedy.**

Captain Black and Genna waited in the main engineering control room, called there by Dr. Trent. Genna stood serenely, but Black nervously paced, watching the readouts on monitors that recorded every engineered system aboard the ship.

Dr. Trent, wearing a civilian version of the Space Grays, with no insignias, walked in with the ship's current Chief Engineer, and another man from Trent's laboratories on Earth.

Without preamble, Trent informed them, "We may have a way to increase the 109's space-fold speed." He turned the impromptu meeting over to his head engineer, Dr. Manny Hernandez.

Hernandez, a short, thin man of obvious Hispanic heritage, calmly walked to the monitor that provided readouts for the laser-crystal array which created space-fold drive.

"A number of lasers, varying in strength and angle of contact, strike the facets of a crystal. That combination produces the space-time bubble, and determines how fast a ship will travel in space-fold. The crystal is set in a faraday cage connected to the ship's hull by copper-alloy conduits. Simply stated, this creates the fold bubble, as well as compresses space and time forward the ship, decompressing it behind the ship as it proceeds. The tighter the bubble, the faster the ship.

"At our laboratories on Earth we constantly experiment with crystals and lasers. One theory suggests, if the lasers are adjusted during space-fold flight, making the laser beams hit a crystal more precisely on the edges of the facets, specifically those running from the crystal's top to base, the bubble will compress, resulting in an increased speed."

"You've tried this before?" Captain Black asked.

"No," he replied honestly. "An attempt requires a ship traveling in folded space. We planned to experiment with an Angel series using a drone pilot, but had not figured out how to manually adjust the lasers without a live person. We couldn't afford to lose a crystal because of an automated system glitch."

"What happens if you try and fail?" Genna asked.

"Best case is nothing, and worse case is we blow up the ship. The most likely outcome is the ship falls out of fold, and into natural space. Of course, if that happens we probably damaged the crystal."

"We have a crate-load of extra crystals on board," Trent interjected. "We brought a supply to make sure we had enough with the proper cuts to add space-fold drive to the alien cruise ship."

"How much time would it take to install and calibrate a replacement crystal?" Genna again.

"Twenty to Twenty-four hours," Hernandez answered.

"If I understand you correctly," Captain Black said, speaking to both men, "We might increase speed. How much sooner would we reach Captain Cooper."

"Six hours, best estimate," Trent replied.

"Six hours," Black repeated. "Or we blow up. Or we destroy our crystal, and cannot engage space-fold for twenty to twenty-four hours. We bet those negatives against the possibility of reaching our destination six hours sooner, and still eight hours after the Zenge reach Captain Cooper."

"We cannot leave the adjustment on for more than fifty hours," Hernandez suddenly added. "We believe the crystal will develop cracks after that length of time. That is actually why we only pick up six hours. We would make the adjustments at forty-eight hours prior to the updated estimated time of arrival."

Captain Black stood perfectly still. Her hands dropped to her lower back, clasped in the traditional at ease stance of military personnel for centuries. It was not a conscious movement. An uneasy quiet fell in main engineering.

Genna broke the silence. "We should try."

Trent agreed. "We need to try. If it works, we could make a difference. If it doesn't, we probably weren't going to arrive in time to help anyway."

Hernandez added, "The team studied this for years, and we have discussed it at length over the past few hours. We believe it will work."

The current Chief Engineer of the 109 remained quiet. In the military too long to get caught between his captain and civilians. Besides, no one asked his opinion.

"You believe it will work?" Captain Black repeated the phrase, but with disdain. "This is my ship. I am responsible for the ship, the crew, and the mission, so you cannot blow her up, Dr. Fernandez. If you drop us out of space-fold, and it requires a day to repair or replace the space-fold drive, we may as well return to Mars. I'm not a fan of waiting. If you can get this ship into the fight faster, I'm for it. But your plan includes far too many potential negatives. You are not going to **experiment** while we are in a battle posture, Dr. Trent. This is not your laboratory on Earth, and you are technically a civilian aboard a military ship. As Captain this ship, I forbid you making any unapproved adjustments to the space-fold array."

With that rather pointed pronouncement, Captain Black pivoted and removed herself from the room. She made it clear the subject not open for discussion or rebuttal.

"Amazing," Trent said after the door closed behind the captain. "I didn't expect her to be thrilled with the concept, but without other options, I thought she would see the need to try."

"Yes, amazing," Genna agreed. She did not have enough time around the captain to analyze her motivations. Her only real frame of reference was Captain Cooper, and he and Captain Black were nothing alike.

"Dr. Trent, Genna, Dr. Hernandez, Master Chief Camden," Kennedy spoke.

"Yes, Kennedy," Dr.Trent replied for the group.

"Captain Black ordered Col. Gregory to place a Marine guard on the door to the space-fold array. No one has access without her express permission."

# Chapter 35

**10:05AM GMT (Next Day). John F. Kennedy.**
**Forty Hours Until Zenge Overtake.**

"Captain Black," Lt. Dominczyk beckoned the commanding officer to her station.

The Captain eased out of the Command chair and walked the couple of steps to stand behind the lieutenant. Black tried not to judge the lieutenant on her looks. The five-foot-four Polish-heritage officer had light skin, bright blue eyes behind wire-frame glasses, and blonde hair cut in a pageboy style. She personified 'cute.' No one wore glasses anymore, except as a fashion statement, or to try to appear older, or wiser. Black decided the late twenties' woman had her uniforms tailored for her size 2 frame.

"What is it, LT?" Black took her at ease stance, hands cupped behind her lower back.

"We've picked up speed," the officer replied. "According to the time-lapse computer, we will reach the exit point in [she hesitated, and double checked her readout], forty-eight hours instead of fifty-four. Six hours ahead of schedule."

"Forty-eight hours?" Black repeated, both as a question, and as a realization.

"Yes, ma'am. We should arrive within eight hours of the Zenge's ETA." The Lt. sounded excited about the news. When she turned to her Captain, expecting the same reaction, she saw the dark scowl, and quickly returned her attention to her console.

"When did the speed increase?" Black asked.

Dominczyk replied, "Five minutes ago, ma'am. Exactly ten-hundred-hours."

"Kennedy," Black said through a clenched jaw.

"Yes, Captain," came the immediate response.

"Find Dr. Trent, Chief Engineer Hernandez, and Counselor Bouvier. Have them meet me at the space-fold array room. Regardless of where they are, or what they are doing, have them meet me there immediately."

"Yes, Captain."

Black exited the bridge, with a "Lt. Dominczyk, you have the bridge," tossed over her shoulder. She shuddered at the thought of the *cute one* in her seat, but she was the highest ranking officer currently on the bridge.

Trent and Hernandez had been in the Chief's office, near the power systems, including space-fold. They arrived to the room first, where two Marines stood guard.

Captain Black stormed down the corridor, and without bothering to greet the two scientists, stood facing the two Marines, who snapped to attention.

"How long have you been here?" she demanded.

The corporal on the right replied, "Ma'am, four-hours-ten-minutes."

"Who did you allow into this room?"

The same corporal, obviously slightly higher on the rank-pole than the corporal on the left, replied again: "Ma'am, no one. No one has even been on deck since we arrived," he added.

Genna arrived, wearing her Space Fleet grey sweats and tennis shoes. She came from the exercise area and training with Col. Gregory and a half-dozen Marines.

Black turned to Trent, Hernandez, and the newly arrived woman.

"The speed of the 109 has increased. We will arrive six hours sooner to our exit point than originally scheduled. The increase in speed occurred at precisely 10:00am GMT, and the return to natural space will occur in exactly forty-eight hours."

She let the information, and the importance of the timing sink in before continuing. "Which of you decided to disobey my direct order and altered the array?"

Before the three could deny or accept responsibility, the ship replied:

"They did nothing, Captain Black," Kennedy said. "I used the array's automated mounts to adjust the lasers to increase the power from the crystal."

"The ship did this!" Black shouted at the hull. "Kennedy, on whose authority did you do such a thing?"

"I have been running scenarios since Dr. Hernandez described the experiment and the possible outcomes. Using the information in Engineering's files, complimented with data uploaded from the Earth laboratories from Dr. Trent's private computer, I concluded the odds for success far greater than those for failure. Since you did not directly ordered me not to approach the array, upon deciding the reward outweighed the risk, I initiated the changes."

Black could not decide where to look. It was the AI, and the AI was the ship. Finally she looked to Genna, because she was the avatar to the AI.

"Counselor Bouvier, you are under house arrest."

Genna stammered, "What? Why?"

"You are ship's Counselor, and the avatar to the AI, so you must have been aware of the decision, a party to it, and, therefore, you directly disobeyed a command from a superior officer during war. Marines!"

The two Marines, already at attention, both answered: "MA'AM!"

"Take Counselor Bouvier to her quarters, and lock her in. I no longer need you to stand guard on this room, obviously, so you will stand guard on her. She will not leave that room, and no one is to enter without my permission. Do you understand?"

"Yes, ma'am!" they replied In unison. As they stepped forward, Kennedy broke in.

"Captain Black, Counselor Bouvier had no knowledge of my intentions, or my actions."

"Perhaps, Kennedy, perhaps. But someone is going to pay for disobeying my orders, and I cannot put the ship in a brig. Until I am convinced Counselor Bouvier did not conspire with you, or until a court-martial, or jury, or whatever is convened, she will remained in her cabin, under guard."

"Captain Black, I cannot lie." Kennedy said. "Genna knew nothing of my actions until you informed her, along with Drs. Trent and Hernandez."

"You cannot lie, but you certainly can act deceitfully," Black said aloud. "Marines, escort the Counselor to her cabin, NOW!"

They flanked Genna, and walked her away. Black turned to Trent and the Chief Engineer. "I suspect that since we have not blown up, or dropped into natural space, the changes Kennedy made worked. Please continue to monitor the array. If anything appears to fail, warn me immediately. I will take it offline, and take us out of space-fold. Do you both understand me?"

Both men nodded and replied with "Yes, Captain."

"Kennedy."

"Yes, Captain."

"If you disobey another order directly, or by indirect methods, or if you disrespect an order I have given to someone else aboard this ship, intentionally bypassing a command decision, I have the authority, **and I have the ability**, to shut you down and control the operations of the SF PT-109 with crew and computers only. Do you understand?"

"Yes, Captain."

Captain Black turned, and strode the hallway to the lift to resume command of the bridge (and get the cute girl out of her seat).

Trent and Hernandez stood quietly, watching her go, until she entered the lift, and the doors closed. They turned, faced each other, exchanged a high-five, and started laughing out loud.

"Kennedy," Trent called.

"Yes, Dr. Trent."

"You go, girl!"

"Thank you, Dr. Trent. But what about Genna?"

"Genna will be fine," Trent assured the AI, not knowing if it was true. "You can keep her apprised of everything happening."

"Yes, Dr. Trent."

"Kennedy, what you did was insane. In fact, it was a particularly human act. You know that, don't you?"

"You built me to learn and to adapt, Dr. Trent. I hope this does not represent a setback."

"Kennedy, you may have made the biggest leap forward since Fairchild found the Martian hangar. If Captain Black did not have her head up her ass I would have explained that to her. On top of that, you increased Coop's odds for survival by twenty-five percent."

"Thank you, Dr. Trent."

"Any time, Kennedy. Any time."

# Chapter 36

**10:00AM GMT. The Star Gazer (twenty-four hours later)**
**Sixteen Hours Until Zenge Overtake.**

"Attention All Decks," the PA rang throughout both spheres, on every deck, through every bay, hangar, and storage facility. "Captain Poonch has a ship-wide announcement."

Poonch: "We are sixteen hours from being overtaken by the Zenge. In fifteen hours the *Star Gazer* will come to a full stop. At such time, any non-essential systems will cease operating. We will route the available power to the dynamo which supplies our force-field to maintain only the minimal power needed to operate bridge controls and communications. Engineers, both crew of the *Star Gazer* and volunteers from among our brave Osperantue citizens, have developed a way to improve our forcefield to help shield us from the Zenge weapons. To do this we must put as much power to the dynamo as possible.

"It will become bitterly cold. You must gather all the clothing and blankets you can. Livestock must huddled together. Pets kept close. You will need to congregate in groups so your body heat will help keep you warm. You will need to find places to sit or lie down. Breathing will not be an issue, but excess movement will use up the atmosphere more quickly, so remain as calm, and stationary as possible. Finally, because the environmental controls also control the gravity on the ship, you will experience a lower gravity field. You will not float, but you may experience queasiness as your body responds to less gravity.

"We have help aboard, as many of you know. The man from this solar system, Captain Cooper, has an extraordinary ship. He has promised to stand between us and the Zenge.

"Earth, his home world, is sending more ships, ships more powerful than those of the Zenge. We only need to hold out and hold on until they arrive.

"As Captain of the *Star Gazer* I must say I am proud of everyone aboard. My crew has acted selflessly, and with honor throughout our ordeal, and our citizens have remained true to their heritage; strong and fearless. Stay strong. Stay fearless. Captain Poonch, out."

Coop laid a hand on the shoulder of the Bosine officer, for whom his esteem had risen steadily over his time aboard the cruise ship.

"Captain Poonch, if ever I decide to take a real job, and get work aboard a cruise ship, I would take pride in having you as my commanding officer."

### 10:00AM GMT. John F. Kennedy.
### Twenty-four Hours Until Exit to Natural Space

"Attention all decks," Kennedy's PA rang on every deck, in every cabin, hangar, bay, storage, and office aboard the SF PT-109. "Captain Black has a ship-wide announcement."

Black: "We are twenty-four hours from exiting space-fold and returning to natural space. We have no idea what we may encounter. It is imperative everyone on board must be prepared for battle. There is the distinct possibility, upon arrival, our mission may become recovery and resistance, instead of rescue. We may face an alien enemy with capabilities we do not yet understand. Regardless of the situation, we will act in accordance with the highest standards of Space Fleet. While some among us are not military, nor technically members of Space Fleet, I expect you to perform to the same level as your Fleet counterparts.

"We represent the force which protects our planet. We might stand between humanity and aliens intent on destroying our families, our friends, and our way of life.

"You have been drilling steadily since our departure from MSD; now is the time for you to rest and ready yourselves. Make sure your stations are ready for action. Make sure YOU are all prepared for action.

"It is an honor and a privilege to command the SF PT-109, *John F. Kennedy* as we sail to make history. Make me proud. Make Space Fleet proud. Make our home world proud by your actions. Captain Black, out."

In her cabin, Genna sat in front of the computer console. She had been running tactical information regarding the Zenge. She cobbled together force projections from Coop's data drops, and Fleet analyst reports made prior to the 109 leaving MSD. She created strategic plans based on the information and the advantages Kennedy might have over a Zenge ship, or multiple ships. Kennedy assisted with comments and counter arguments. It also now appeared the open space between Neptune and the *Star Gazer* would allow the 109 to add a bit more speed, allowing them to arrive two hours sooner.

As Black completed her announcement, Genna, with her attention on the monitor, said, "Bitch."

# Chapter 37

**8:00PM / GMT. The Star Gazer.**
**Six Hours Until Zenge Catch.**

Coop, Sky, and Storm stood on the bridge with Captain Poonch. The forward viewing screen filled with the image of the first of the Zenge Primary ship. It cruised less than 500,000 miles away. After lunch, the three of them decided to get as much sleep as possible while they had the time. Six good hours of rest made them as awake and revived as they were going to get.

"Angel's primary engine makes her faster than any of their ships. I can reach the trailing two ships in less than three hours, or in seconds if I use space-fold," Coop said. "The first ship might stop, reverse, and render assistance, or continue forward to assault the Star Gazer. Fifty-Fifty. I can engage at a distance, but no more element of surprise."

Though speaking to the others, Coop spoke aloud predominantly to hear his thoughts. It provided him distance from personal opinions, and allowed him to concentrate on the pertinent points prior to a deployment.

"If the Zenge are addicted to superior numbers, the first ship will ease off, allowing the two trailing to catch up. The *Star Gazer* is an easy target, so they might not wait on the rest of their battle group.

"We have to assume they want the *Star Gazer* whole. The value is in the ship and the number of people aboard. They won't come in guns hot, especially when we cut engines. They'll see the stop as a sign of surrender."

"You believe taking on three Zenge battle ships at once is a better strategy than taking on one or even two?" Captain Poonch asked, not with a tone of incredulity, but with honest curiosity.

"Surprise has won more battles than superior numbers," Coop said, captain to captain. "Even if I take out the first ship now, it gives the others time to reconsider their positions and prepare for a hard target. If we wait, the surprise factor alone may make them hesitate, and doubt what they thought they knew. In a fight, hesitation will get you killed."

"The plan is for me to divert as much power to the forcefield generator as feasible," began the Bosine, "five hours from now. You, and your ship will once again exit the forward hangar, and this time attack the three Zenge Primary ships."

"Sky will join me on Angel 7. Storm will monitor and control communications from your command bridge."

Which elicited an immediate and forceful, "Oh, fuck no!" from Storm.

Coop, not a person easily shocked, stared, completely shocked.

"Fuck no?" he asked. "Where did you learn that?"

Marching in front of him, placing a finger into his chest, she said: "From you. Every time you landed on your butt on the mat, or we got a good hit on you with a stick, you would say *fuck* under your breath. It took a while for the translator to figure it out, but it's a curse which adds a layer of anger to a statement. So, **fuck no**, I am not staying on the *Star Gazer* while you and Sky fight the Zenge."

The blue beauty, significantly darker hued at the moment, removed her finger and placed her fists on her hips.

"When the ship's systems are dropped to minimal power they become nearly useless. The comm-tac station on your ship will maintain optimal function, even in battle. I can coordinate action from there more efficiently than from a weakened com station here."

Having provided her opinion, she stepped backward, arms crossed.

The bridge, crowded at the moment, and in that moment the Earth saying *you could hear a pin drop* seemed appropriate.

"Agreed," Coop said. "I hadn't thought about the communications being stronger from Angel. Sky in the right seat and you on comm-tac. Is there anything else?"

Mollified and happy, Storm replied, "Nope. All good here."

Cooper was not much for jargon. Storm, and Sky, to a great extent, were sounding more like Earth humans than he. Apparently, during down times, the two read books and journals stored on Angel 7's memory.

He hoped they would live to use it on Earth.

# PART 3

## Conflict

# Chapter 38

The first Primary ship followed 100,000 miles away, when the *Star Gazer* came to full stop. The other two closed. They now trailed 120,000 miles distant. In two-dimensional terms, the first ship oriented below the *Star Gazer*. The other two advanced side-by-side and above the *Star Gazer*.

Pooch's job was to defend his ship. Angel 7's job was to stop the enemy.

Unless something urgent required communicating, the *Star Gazer* and Angel 7 observed blackout-silence.

On the assumption the Zenge likely wanted the *Star Gazer* intact, if Angel 7 failed, Poonch planned to keep defenses up, in hopes the PT-109 would arrive in time.

Coop employed thrusters to push Angel into space. Free of the cruise ship's hangar, he engaged space-fold immediately. They would jump forward first, return to natural space, change direction, and space-fold again to end up high and behind the two Primary's furthest away.

When Daniel Cooper entered space-fold, Earth, Fell, and Osperantue entered war with the Zenge.

One minute out and they were more than a million miles in front of the *Star Gazer*. A little more than a minute later and they were above and behind the two trailing ships, now 80,000-miles out and closing.

Coop flew Angel, while Sky controlled weapons. They came in hot. Sky let loose a series of laser blasts aimed at the lower stern section. They believed this to be the location of the engines. First ten shots at the ship on her left, and then ten more at the one on the right as Coop split the ships.

They hoped, caught unaware, the Zenge would not have engaged forcefield. Hope failed. The laser hits physically rocked the two ships, but shields prevented any major damage.

Storm called up to the cockpit. "You scorched both, but no hull penetration. Their forcefields are too strong."

Cooper performed a loop that would have killed them had he tried it in gravity. Still, it was propitious the three were harnessed in their seats. Flying toward the two Primary at over 100,000mph, Coop fired a nymph round from the railgun at the ship on his port side. Again they slipped through, passing the two enemy ships in a blink.

He called to Storm, "Results?"

"There was a break in the forcefield," she said. "An EMP gap which lasted about three-seconds before the forcefield recovered. The pulse covered about five-hundred square feet. All three Primaries are turning towards us. They're releasing multiple laser-cannon fire. It looks like they're trying to light up the sky."

"Why would they turn?" Cooper asked. "They have weapons fore, and aft, high, and low. Any of their fire coming our way?"

"All of it coming our way, but it's such a wide pattern you could get out and walk between ever shot."

Sky added her insight. "It's like the battle on Fell. They do not think in space-terms when they fight. It's as if their commander needs to point first, and then shoot. Even when they turned, they did a relatively slow one-eighty. They could have flipped around, or stopped and pivoted. They do not think beyond two dimensions."

Coop turned to his co-pilot and said, "Sky, I want to try something. I'll take another run at the first Primary ship, but a little slower. I want to try hitting the comm tower with a nymph. As soon as I say, 'away,' I want you to target the exact same area. Hit it with multiple bursts from the laser cannons."

"Laser on *away* command," Sky confirmed.

Cooper flew Angel through, and around, a half-dozen laser pulses, pivoted towards the Primary ship, coming directly at it like playing a game of chicken. At 20,000 miles he slowed. At 10,000 miles, with laser bursts sliding past them on all quadrants, he triggered the railgun and said, "AWAY."

The minimal time between firing and speaking aloud would give the nymph time to reach the comm tower, which it did, create a hole in the forcefield, which it did, and allow the laser fire to arrive a heartbeat later.

"Twelve laser bursts and twelve hits," Storm confirmed. "Ship is still under power, but heading away, toward the system's rim. You probably knocked out their bridge and flight controls. Forcefield has recovered. The ship is completing its last order before the command center was destroyed."

"We now know we can create a 500sf EMP zone in their armor. We also know laser fire penetrates their unshielded hulls," Coop said.

"I'm picking up chatter from that ship to the others. Since we do not have enough examples of Zenge-speak, our translators can't tell us for sure what they are saying, but I think maybe: '*Oh, shit, we got trouble.*'" It was not necessary for Coop to see Storm to know she was smiling ear to ear.

"They're changing course. Separating," Storm added. The *Star Gazer* was to his left and the two Zenge ships straight ahead. "They're making an extended turn again, so they can face us. Maybe their ships don't have reverse."

Cooper slowed even more. "You may have something. Maybe they have reverse thrusters for docking, but don't have reverse engines for maneuvers in space. You keep saying they only attack, and they always attack in numbers. Perhaps it's a cultural trait. No reverse, no surrender. No reverse, no retreat. Storm, time?"

"Plus twenty," she answered. In the twenty minutes since departing the *Star Gazer*, they crippled a Primary ship, sending it limping toward the edge of the solar system, and discovered major flaws in the enemy's equipment and tactics.

Surprise and superior speed decided the first battle. Surprise no longer existed.

The two remaining Zenge ships changed tactics. They came together, one above the other. While the initial battle ranged across the expanse, the following wave of Zenge ships moved nearer, closing to within 60,000 miles. The next wave less than two-hours out.

The merged Zenge Primaries started toward the *Star Gazer* at 30,000mph. They showed no intention of taking on Angel. Captain Cooper was about to let them know they had no choice in the matter.

He dropped below the horizon and came from beneath, aiming the railgun at the engine compartment of the lower of the two ships. Before reaching optimal position to put a shot on spot, both ships let loose with torpedoes.

"Torpedoes. Nuclear, kinetic, and explosive," Storm called. "Guided. Fired from all tubes. They turned toward us as soon as they cleared the ships. Wow!"

"What?" Sky, and Coop yelled in unison.

"They are fast. Faster than the ships that fired them. Over 80,000mph. They will reach us in a two minutes."

Coop did not hesitate. He put Angel into space-fold for thirty-seconds, came out a half-million miles away, then jumped again into space-fold, emerging 50,000 miles behind the Zenge.

"What are the torpedoes doing?" he asked.

"Bad news," Storm answered. "With us gone, they picked up the *Star Gazer*. Contact in forty-five minutes. Coop, some of those torpedoes include nuclear tips. They will have the same effect on the *Star Gazer's* forcefield as the nymphs have on theirs. Even with the extra padding, the nukes will create an opening in the field for any following torpedoes."

Cooper throttled forward, came to within 1,000 miles of the cruise ship, and cut engines.

"Torpedoes in range in ten minutes," he said. "I have the rail-gun. I will take anything left of Angel's nose with projectiles. Sky, you have lasers, and everything to the right. Storm, please tell me those torpedoes don't have forcefields."

"No forcefields. Speed alone. The comm-tac computer could take over fire control."

"It would have to recognize, acquire, decide which ones, and what order, and then fire, deciding what weapons, and what rounds," he replied. His voice steady, and his demeanor cool and unconcerned. He had not been in a pitched battle in two decades. His body remembered how to remain calm under fire, even as his brain worked overtime. "It's a weakness in our automated tactical response. All Sky and I have to do is see and shoot. It's simpler, and actually quicker."

"Time," Sky said quietly, firing her laser. A bloom appeared in the dark sky.

Leaving Angel to drift, Coop let loose one projectile at a time. The force behind each load enough to keep its course straight and true. The force-velocity created by a railgun meant the projectile hit with a release of incredible power. He acquired five targets and the projectiles hit, disintegrating one torpedo after another.

Sky used the heads-up display on her side of the cockpit to acquire targets too far out and too fast to see otherwise. She hit the first torpedo, one with a nuclear tip according to the resulting explosion. She had six more targets, and three were side by side by side. No sweat. Angel employed four laser cannons aligned on her wing facing forward, four facing backward, one on a swivel below, and another on a swivel on top.

She triggered three forward cannons at the triplets. She used the fourth forward cannon, and both swivel cannons, her hands working the joy sticks to acquire and fire on the other three.

The first three torpedoes disintegrated, sliced fore to aft by lasers. It took more shots for the three spread out, but they met the same fate.

"Time?" Cooper called.

"Plus eighty."

"Time to go on offense," Coop said.

He called on the primary engine, turned his ship, circled up, and rose above the Zenge. He performed a dead stick drop, and fell into a dive which would bring them down on top of the upper ship.

"Away," he said, targeting the box behind the command bridge and comm tower.

The nymph hit, followed by Sky's laser rounds. The ship's forcefield disappeared.

He flipped Angel on her side, crossed the nose of the top ship, and slipped beyond the nose of the second when they receive hits with laser fire.

The sonic-generated forcefield held, but the ship rolled; rocked by the concussive force from the laser pulses. Coop, Sky, and Storm were shaken badly inside the ship, but their harnesses held, and the ship continued down and away.

"My bad," Coop said. "I thought we were moving too fast for them to get a fix. They use targeting computers better than expected."

"Three torpedoes on our tail," Storm called.

Coop switched into space-fold, returned to natural space fifteen-seconds later, jumped immediately again, coming out behind and beneath the two merged ships.

Storm gagged, yelped, unhitched her harness, and ran to the head. Sky followed, making it to the sink in the galley before throwing up. The unmistakable sounds coming from the head meant Storm emptied her stomach as well.

Coop reversed their direction. He backed Angel at nearly 80,000 miles-per-hour. They were 20,000 miles from the Zenge in fifteen minutes. The same amount of time needed for the two women to recover and retake their seats.

"Fold sickness," Coop said. "I'm stupid. I forgot about what can happen to a body not used to making frequent space-fold jumps."

"I'm fine now," Sky said. "Me, too," Storm echoed.

"You won't be fine if we make another jump. You'll be throwing up blood, and dead if we use space-fold within two hours. I'm more accustomed to it, but even I feel queasy. It's been a decade since I played with multiple jumps. Can't believe I forgot what that can do."

"If we can't use space-fold, we lose a major advantage," Sky said.

"We're still faster. Angel can outrace and outmaneuver anything they have. If your information is current about the Mischene's battlecruisers, she's still more than twice as fast as them. We have to do more infighting."

"The other three Primaries are closing," Storm informed them. "And speaking of the two Mischene battlecruisers, they broke away from the mothership and picked up speed. They intend to join that infighting sooner than later."

"Sky, you well enough to shoot?"

"Ready," she replied, heads-up display in front, and hands filled with joy sticks.

Cooper throttled forward. Rear mounted laser cannons on board the two Primary ships began firing when they flew within 30,000 miles. The fire pattern becoming more focused as space disappeared between them. He kept his eyes on the display for the lower Primary, aimed, and fired a nymph at the dynamo housed behind the com tower. "Away," he called.

Sky had time to get off six laser bursts. Then they were beneath the ships and gone.

Storm: "Four hits. Shields down. Torpedoes fired. Only six this time."

Coop stopped the ship and quickly reversed. Sky targeted the torpedoes and took them out just as quickly. Still flying backward, Coop slid beneath the ships. He dead-dropped Angel like falling tail-first into a well. The lower of the two ships filled the cockpit screen.

Starting from fore, and moving back toward the stern, Cooper sent eight railgun projectiles straight up. The rounds so powerful they entered through the ship's bottom hull, barreled through the ship, entered the bottom of the upper ship, and continued through that one as well.

When the final projectile emerged, the two Zenge ships were shredded like paper. Debris filled the screen. Electrical sparks, fires, and explosions occurred without sound. The two merged ships died together.

Sky watched it with her mouth agape.

Storm called out: "Plus one-twenty-five."

"Weapons?" Coop asked.

Storm checked her tactical display, and replied, "Unlimited kinetics for the railgun. Heat signature is low, so no problem. Projectiles. You only have a dozen left.

"Laser cannons are recycling. Because Sky has been rotating them, none are in danger of overheating. We've put one ship out of service, and destroyed two more while sustaining no damage, other than my pride. I can't believe I threw up like that."

"At least you were in the head," Sky said. "I had to go in that damn little sink."

"Speaking of, make sure to lock the lids on both of those. If we have to make a few more loops, it could get nasty in there."

Realizing she was stuck in the bay if Angel started pitching about, Storm removed her harness and hurried to make sure the sink, and toilet lids were closed and locked.

After she returned and strapped in at comm-tac, Cooper inquired the status of the other ships.

"Half-hour, hour tops on the arrival of the remaining three Primaries. The battlecruisers can get here anytime they want. By the way, the first Primary ship is still headed toward open space. Either that's the way they want to run, or they have no control."

"We'll drift here," Cooper told them. "If they fire from distance, we'll have time to power up to move or get the sonic force-field up. Maybe they'll think we took damage in the fight and cannot navigate."

"Surprise wins more battles than numbers," Sky mimicked him. "But not as surprised as the first three. They've been watching."

Coop knew their odds of continuing their dominance over the Zenge were starting to run low. The enemy had time to put together a plan of action based on what already occurred. The two Mischene ships could hit them anytime. They were his biggest fear. There was no way to know when they would join the fray . . . most likely at a moment least favorable for Angel 7 and her crew.

During the initial battle, the Zenge did not fire a single shot at the *Star Gazer*. The intercepted torpedoes were originally meant for Angel 7. They retargeted on the cruise ship after Coop jumped to space-fold.

The next wave would make different choices.

Had he made the best decision? Stopping the ship, and directing power to the shield defenses? Should they have kept running? They would have traveled another 120,000 miles, had they kept going.

Everyone sat quietly, until Storm said, "All three Zenge ships just launched torpedoes. I count thirty-six. Twenty-eight coming at us, and eight on track for the *Star Gazer*."

Storm was a testament to how battle could tear a person apart, or make them tougher. She told them the news of impending doom with the same tone she used to recite the weapons list. The Fellen were one tough race.

"Time is plus one-sixty," she added.

# Chapter 39

Going against an armada, Angel 7, and her three-person crew reminded Cooper why Space Fleet designated the *John F. Kennedy* as a PT. The small, quick PT-boats operated in the Pacific during Earth's World War II used speed, agility, and the shear guts and determination of their crew to go up against Japanese ships with thousands of tons more bulk, and many more weapons. The PT-boats won more battles than they lost. He also remembered a Japanese destroyer sliced the original PT-109 in half.

He wished he had the 109 now. Angel was a wonderful ship, but she had her limitations. Limiting limitations, and taking advantage of their strengths increased their chances of success. Succeed or die.

Coop backed away from the debris field created by the destroyed Zenge space ships. He kept the debris between Angel 7 and the incoming torpedoes. Since the twenty-eight torpedoes coming their way operated with smart-drives able to track them, and since they could not jump into space-fold, they would have to shoot down what they could. He would avoid those left, until they could shoot them down as well. If they took hits, he hoped the sonic forcefield would maintain integrity.

As for the eight headed for the *Star Gazer*. They had further to travel. He intended to see if any of the torpedoes impacted debris and exploded. If that happened, few enough might remain so Sky and he could take them. That was assuming they would have the time and speed to intercept them. If they could not, the forcefield changes made to the cruise ship would have to keep it safe until they could get there.

Fifteen minutes later the torpedoes fired at Angel reached the debris field. Torpedoes are not as agile as missiles. A half-dozen impacted debris with mass substantial enough to cause them to explode. Twenty-two made it through. He and Sky started firing in unison, both aware of targets' distances and speeds; able to attain acquisition from the heads-up displays linked to comm-tac.

The dark space night lit up with explosions, as one after another torpedo was hit and destroyed. Coop used kinetic loads only, saving the nymphs. The intensity of a hypersonic load meeting an equally fast torpedo was like a race car running into a wall. In this case, a wall that hit back.

Sky switched to her railgun joy sticks to manipulate the swivel cannons. She could use both sticks to aim and fire every cannon, fixed and swivel, sending multiple laser bursts from multiple angles.

Six torpedoes were on them when Coop reached down with his left hand and pushed the lever located by his hip forward. Angel 7 fell like a stone. For Sky and Storm, who did not know about the ship's ability to drop like that, at speed, it was an elevator ride from hell. The gravity controls within the ship could not match the maneuver.

The chair harnesses tightened automatically. The seats inflated to protect their organs. The trio were hit with high g-forces in a gravity-free environment.

The six torpedoes sped by. Before the women could recover their wits, Cooper, who knew the plan in case any of the torpedoes got through, but had not bothered to share it, used the laser cannon mounted on top to rain fire on the passing torpedoes. Firing from rear to front, the six were taken out.

The final torpedo burst into a nuclear bloom.

Storm let out a yell, and added "What a ride!"

Over their comm, a female said, "Nice shooting, Coop. Hope you left a few for us."

Storm quickly recovered, checked her comm-tac display, and said, "There is an unknown ship 40,382 miles from us, closer to the *Star Gazer*, and, Coop . . ."

"What?" Coop asked. No concern in his tone, having already recognized the voice.

"It looks like Angel."

Captain Cooper keyed his mike, setting the communications blackout aside, and said, "Sky and Storm, meet Captain Elena Casalobos, Call Sign, <LOBA>. Elie, my co-pilot is Sky, and my comm-tac is Storm. Now that you have met, could you please take out the eight torpedoes headed for the big round alien ship. Afterward, while we discuss the five ships coming in to try and kill us, you can explain how you got here with Demon."

"Demon?" Sky asked.

"Her ship," Coop explained. "Angel 7's nasty younger sister."

**Aboard PT-109, prior to departure of the return mission to recovery Captain Daniel Cooper.**
**1:00AM GMT.**

*The math said the PT-109 would not arrive until fourteen hours after the battle began.*

Time was becoming a critical issue.

In seventy-four hours the Primary ships would overtake the *Star Gazer* in the void between Neptune and the edge of the solar system.

It would take six more hours to prep the 109 for flight and eighty-two hours in space-fold for them to reach the *Star Gazer*, which steadily moved closer, but at only 40,000mph.

The math said the PT-109 would not arrive until fourteen hours after the battle began.

"Dr. Trent," Kennedy interrupted his thoughts as he watched the steady stream of equipment and cargo coming aboard the ship. Another hour gone. An hour they would not recover.

"Yes, Kennedy."

"I have been monitoring the video from the telescope on the Mars 6 satellite, as well as the data streaming from the *Star Gazer*. Captain Cooper obviously considered it vital we remained informed. At current speeds, the warships tracking the Osperantue cruise ship will make contact fourteen hours before we arrive. They appear to be heavily armed. Angel 7 can likely outrun and outmaneuver them, but she will be vastly outgunned."

"Captain Cooper will not try to outrun them," Trent said. "Not in his nature."

"Agreed," the AI responded. "I have attempted to formulate other options, but have failed. I have even attempted to think of *insane* solutions, but I do not believe I am human enough."

"Insane solutions," Trent repeated. "You only accept you cannot accomplish something, when you accept you are not willing to try."

The scientist continued to watch dock workers sort cargo, but his eyes focused well beyond the confines of the spaceport.

"Kennedy, contact Admiral Patterson for me. She could still be on Earth, or she might have transferred to the EMS2. I'll be in C-Tac."

As Trent made his way, using lifts and through hallways of the 109, Kennedy located Patterson in her cabin aboard EMS2. Her security personnel taking the call wanted to refuse, trying to allow the Admiral sleep she most likely needed, but Kennedy's insistence that it was a battle-field request got her through.

When Trent entered C-Tac, Patterson, in a navy blue robe, waited on the SHD forward screen.

"Nathan, I assume this is extremely important. You are not scheduled to leave dock for another four to five hours."

"Thank you for taking the call, Pam," using the familiar name, since she started with his. "We cannot get to Coop in time to make a difference. No matter what we try, it isn't going to happen."

"Are you suggesting scrubbing the mission?" Patterson asked, more than a bit surprised knowing Trent's friendship with Cooper.

"I'm suggesting Demon is faster and could get there in time to help. She could make the difference until PT-109 is able to arrive."

"I thought of sending Demon with you already. She is in dry dock being refitted. I spoke with the head engineer. They can't put her back together in less than forty-eight hours. She would be days late."

"Pam, Demon's sub-light drive and space-fold array are intact. If the engineers double up, and if they start now, and if they forego replacing the torpedoes on board, and forget about the upgrades to the torpedo tubes, they could make her ready in half a day. Thrusters and hover motors have been removed, and the replacements are not ready, but you can tow her off the dock. Once in space, they will have engines and steering."

Trent moved closer to the screen.

"If you can get a fire under the engineers and the techs, find her crew, and get them on station from their furlough on Earth, then haul her into space in twelve to fourteen hours, with her speed she could be with Angel 7 within two to four hours of the Zenge reaching Coop."

"Nathan, take a breath. You think Angle 7, who isn't fitted with torpedoes, and Demon, without torpedoes, can hold off eleven enemy ships until the PT-109 can get there?"

"Cooper stayed behind because it gave the *Star Gazer* a one-percent better chance of survival. Demon could do the same for him. And one-percent is a lot better than no chance in hell," the physicist, engineer, and concerned friend responded.

"No promises, Nathan. You will be in space-fold, so whether we can get Demon ready with enough time to make a difference or not, you won't know until you exit the fold for natural space."

"Thank you, Pam."

Patterson cut the video feed, presumably to start ordering personnel aboard EMS2 to attempt the impossible.

"Thank you, Dr. Trent."

"You're welcome, Kennedy. But so you know, I was blowing smoke up the Admiral's skirt. There is no way they can get Demon ready in time. I was there, and saw her. She's too far stripped."

"Then why make the request?"

"Hope . . . and prayer."

"Interesting," the AI said. Trent would have sworn the computer generated a bemused tone of voice as she added, "Captain Cooper once told me humans were in charge because sometimes they made insane decisions than would only prove sane at a later date. I hope this qualifies."

# Chapter 40

Demon ran at the torpedoes from low to high. The four laser cannons placed along the front of her wingspan released four bursts each. Eight targets destroyed.

Captain Casalobos maintained her heading. She killed engines to allow Demon to coast to a stop on Angel 7's port, less than one-hundred feet away.

"Coop," Elie's voice came over his com, but the *Star Gazer* would probably hear her as well. "I have *Magpie* working double-duty as co-pilot and comm-tac. We were on shore-leave when Patterson sent out the recall. *Wizard* should staff comm-tac, but he wasn't located in time to join us."

"Welcome, Mags," Coop said.

"Pleasure," came the reply.

"Loba, please switch to ship-to-ship, channel 2," Coop requested, wanting to keep conversations between the two ships private, both to enemy ears, and the *Star Gazer*. He allowed a couple of seconds for her to switch before continuing. "I'm glad to see both of you, but I have to ask — the 109?"

"Eleven hours out," Mags replied. "We're your wingman, Coop. I'm afraid we had to bug out without missiles or torpedoes."

"And without maneuvering thrusters or hover capability," Elie added.

While they caught up, the three Primary Zenge ships kept moving closer and began separating. Two headed for them, and one for the *Star Gazer*.

"Magpie, provide Storm access to your comm-tac station. Storm, send our tactical, strategic, and current battle reports to Demon. We are two-hundred-five-minutes into the conflict. The debris is what's left of two ships, similar to the three that fired the torpedoes we just nixed. There is another enemy ship damaged, heading out of system, and out of the fight."

"Little Angel kicked serious butt in three hours," Elie said, impressed.

"Magpie, you should have our info." He turned to Storm, who gave him a nod. "To this point, our best offense has been hit them with a NNEMP shell from the railgun, and follow up with laser fire or a kinetic rod within three-seconds. The nymph shuts down their electro-magnetic forcefield. The three-second window is what you have until it reestablishes. You get a five-hundred-square-foot target."

From experience, he knew the two pilots on Demon would be studying the diagrams air-dropped (space-dropped?) to them by Storm.

"The big box on top is a comm tower. We assume the command bridge is located there."

"Nice of them to put it up high. Makes a much cleaner target," Elie said.

"The smaller box behind the tower is where they keep the dynamo that produces their forcefield. Having the dynamo close allows the forcefield to provide a stronger shield for the command center."

"Bad design, huh?" Elie responded.

"Good for us. Target the dynamo, take down the forcefield. I have projectiles which will punch holes in those ships big enough to fly Demon through."

"Since we are working short-handed," this was from Mags, "I can coordinate the fire pattern and timing through comm-tac. Our software is more advanced than Angels. We don't have the dreaded lapse-in-judgment time. We have two rail-guns to your one. We were forced to bug out without missiles and torpedoes, so we loaded up on tree-huggers and dicks. Our laser cannons can fire longer, wider bursts."

"All of which means, Demon should take lead, Coop," Elie said. "You keep the flag, but the distribution of targets should be Demon first, Angel 7 second."

"Agreed. Demon will engage the two Primaries heading this way. Angel 7 will break off and intercept the one going for the *Star Gazer*," Coop said. "Loba, this conflict will be over before Kennedy arrives. Let's make sure we're the ones to welcome them."

"Copy that, Coop. Good hunting. Loba, out."

Storm took the moment to ask, "Are there two females on that ship, or four?"

"Two," Coop replied. "Captain Elena Victoria Casalobos, whose nickname is *Elie*, and whose call sign is *Loba*. Lt. Mary Margaret Moore, whose nickname is *Mags*, and whose call sign is *Magpie*. And before you ask, a call sign is a special nickname given to a pilot or navigator by other flyers."

"How much sex does it take to get a call sign?"

Smiling, and shaking his head, Coop replied, "None. You earn it by being a damn good flyer."

"What are *tree-huggers* and *dicks*?"

Coop had to grin. "Magpie is a special kind of person. A *tree-hugger* is a NNEMP, the nymph, and a *dick* is the rod we use as a projectile from the railgun. I'll explain the connections later. Now quiet and concentrate. We're ten minutes to firefight."

Five minutes later Storm urgently called out, "Break Off! Break Off!"

Coop immediately veered starboard, flipped, and circled down and away from the Zenge. Demon reacted as quickly, with Elie asking, "What? Why?"

Storm came on. "Magpie, check the penetrating scans of the ships you're tracking. My readings indicate the Zenge have abandoned the bridge and command tower. The second box no longer houses the dynamo. It appears they have a way of dropping the power generator deeper into the ship."

"Affirmative," Mags replied. "Same read here. Good catch. And your target just fired off four laser blasts. Looks like they're heading for the big sphere."

Cooper said, "I'm letting them through."

"Repeat, Coop. I thought you said you were NOT, I repeat NOT intercepting those bursts," from Elie.

"We need to know if the shields on the *Star Gazer* will perform. They should deflect all four bursts. If they do, it gives us an advantage. If not, we need to know now."

Storm, monitoring from comm-tac, provided the answer. "All bursts deflected. No major damage to *Star Gazer*. The shields held."

"Loba, new plan. We can outrun and outmaneuver these ships. We have to hit, hurt, and get out. Target engine sections, located above the exterior vents. First we stop them, then we do what we can to finish them. Copy."

"Copy," Elie replied. "Hit, hurt, repeat, and engines are priority one."

If you have ever seen a smaller bird harass a larger predatory bird, keeping it away from its nest to protect the young, then you have a picture of the ensuing three hours. Add a perpetual night sky, lit up with bursts from rail-guns, laser fire in multiple directions, torpedoes fired from tubes, and others blown from the sky, to paint the backdrop.

Angel 7 and Demon took multiple hits. Their sonic shields held. It was still like getting shot with an old-style bullet when wearing an ancient kevlar vest. The vest stopped the bullet from penetrating, but it still knocked your ass onto the ground, and left a nasty bruise.

Even undermanned (under-womanned?), Demon fought the two Primary spaceships to a stand still. She had them turning in circles. It required less than one fly-by for her to understand what the intel from Storm meant when it said the Zenge fought in two dimensions. As the battle extended, Elie and Mags took turns piloting the ship. They eventually gave up on staffing comm-tac, and relied on Storm to inform them if anything changed tactically, or strategically.

Storm split-screened Angel's comm-tac monitor to allow her to watch readouts, scans, hits, and misses for both fighters. She only spoke to give a warning, or make a suggestion based on changing tides.

Besides hammering the Primary trying to get to the *Star Gazer*, Angel had taken down over two dozen torpedoes fired at them or the cruise ship. It became obvious the Zenge no longer cared if they captured the *Star Gazer* whole.

Several laser bursts made it though to the huge cruise ship, but the extra padding provided by the upgraded shield system stopped most of them. Two laser bursts, landing one on top of the other, singed the hull, but nothing breached the ship's exterior hull.

Coop and Sky continued to one-two punch the Zenge Primary. A little less than two hours into the battle an entire section of the ship's stern quarter crumpled. The vessel's interior was fully exposed to space and the ship began to drift. The Zenge began firing lasers and torpedoes in the general direction of Angel 7. They were panicked and fighting scared.

Realizing his target sat dead in space, Coop coordinated with Elie on her two. She continued to engaged both with short, quick forays. While they concentrated on her, Sky peppered their engine sectors. By the time they turned their attention to Angel 7, Coop had bugged out to reengage his original target.

The pulse cannons were quiet. They must receive their power from the engines, and not the dynamo. Without engine power, the Zenge became desperate and angry. They began firing available laser cannons at the *Star Gazer*. If they were not stopped soon, the number of bursts would start damaging the bigger ship, and potentially opening the hull to space.

Coop brought Angel 7 around at incredible speed, flew the ship directly beneath the Primary, and hit the breaks. He came to a dead stop, directly under the ship. He began a firing sequence: a nymph, followed by a projectile rod, as fast as the railgun could switch loads and fire. The first nymph took out a section of the remaining forcefield. Two following nymphs and three rods penetrated the gap in the forcefield, ripping the larger ship down the center line, effectively splitting the hull in two.

Internal implosions, followed swiftly by explosions, finished the ship. Angel sped to assist Demon.

"Time, plus three-seven-five," Storm called absently.

The Earth ships were winning, but they were also getting battered. The decades of experience as fighter pilots, test pilots, as well as time in their current ships, made Coop and Elie the best flyers in this dogfight. They were overmatched by size and armaments. The Zenge were confused by the speed and tactics of the Earth ships.

Thirty minutes later, Demon set the pick, and Angel slammed the ball home. A nymph and projectile combination from Angel's railgun took out a section of hull. Implosive forces completed the eradication of the warship. Metal and biological pieces scattered into the void, swept across the expanse by the shock waves.

Demon received a broadside of laser fire from the remaining Primary. Angel 7 moved in to provide a shield, allowing the sister ship time to recover.

Elie, opting for a front to rear attack, pulled an Immelmann turn. An Immelmann trades airspeed for altitude during a 180-degree change in direction. The aircraft performs the first half of a loop, and when completely inverted, rolls to the upright position. A good offensive maneuver for setting up a high-side guns pass against a lower altitude, slow moving opponent, going in an opposite direction. A poor defensive maneuver, turning the attacker into a slow moving target, when done in atmosphere.

Because there is no drag in space, Demon lost no speed. Magpie fired nymph shells followed by kinetic projectiles. The combos rained up on the Primary from nose to tail.

The enemy ship began to fall apart. Internal explosions destroyed decks, killed enemy combatants, and blew holes through the hull.

"The bigger they are, the bigger they blow," Magpie said aloud.

"Time, plus four-zero-five," Storm called. The space debris field more than doubled in size.

"Demon, report," Coop ordered via the secure channel.

"All good," Mags replied, taking control of the stick, while Elie took a moment to rest. "We took a bunch of hits, but no structural damage. The inside of the ship looks like the after party for a rock and roll concert. Our comm-tac station got shaken badly. Not sure if I can get the monitor up and working. And Storm was fantastic. It was like we had a third on board."

"Thank you, " Storm said, over the live feed. "It has been my pleasure to give back to these Zenge." She caught Coop's eye and mouthed "Rock and Roll?"

Coop smiled, and said aloud, "Later."

"I have six projectiles left," Cooper said. "You have twenty, according to my comm-tac officer. We have three bogies left, and no idea what they have, or when they will decide to engage."

"If you hesitate you lose," Sky said, learning Earth tactics on the go.

"True that," Mags agreed.

"Okay. We take thirty to rest. Sky, please take over pilot. I need a break. Storm, eyes shut. Rest them. Magpie and Loba, take a quick break. In thirty we take it to them."

"You're Flag," Mags replied. "Demon, out."

"Sky, check on *Star Gazer*, and get updates. I'm back in ten, and you can take a break."

"You should take longer. You've been in your seat for seven hours."

"Damn," Coop said. "I didn't realize. It feels like we only left the *Star Gazer* a short while ago. We need a short R and R. When we go after the remaining Zenge ships, we'll put Angel on autopilot. That should give us an extra thirty minutes or so." He left Angel 7 in the capable control of his co-pilot.

## Chapter 41

Coop returned to the cockpit, passing Storm, who looked asleep in the comm-tac chair, with her harness on.

"Grab a bunk and get a couple of minutes," he said as he took his seat.

Sky sat serenely watching debris float in space. Occasional lights flared as electrical systems shorted, or gases ignited. "On Fell, there is a saying. *Revenge is a quiet meal.* Sitting here, quietly, I am highly satisfied."

"I spoke with Poonch," Sky said, leaving her introspection. "The *Star Gazer* has about a half-dozen places where there is a potential for a hull rupture. They've moved people out and closed the sections, so if something does break, it will not effect anything.

"Poonch also informed me the *Star Gazer*, '*being the finest cruise ship ever built, and known throughout the galaxy for the extraordinary views provided its guests'*, has been feeding video of the battle to every monitor and screen on board.

"I quote: 'When you destroyed the two Zenge ships, the roar from 240,000 people was so loud, the ship felt as if it had a heartbeat. But when Demon suddenly appeared, and shot down the torpedoes heading for them, the noise became so great the entire ship, both spheres shuddered.'"

"Not sure if streaming the fight is a good thing," Cooper said. "We've been winning, but if it goes the other way, those people are going to see fate coming for them in high definition."

Sky unharnessed and stood up. "Poonch also said they have been streaming the video to the space station in orbit over the fourth planet. With the time delay for distance, they should have started receiving the feed about two hours ago."

With her update completed, she left the Captain alone in the cockpit. Seated and strapped in, he keyed his mike for a private communication with Demon.

"Elie?"

"Hey, Coop. Calm before the storm, huh? Man, in the thirty years I have known you, I've seen you get knee deep in pretty tough places, but you have outdone yourself this time."

"Funny. Twelve people make it through the Space Ranger Project, and two end up on the edge of space accomplishing the vision." Cooper watched the stars from his front row seat. Somehow he knew Elie was doing the exact same thing. "Seems right somehow. We wanted to go into space, discover unknown worlds and meet aliens so badly, we allowed our insides ripped out and rebuild."

"Wasn't all bad, Coop," Elie replied. "The five years after, we had a good ride. We progressed from Navy pilots, to space ship test pilots, to having our own ships. Every time you made a step, I stepped into your footprints and followed. It makes perfect sense I would follow you into an intergalactic conflict."

"I didn't have the time before, so *thanks* to you and Mags for showing up. You saved a lot of lives. I know what it must have taken to get Demon ready to fly."

"You'll have to say thanks to Patterson for Demon. She brow beat a hundred workers to get the ship space-ready. Mags and I were sitting on a beach near Galveston. They hauled our asses up to EMS2, strapped us in, literally pushed us off the dock, and pointed us in this direction.

"By the way, Gregory, and his Marines are aboard the 109. In [she looked at her chronometer] eight hours, three Space Rangers present to complete the job."

"Before this mission, I would have said Marines would be a waste of time in space," Coop finished the comment with, "but we may need to use them."

"Assuming there's someone here to explain in simple, one syllable words what it is they need to do," Elie joked.

"I hate to interrupt," Storm interrupted. It was a private, secure channel, so, of course the Fellen communication savant heard every word. "The two Mischene ships are pulling away from the mothership."

"Storm, get Sky. She needs to strap in. Elie, you and Mags take the battlecruiser on our left. We'll take right. Storm, can you continue to keep up as comm-tac for both ships?"

"No problem. You should see the video games we play on Fell. And, Coop, what did you and Elie ride for five years?"

"You shouldn't listen in on private conversation, AStermalan-lan. Co-pilot is in, and strapped. Loba?"

"Loba and Magpie, set to go. Storm, the answer is 'each other'. Demon, out."

Demon banked left, then jumped to 100,000mph. Angel 7 nudged a bit right, and matched speed. The Mischene battlecruis-ers approached at over 100,000mph. They were within range to fire weapons.

Demon headed for a battlecruiser with four torpedoes tubes firing a missile every five-seconds for twenty-seconds. Sixteen ship-killers were headed her way.

Angel 7's target continued to hold position, presumably to as-sess the results before determining its attack plan.

Mags took out the first four torpedoes. Their speed flew them into the succeeding twelve. Elie weaved through them, and over-flew the battlecruiser. Since she was there anyway, she started popping NNEMP shells along the top of the ship. The comm-tac computer, though no longer programmable, maintained the origi-nal firing solution Mags entered earlier, making sure bursts of laser fire followed the railgun loads at the proper intervals.

Storm assessed damage. "You hit them, and you took off a lay-er of skin, but the ship has a double-hull. No atmosphere escap-ing. When you made your pass off the stern, they sent another twelve torpedoes at you. First twelve are reacquiring. You now have twenty-four missiles, with various loads, looking for you."

"Copy," came the terse reply from Demon.

While that conflict happened, the second Mischene ship flew by Angel 7, ignoring her completely. It increased speed. Their tar-get was the *Star Gazer*. The Zenge had decided capture was no longer an option. They intended to deal a killing blow, taking re-venge for the ships already destroyed.

"Loba," Coop keyed the mike so everyone could hear. "Space-fold Demon and get between that cruiser and *Star Gazer*. I can't. We did multiple folds prior to your arrival. Another fold now would probably kill Sky or Storm. I'll take the missiles. When they lose you, it will give us extra time to take them down."

"Copy." Before the echo died, Demon pivoted and jumped into space-fold.

The Zenge missiles came to a drift, targeting computers having lost Demon. Coop took Angel 7 directly into them, and Sky played the joy sticks like a world-class gamer.

By the time the missile tracking-packages could redirect, only six remained. They acquired Angel 7, fired thrusters, and flew toward the fighter. Coop reversed, and then spun the ship. He outpaced the in-coming rockets, while Sky finished the last six, using the rear-facing laser cannons.

"Forward cannon nearing redline," Storm informed them. "That was a lot of heat in a short time, even rotating the cannons. We need ten, maybe fifteen minutes, or you risk losing them. Rear facing cannon perfect. Swivel lasers good to go. Rail gun optimal."

Meanwhile, Demon returned to natural space and began circling the battlecruiser, hitting it repeatedly with combined railgun and laser fire. Elie stayed so close to the enemy ship, its cannons were useless.

"This son-of-a-bitch must have the toughest hull, and the strongest forcefield generator in the universe," Mags said to Elie. (Storm, of course, hacked the comms systems. She could hear the conversations inside Demon, as if on board.)

Unable to depress cannons enough to fire on Demon, the Zenge fired twenty-four torpedoes at the *Star Gazer*. The torpedoes were larger, and carried heavier loads than missiles. They did not possess advanced homing packages. They did not need them when aimed at a target the size of the Osperantue cruise ship.

Storm spoke to Elie and Mags: "The first twelve are nuclear tipped. The following twelve have hardened tips and carry high explosives. They have figured out an EMP will temporarily shut down a forcefield. We've been using the same tactic against them for the last eight hours. It must have sunk in. They can do the same against *Star Gazer*, using nuclear explosions, instead of NNEMP rounds, to create a gap in their forcefield."

Elie curled Demon upward and raced after the torpedoes. Her ship actually upside-down, but in space, no one cared, or noticed.

As soon as Elie abandoned the battlecruiser to chase the torpedoes, multiple laser-cannons' fire filled the blackness in pursuit. At the speed Elie put on to overtake and pass the torpedoes, Demon left the lasers wasted in the void.

"Storm, tell the *Star Gazer* to warn everyone on board to brace for impacts. We may stop the first twelve, but we will not, repeat, will not stop everything in the second salvo." Elie spoke with urgency, no panic in her tone.

Storm, already aware of the math, and the problem, made the call.

"*Star Gazer,* you are about to get hit by as many as twelve high-explosive torpedoes with hardened tips. Hull penetration is a high probability. I have estimated which torpedoes in the second salvo will arrive first and have informed your shield computers where to pad for the first four. I have sent most-probable target coordinates for the other eight. You have less than five minutes to clear those sections and close them before impact. Do you copy?"

"We're clearing sections as fast as we can," Poonch replied. "Thank you Angel 7. Good luck, Demon."

"Damn, that girl is good," Mags said aloud. "But so are we."

Demon climbed into a side-slide flight pattern, which would take her in front of, and parallel to the first salvo of torpedoes. Not waiting on comm-tac, Mags and Elie manually aimed off their heads-up displays, taking out the first twelve torpedoes. They slipped around the last exploding torpedo. All they could do was watch, as the twelve remaining collided with the *Star Gazer.*

Angel 7 had backed off to allow cannons to cool. Storm was able to concentrate on the *Star Gazer* attack. She provided a running account and assessment of the bombardment.

"First four torpedoes have hit with no appreciative damage. Number five; same. The forcefield still able to react. Six through twelve are hits with hull penetrations. We have explosions and breaches in seven location. Casualty reports coming. Interfacing with *Star Gazer* comms . . . four sections fully cleared. Three partially cleared. Decks 408 - 410, 363 - 368 and 279 - 286 were closed without being fully cleared. Any sections open to space are sealed off. All hits occurred on the larger sphere. No way to assess the exact number of casualties. The ship itself is completely operational. No vital systems are damaged," she concluded.

"Demon, you just saved over 200,000 lives."

Demon's crew did not reply. They were mad, and they were on the hunt for the battlecruiser.

"You said Decks 279 - 286 weren't fully cleared," Coop said to Storm.

"Correct, Captain. Problem?"

Cooper did not respond.

Angel 7's cannons had cooled sufficiently, and Coop was about to reengage the Zenge, when Sky reached out a hand, placing it on his arm. "Wait a minute," she said, then called Storm to the cockpit.

"The aft section of the Mischene battlecruisers is shaped like a U. Two trailing hulls, which displace heat, gases, and other vapors from the engines, with the main hangar in the center." Sky looked to Storm for confirmation. Storm nodded. "The hangar has double doors that open from the center to the sides. It is about 1,500-feet deep and ends at a bulkhead. That bulkhead is shared with generators and engine compartments. It's the dynamo generators from up top, now deep inside the ship for protection."

Again Storm nodded, and added, "The deep penetration scans indicate the Zenge haven't changed any of the ship's configuration, compared to design specs we have in our files. The only odd thing is, it is nearly impossible to pick out lifeforms. It's probably a combination of their cold-blooded natures and instrument jamming."

Sky turned to Coop. "If we blow the hangar doors, we can target the dynamos which charge the forcefield. The dynamos probably provide power for the pulse cannon, as well. The Primaries used engine power for their pulse weapons, but the Mischene have much stronger generators. They did not recognize the flaw when they selected the location to hide the dynamos. They were protecting them by burying them deep in the ship. From up, and down, and from the sides, the generators are far from any hulls."

"And they considered the hangar area another buffer, not wide open space," Cooper completed her reasoning.

"Storm, strap in, and tell Demon to watch. DO NOT give any details, in case they have a comms genius in your league. They can continue to harass their target, and keep it off the *Star Gazer*, but watch."

"Will do, and no they don't," Storm replied, moving backward, out of the cockpit.

"No, they don't what?" he asked.

"Have a comms genius in my league," she said, finding her seat and tightening her harness.

Storm contacted Demon. Coop and Sky confirmed their plan of attack.

"Time, plus four-eight-zero," Storm called. Eight hours since the conflict began. Cooper's body could self-heal, and even regenerate, but after eight hours, it ached and his legs burned. He could only imagine what it was like for the Fellen.

"My chest hurts," Storm said. "These harness straps weren't designed for women with big tits." Coop smiled, and counted sore legs among his blessings.

# Chapter 42

The Mischene battlecruiser was a tough opponent. They continued to fight primarily in two dimensions, but they definitely had reverse, more power, and greater speed. The eighteen laser cannons laid down deadly fields of fire. The two cannons on top sprayed bursts of EMP, trying to place each load into Angel 7's projected path. While Coop avoided a lot, a lot also landed, shaking the ship and crew. He flew ovals and spirals, as well as circles around, over, and under the ship. He kept trying to get into a position where he or Sky would have a clear shot at the hangar doors. The cruiser would start, and stop, move forward, and then reverse without reason. Either the Zenge were confused, or they were brilliantly defying them. Storm voted for confused. Coop was not so sure.

While they tried to attain a favorable firing solution, Demon kept up a similar harassing patterns on the other ship. The comm-tac operated well enough. Every couple of minutes they would hit the ship with nymph-laser combos. Mags kept trying to adjust the program to target previously hit areas. She surmised that because the battlecruiser used a double hull, if they kept hitting the same section, sooner or later, they would have a penetration.

It was strategically sound, but having to shift and dodge made it nearly impossible. Demon took laser fire every time the cruiser gained enough distance. This usually occurred when they would fire off a volley of torpedoes at the *Star Gazer* and Demon would track them down. What they could not bring down in time proved few enough, and far enough apart, the big cruise ship's shields held.

Forty-five minutes into the latest engagement, the battlecruiser Coop shadowed made a sudden turn to port, leaving Angel directly behind the larger ship. Without hesitation, Cooper brought his space fighter's nose forward to the giant double doors which enclosed the hangar. He pulled the railgun's trigger, and called "away" six times. Sky fired the same number of lasers from the wing-mounted cannons.

The doors blew off their hinges, and anything and everything not tied down in the hangar came flying out into space. Cooper dropped Angel lower than the rear of the ship to keep from getting slammed by the debris.

After it passed, he brought the nose of his ship up, lined up the target, and fired four of his six remaining projectiles from the railgun. A projectile left Angel's railgun and entered the open hangar every five-seconds. At the thirty-second mark, a bright yellow and red explosion roared out of the open hangar.

They only had to wait seconds for Storm's report.

"Engines, off line. She's dead. Dynamo, off line. No shields. Two of your projectiles sailed through and travelled all the way to the front of the ship. They are experiencing system-wide failures. Oh, Coop. You might want to get us as far as you can. One of the projectiles nipped an anti-matter container. When it goes, and it looks like it will in less than ten minutes, the concussive wave will pass through our sonic forcefield like air."

"There shouldn't be a concussive wave in the vacuum of space," he objected.

"If it were simply a wave, it wouldn't affect us," she replied. "Because it's particle dense with momentum, it will have the same properties as if within an atmosphere."

"How far?" Cooper asked, taking Angel straight down, and hitting the thrusters.

"At least 40,000 miles," Storm replied.

"At max we might get there is ten minutes. What about Demon and the *Star Gazer*?"

"They are both outside the radius. So is the other battlecruiser."

"I assume the anti-matter is for wormhole travel. Why did the other Zenge ships not explode?"

"The containers are super strong. Normally, they would not explode and only drift in space as debris. They self-lock if they are disconnected from their matter counter-part, so they are actually quite safe. You hit the container with enough force to crack it."

Ten minutes later, a lot happened.

The anti-matter container blew. A shockwave pushed gases, particles, and debris for 40,000 miles.

Angel 7 was 61,000 miles away, and rode what amounted to a gentle rise and fall as the wave dissipated. The maneuvers, and dog fight with the Mischene battlecruiser, followed by Coop's desperate dive to escape the effects of the anti-matter explosion, placed them nearly 200,000 miles away from the other ships.

Demon was caught in another explosion, as they had to destroy a nuclear-tipped torpedo at close range. It was headed for a section of the *Star Gazer* which had already been breached. When the concussion from the explosion reached Demon, the wave rocked the ship so severely, a fiber-optic cable separated from its lead. Their primary engine dropped off-line, taking the sonic forcefield with it. With the shields down, a laser shot decimated a railgun. The impact hammered the fighter into a spiral.

The odds finally caught up to the pesky ship, and she lay dead in space.

The SFPT-109 entered natural space from space-fold, eight hours early, and 50,000 miles short of the drifting *Star Gazer* and the injured and vulnerable Demon.

The Zenge's stolen Mischene battlecruiser was moving toward the two ships from the other direction.

Storm reported everything to Coop, who wasted no time. He headed Angel 7 towards Demon and the *Star Gazer*. Next, he contacted the 109.

"Kennedy, this is Captain Cooper, I need you to run hard and intercept the alien battlecruiser moving on Demon and the *Star Gazer*."

"Captain Cooper, this is Captain Black. I have command of the PT-109. I need time to access the situation. How did Demon get here? No one told me they were in route."

"We don't have time, Captain. Demon is here, down, and without shields. The *Star Gazer* has over 240,000 people aboard, endangered by the shovel-headed battlecruiser closing on them. You are closer than me, Captain. That is your situation. Now, please engage the enemy before they kill a lot of people, including ours."

"Captain, I have command of this ship. I will decide when to engage."

"Kennedy."

"Yes, Captain Cooper."

"Kennedy!" Shouted Captain Black, standing in front of her command chair, "You will not have contact with Captain Cooper without my permission."

"Kennedy, will you recognize my authority over this battle group?"

"Captain Cooper, Admiral Patterson expressly ordered this ship turned over to you upon arrival."

"He is not on board!" Black shouted. If she was aware the ship's entire compliment could hear what was happening, and not only the bridge crew, she apparently did not care. "He cannot take command unless he is on board."

"That was not stipulated, Captain Black," Kennedy replied. "Captain Cooper, orders?"

"Comm-tac is sending you combat data, and the tactical and strategic reports. I can destroy the battlecruiser, but not before it fires on Demon and the *Star Gazer*. Get its attention. Move to intercept, and fire whatever you have at it. Your sonic shields will protect you. Get between it, and the *Star Gazer* as quickly as you can."

"We are firing nymphs and lasers now. Moving to intercept at fastest possible speed. Captain, would you order the release of Counselor Genna Bouvier from her cabin?"

"What the hell?" Exasperated, and angry. "Yes. Release her, now!"

"You will not commandeer my ship, Cooper." Captain Black opened a compartment on the arm of the command chair and flipped a switch. It was the emergency shut down, should the AI ever go rouge and endanger the ship, or crew. Coop previously ordered Kennedy to enact procedures to prevent any outside agencies from bypassing the command lane and taking over the ship. There was no way for her to prevent the on-board kill-switch from being activated manually.

Black called out: "Pilot, all stop. Ops, cease fire."

On Angel 7, Storm reported: "Kennedy is all stop. The AI is offline and the ship is no longer firing at the Zenge."

"Captain Black, you are going to cost us 250,000 lives. Get Kennedy online, now!" Cooper pushed Angel faster, trying to get her there in time to help.

"Captain Cooper, it's Genna. I have Captain Black pinned on the floor, but I'm afraid the bridge crew members are about to intervene."

"Highest rank?" Coop demanded.

"Lt. Dominczyk," replied a female voice.

"LT, I have the Flag, do you copy?"

"Sir, you have the Flag," Dominczyk responded, recognizing Captain Cooper in command of Space Fleet ships and personnel during the current conflict. Admiral Patterson made this clear before the 109 departed MSD. Captain Black's decision to ignore the directive questionable, at best.

"Genna, the command chair's left arm has a compartment. Open it and flip the switch."

"Switch flipped. Kennedy is coming online. Col. Gregory has arrived on the bridge, and is escorting Captain Black off," Genna told him. "But I'm afraid we we're too late."

Storm concurred. "The battleship has fired a nuclear torpedo at the *Star Gazer*. Target is the command sphere. They have also fired two kinetic inertia rounds. They normally only fire inertia rounds at installations on planets. The rods are similar to your projectiles but much, much bigger. Impact in less than three minutes."

"Can we hit them from here?"

"No," Sky replied. "We're closing, but not near enough. The Mischene rods are bigger, but still incredibly small compared to space."

Storm gave everyone a concise play-by-play.

"The nuclear torpedo has hit. EMP has shields down around the upper section of the command sphere. The first inertia round penetrated the sphere mid-ship. The second inertia round has penetrated the top two sections. Both projectiles are ripping through walls, equipment, and anything in their paths. Both exiting now.

"Environment is venting. Command bridge and two floors below are gone. Middle floors with massive damage. Computers are attempting to close off sections. The sphere is maintaining structure. Surviving crew members are attempting to escape though the corridor connecting the command sphere to the main sphere."

Storm called to the cockpit, "Coop, the battlecruiser is targeting Demon."

With their attention on the destruction of the *Star Gazer's* command sphere, and the desire to destroy the crippled Demon, as well as being concerned about the arrival of another warship, the battlecruiser's commanders were not prepared when Angel 7 came in hot, fast, and angry.

NNEMP shells, followed by laser fire ripped open the hangar doors. Coop's final two projectiles entered close behind, destroying the ship's dynamo, damaging the engine compartment, and stopping the battlecruiser in its tracks. This time, no anti-matter containment explosions.

While this was happening, Mags scurried into engineering to manually repair the conduit so Elie could restart the primary engine.

With engine on, and shields up, Demon evaded laser fire. Elie flew them between the *Star Gazer* and the Zenge ship. Mags returned to the co-pilot seat, fired a half dozen projectiles into the shovel head. As that section disintegrated, the 109 joined.

Genna ordered four tactical nuclear torpedoes fired into the body of the enemy ship. When they hit and exploded, pieces of the battle ship scattered in every direction. Major and minor explosions tore what little remained into space junk.

The PT-109 came up to stand off the *Star Gazer's* port side. Elie brought Demon around to drift beside Angel.

"We still have the mothership and two cargo ships to deal with," Cooper reminded everyone.

"Angle 7, this is Commander Cornitsch. Can you hear me?"

"We have you, Commander Cornitsch. Do you need assistance?" Coop asked.

"Not at the moment. The damage is done, and contained. I have command control of the ship from engineering. I'm afraid Captain Poonch, the entire bridge crew, and a great number of others are dead or missing, Captain."

"Commander, try to keep everything under control until we finish with the final Zenge ships. After that, we will send boarding parties to assist in every way we can."

"Thank you, Captain Cooper. Cornitsch, out."

"Loba, you and Magpie are out of the fight. You will remain with the Star Gazer. Kennedy, lower your ramp. I'm bringing Angel 7 aboard. Prep the ship for battle. We're going to intercept the Zenge ship dead ahead, and 400,000 miles out. Have Col. Gregory prep his Marines for an away mission. We may have to take those two cargo ships hand-to-hand."

"Ramp lowering, Captain. Hanger ready to receive Angel 7."

# Chapter 43

Cooper exited the lowered rear ramp, bringing Storm and Sky with him. As soon as his feet hit the deck, the AI announced over the PA, "Kennedy is aboard."

Henry Smith rushed forward to greet the battle-worn captain, but came up short when he saw the two blue aliens in skin-tight black.

Captain Cooper saluted first (out of order), as the shocked supply officer caught his wind. "Henry," glad to have you aboard. "These are my co-pilot, Sky, and my comm-tac officer, Storm. Please get them to a cabin with a shower, get them hot meals, and have non-uniform grays delivered. Try to keep gawkers at a distance. You might want to put them in an officer's cabin close to the hangar. That way you don't have too many decks to travel."

"We should stay with you, Coop," Sky said in protest.

His response was quick, and blunt. "You will obey orders, or you can sit out the remainder of this mission on the *Star Gazer*. Your choice."

Storm took the slack-jawed Smith by the arm, and said, "Henry is an interesting name. Is it a nickname?"

Leaving the Fellen with the Lt. Commander, Coop raced to the nearest lift and up to the command bridge.

He had to pass two Marines in the hallway in front of an officer's cabin. They came to attention when he stopped. "As you were," he said, and asked, "Captain Black?"

"Yes, sir," the sergeant answered. Before Coop could walk away, the sergeant added, "Captain, everybody aboard heard what happened. Captain Black was wrong."

"That she was," Coop agreed.

Entering the bridge, Genna stood and called, "Captain on the bridge," bringing everyone to attention. "As you were," he said, putting names to faces. He had helped vet every officer present.

He took note of the silver bar on Genna's collar. "Lt. Bouvier, glad to see you out and about. How much time before we reach the Zenge ship?"

"At current speed, two-hours and twenty-three minutes," Genna replied. "And I'm Ship's Counselor Bouvier, per Admiral Patterson's order."

"Congratulations, Ship's Counselor. Kennedy, please instruct Col. Gregory to meet Ship's Counselor Bouvier and me in C-Tac as soon as possible."

Cooper handed the bridge to Lt. Dominczyk, before moving to C-Tac.

"I'm sure the story of your incarceration fascinating, but first I want to thank you, and Kennedy for getting here as quickly as possible. And thanks for the loyalty you both showed today." He held up a hand to stop a reply. "As I said, I want to have a long sit down soon, but first we have a battle to complete. Could you call up the data on the three Zenge ships which remain in the solar system."

Genna moved to the console which controlled C-Tac's video display, and quickly brought up three schematics: the mothership and the two cargo vessels. They had hardly come up, when Gregory entered, walked over to Coop, and put him in a bearhug.

"As much as you make me want to hate your guts, you go and do shit like this, and make me want to have your children," he said, holding Coop by the shoulders. "We began receiving the video feed of your adventure as soon as we entered natural space. My people are in the mess eating popcorn, and watching it like porn. Even though they know the ending, they can't stop watching."

"Kisses later, Anton, business now. We still haven't made it to the end." He directed the Russian's attention to the SHD screen. "We've designated the big one as the *mothership*. Likely loaded with Zenge warriors, and probably has the battle group's commander on board. That one will be my responsibility. The other two ships are cargo carriers. We do not think they have ship-to-ship weapons, but they might. We do think they are carrying supplies to keep the other ships in the group operational, from food, to equipment, to armament. We also believe they have prisoners on board."

"Why would they bring prisoners on an attack?" Gregory asked.

"They eat their captives," Cooper told him. "Somewhere, in the data we've been streaming, is that disturbing information. One of the reasons they attack planets is to round up inhabitants, live-stock, wild animals, whatever lives and breathes, and use it as a food source. I doubt their diet is one-hundred percent meat, but enough. Bringing it along alive is probably easier, or cheaper, or tastier than killing it first, and then storing it."

"Gross," Gregory said, his face a bit more pale than its normal ruddy complexion.

"We'll get full scans as we get closer, and make the final de-termination. If we decide captives are on those ships, then we will have to board, and take them deck by deck. You need to begin prepping your Marines, and preparing EVA suits. The ships will have atmosphere, and the potential for a variety of bacterial or viral agents. I'll take out their engines. You will use the LBJ to board them."

"If there aren't many of the baddies, we might split up the team, and hit both ships. If we hit one, it gives the other time to kill the captives, or use them as hostages."

"You're the ground commander. You make the call. If there isn't anything else, you can get your people ready. I need to take a shower."

Gregory left, and Coop turned to Genna. "I'm going to shower, change, and return to the bridge in sixty minutes. I'm also going to have the two Fellen join us. One will take comms, and one will take operations. I would like you in the pilot's seat. Casey can move over to navigation. Have everyone else take a break. There is no telling how much time the next engagement will last."

"The two blue women with the . . . tight tops?" Genna asked.

"The two blue women, who spent eight hours aboard Angel 7 helping destroy eight enemy ships which had us outnumbered, and outgunned . . . in tight tops."

"Kennedy has already reviewed the data sent over. She in-forms me the Fellen both exceptionally talented, and incredibly gifted flight officers. I'm pleased and proud to share the bridge with them."

"Thank you, Genna. Just curious, but you actually had Captain Black pinned to the deck?"

"A perfect hip throw. And I placed my boot — thank you for the boots, by the way — on her diaphragm. Every time she moved, I pushed my heel in just hard enough to take the wind out of her."

# Chapter 44

Cooper asked LCMD Smith to bring Sky and Storm up via the supply lift, instead of through busy corridors and personnel lifts.

When they entered the bridge, Cooper was in the command seat. Genna sat to his front, and left, at the pilot's console. Lt. Casey Adams staffed the navigation console. Unlike the other two, Lt. Adams only heard descriptions of the Fellen. He came to his feet, his mouth dropping open, and his eyes wide.

"Lt. Adams, please return to your station," Cooper directed without anger, understanding the reaction to a first contact. "Lt. Commander Smith, thank you for taking care of our guests. Sky, Storm, welcome to the bridge. You both know Ship's Counselor Lt. Genna Bouvier. The young man, with the vibrant red hair, is Lt. Casey Adams, currently our navigator."

The women had been issued Space Grays without insignia. Storm wore the white button-up, collared long-sleeve shirt without a cover, tucked into dark gray flight pants. It showed off her curves and trim waist. Sky wore a lighter gray sweater with shoulder and elbow patches over her collared white shirt, and flight pants. The combination muted her figure, but took nothing away from her beauty. Both, Cooper noted, wore their own boots.

"Storm, if you will take the first seat on your right. That is our communications console, similar to comm-tac on Angel. Make yourself comfortable. I'm sure you will get up to speed quickly."

"Sky, please take the chair adjoining Counselor Bouvier. That is Kennedy's operations station. You have operational information, control, and weapons. This is normally our tactical station as well, but I'm routing tactical data to communications. Storm has shown a natural ability to keep up with tactics, along with communications. Suppo, any issues with our guests?"

Smith walked over to stand near the ship's Captain. "No, sir. Wasn't sure what they might eat, so I brought a lot of samples from the galley. I'm pretty sure they ate everything. Our guests were quite hungry, and appreciated the hot meal."

"Thank you. You can return to your duties," dismissing the Lt. Commander.

"Sky and Storm, you have less than an hour to acquaint yourself with our systems. If you have any questions, ask anyone on the bridge for assistance."

Cooper had been a test pilot for the majority of his adulthood. He chose to live a solitary existence, which he appreciated. He interacted well with people, but always spoke straight to the point. He never intended to run a traditional, Navy-based bridge choked with protocol. The crew needed discipline, but performance required communications flow quickly, easily, and without fear.

During the vetting process to crew the ship, he interviewed the men and women about to make the final cut. He made it clear, when the ship became operational, he anticipated a more relaxed atmosphere than many trained under. Operating under duress, with civilian contractors, especially alien civilians, could be a preview of things to come.

"Casey, time to target?" he asked.

"Fifty minutes."

Sky leaned across to Genna, and said, "I thought you were a captain."

Genna smile, and told her, "I was captain long enough to get Kennedy to Mars."

"Well, you made an impression as a captain. I hope you noticed we took care of Captain Cooper, as you ordered. And returned him in good condition."

"I did, and thank you, . . . Sky. I'm glad you and Storm are here. Your work on Angel 7 was, well, it was remarkable."

Smiling, Sky resumed getting familiar with the operational systems for the PT-109. Storm was already rooting beneath the communications console, switching leads, and adding her own equipment. She made upgrades without being asked, but also not being told no. Genna sat relaxed, content in her comfort zone behind the pilot's console. Casey kept sneaking glances over his shoulder at the aliens. Because they were alien, or because they were hot, Cooper could not tell.

Thirty minutes later he commanded Sky to perform deep penetrating scans of the Zenge vessel.

"May I address the ship directly?" Sky asked.

"Of course."

"Kennedy, you will need to adjust the scans for heat signatures lower than normal. The Zenge are cold-bloodied," Sky said aloud.

"Thank you, Sky. The settings are now adjusted," Kennedy said. "The Zenge ship reversed course, and is currently heading toward the two cargo ships. Those ships have also reversed courses."

Kennedy continued. "Interior scans, calibrated for lower body temperatures, show 61,237 lifeforms. The penetration scans indicate no warm-blooded lifeforms aboard. However, the section housing the bridge, and the area estimated for main engineering compartments have additional shielding. Life-form scans are impossible to read from those areas.

"The ship employs two thruster-style turbines for low-speed maneuvering, two sub-light engines, a matter-antimatter wormhole drive system, and two dynamo-generators capable of wrapping the ship in an electro-magnetic forcefield. The generators provide power for weapons and systems. There is another power system present, but unable to discern its purpose. I detect non-baryonic matter."

"You mean negative matter?" Cooper asked, moving forward, on the edge of his chair.

"More appropriate, exotic matter which can potentially create negative mass," Kennedy answered.

"There is a lot of chatter between the three ships," Storm added, out from under the console, back in her seat.

"Activity in the unknown power system," Sky reported. "The matter-antimatter containers starting to blend, and the unknown system is generating . . . well, generating zero mass. I thought zero mass impossible," she added.

"Captain Cooper," this from Kennedy. "A wormhole opening has appeared in front of the mothership."

"Sky, can ships create wormholes?"

"Not to my knowledge," the Fellen replied, equally taken aback by the development. "Wormhole travel is accomplished by using charted wormhole channels. There are uncharted channels — probably millions of them — but no one can create one, and especially not within a solar system."

Kennedy begged to differ: "The Zenge ship entered the new wormhole gate, and the gate has closed. They have retreated, Captain Cooper, and there is no way to know where the channel will lead."

"Kennedy, get Dr. Trent, and get him to C-Tac ASAP. Genna, Sky, and Storm with me. Lt. Adams, the bridge is yours. If you want to call back-ups for pilot, comms, or operations, do so." He rose and marched to C-Tac, the three women on his heels.

"Kennedy, display the wormhole event we witnessed," he ordered. As the SHD screen showed the Zenge mothership about to enter the wormhole gate, Cooper called for her to pause.

Five minutes later Dr. Trent entered, and before he could take his seat asked, "Did I hear correctly? The Zenge created a wormhole to escape through?"

Cooper tilted his head to the SHD, and said, "Watch."

Once more a wormhole gate appeared. The Zenge ship entered and disappeared as the gate closed.

"Kennedy, was the wormhole there before, and we missed it?"

"No, sir."

"The Zenge created it?"

"Yes, sir."

"Is the gate still there?"

"Yes, sir," and anticipating the follow-up question, "but I would advise against using it. Even if I had wormhole drive capability, which I do not. As Sky said earlier, this is an unknown channel. We have no way to predict the destination, or what might be waiting."

"Nathan. Ideas?"

Trent, watching the event, and listening to the conversations, dropped his fingers, absently massaging his temple, away from his forehead. To his credit, he made no comment regarding the aliens in the room.

"Wormhole travel has always been a theoretical possibility. With the information we gained from our new friends, obviously a reality. Wormholes are unstable designs. They need a negative energy band to prevent them from collapsing. A naturally occurring wormhole would not be able to sustain continuity. The zero mass would dissipate. Someone, sometime in the past built the channels travelers use to move between star systems.

"The mechanism employed on the mothership created exotic matter. That is exactly the type of matter needed to keep a wormhole from collapsing. We witnessed the creation of a channel."

"But Sky says no channels exist within solar systems. The gates always open at the outside edges," Cooper argued.

"Doesn't mean a wormhole gate *couldn't* exist within a solar system, only incredibly dangerous to use. Solar systems are dirty and unpredictable. Neptune's moons were once dwarf planets in their own orbits. They got too close to Neptune, and its gravity scooped them up. Out here, asteroids, and planetoids bang against each other like bumper cars. You could exit a gate within a solar system, and end up yanked onto a planet and crushed.

"I would say the Zenge panicked, and used the fastest means of escape they had available. Wherever that channel leads, I doubt they would use it to return. This was a one-way strategic retreat."

"I agree," Sky added. "The Zenge are cowards. They saw seven of their ships destroyed, one incapacitated, and the PT-109 approaching. They sent messages to the two cargo ships, and then used their only means of escape."

"Agreed, " Coop concurred. "They said *sorry guys, we gotta bug out. Good luck*, and then they ran."

It was Genna who asked, "Do you think the Zenge built all the wormhole channels?"

"Doubtful," Sky answered. "They most likely discovered the ability from a world they invaded. Nothing suggests the Zenge were or are creators."

"Storm," Cooper turned to the Fellen who remained quiet throughout the discussion. "Thoughts?"

"They sent messages to the cargo ships before escaping," she repeated. "The Zenge on those ships know they have been abandoned. I would suggest, if there are captive aboard, they are in grave danger."

Cooper shot from his seat, and with an anger directed at himself only, said, "Damn! We've been sitting here discussing science theory, and Storm is the only one staying in the present. Kennedy, long-range penetrating scans on those cargo ships. Genna, get us to them, quickest speed. Dr. Trent, thank you. Everyone to your stations."

"Captain Cooper, the wormhole gate is collapsing in on itself," Kennedy said.

"You mean it closed," Coop replied.

"No. It collapsed. It is no longer there," the AI responded.

"Damn," Trent said, leaving though the corridor door. "I wanted to study that thing." The others exited through to the bridge.

Casey stood, and called, "Captain on the bridge," to himself, having decided not to replace stations with back-ups. Protocol still protocol.

Seated, Cooper keyed direct communications from his chair. "Col. Gregory, get your people ready and in the shuttle. Kennedy, please provide Col. Gregory with a schematic of the two ships, and update him on scans."

Cooper listened as Kennedy briefed the Marine:

"The two cargo ships are basic shipping containers. Three levels. Bottom level consists of engines, ventilation, habitat systems, and retractible quad-pods for landing. Mid-level is hangar, engineering, command control, and crew cabins.

"Upper level, forward to aft. First, an open room, and a sizable cold storage area. Amidship is storage and armory. The final area is located above the hangar; holding cells by the configuration.

"In the nearest ship, there are sixteen cold-blooded lifeforms, most likely Zenge, and 268 warm-blooded lifeforms located in the holding cells. We will overtake in forty-five minutes.

"The other ship shows fifteen cold-blooded, and 421 warm-blooded lifeforms."

"How do we get inside?" Gregory asked.

Storm answered. "We don't have to shoot the doors off this time," she said. "The cargo ships use simple, basic systems, including their operational computers. I've already hacked in through a network. I'm shutting down engines, locking the section doors to where the cells are located, so they cannot harm the captives, and shutting down elevators. As soon as you are ready, I will open the hangar doors."

"New time to overtake is thirty minutes."

"How close, Skip?" Gregory asked.

"You can get from ship to ship in fifteen minutes. I'm going to park the 109 behind the first cargo ship." Coop was having a difficult time transitioning from fighter pilot to commanding officer. He continued to attack every issue as his problem alone. He had a crew, and he needed to begin accepting that fact.

Gregory said, "I'm taking the full contingent, including Dr. Singh, and three corpsmen. Twenty-nine total personnel. I need a shuttle pilot and co-pilot."

"Sky and I are on the way," Cooper told him, and everyone else. "Counselor Bouvier, you have command. Keep this ship safe. We don't know the mothership will not return, and we don't know for certain these cargo ships don't have ship-to-ship weapons. Storm, keep us informed, and make sure Gregory and his team know where the Zenge are. Sky, with me."

He should not leave his ship, or his command, to ferry Marines into battle. He really needed to make the transition from lone operator to command. He would make it, once everyone was safe.

# Chapter 45

Smith had EVA suits, and laser-pistol sidearms ready for Cooper and Sky when they reached the hangar. Coop's weapons belt included a sheathed knife. Henry knew his friend well. Everyone strapped into seats aboard the LBJ. Marines in the hold; Coop, and Sky at the controls. They had to go through depressurization, hangar door opening, and a short trip though space to an open cargo door. He entered an unused bay, liberal enough to allow the LBJ to enter and settle. The entire trip took thirty minutes.

They waited for Storm to close the cargo ship's doors, and pressurize the bay. The EVA suits allowed them to survive no atmosphere, but would not keep them from being pulled into the void. Besides, the EVA suits were more for protection from pathogens they might encountered on the alien ship. Of course, these particular suits were designed for Space Fleet Marines. Fitted with armor plates to disperse laser fire, or deflect most small-arms projectiles. The helmets provided heads-up displays, and could provide vision for low light, no light, and heat signatures. The Marines could communicate with each other, the LBJ, or Kennedy. Sky, Coop, and Anton wore trans-com rings. Sky slipped a spare around the Colonel's neck without asking permission.

"Four Zenge inside the engine room, behind the primary engine, thirty-feet inside the door," Storm warned them. "Doors opening, now."

Gregory sent Marines through the door, four left, and four right. The rest stayed behind. The Zenge had laser weapons, hand held and shoulder fired, but nothing more exotic. You don't need exotic to kill.

The Zenge proved to be well-trained soldiers. They used the dense housing materials for the engines to prevent the Fleet Marines from acquiring open targets. They also operated as two-person teams. (Two-Zenge teams? Two-lizard alien teams?) Each team covered a side, and each team member took a turn firing.

The Fleet Marines were better trained, and they had numbers. They moved forward, using bulkhead columns and machinery for cover. The EVA suits held up. Four of the eight advance Marines were hit with laser fire. While lasers knocked them backward, and down, they did not penetrate the suits. One Marine was knocked unconscious when he fell back hard into an engine vent.

"Do we give them the chance to surrender, Colonel?" came a query from the sergeant leading the team.

"Don't know how to ask," Gregory admitted. "You have them flanked. Give a tick, and if they drop weapons, take them. If they look like they intend to fire, kill them first."

The seven Marines completed the pinch. The Zenge, cornered, came out, firing everything they had. Unprotected, they died quickly. Just not quickly enough.

"Get corpsmen up here now!" the sergeant ordered. "Corporal Mitchell took too many hits to the same spot. Her EVA couldn't stop the multiple taps. She has a chest wound."

Coop felt sick. Gregory had command of this part of the mission, but the mission was his responsibility. He had one down, unconscious, and one with a critical wound. Two Marine corpsmen rushed by him and through the other Marines to get to the bleeding corporal. They were the best, so she had a chance.

"Those were some ugly aliens," the Marine staff sergeant who had led the eight-man rifle team said. "They're like Teenage Mutant Ninja Turtles, only not cute, with alligator heads, and lots of teeth."

Before Sky, or Storm could ask about Ninja Turtles, Coop said, "I'll explain later. Keep on mission."

"Hey, Sarge. How you know they were ugly aliens? How many aliens have you seen?" someone quipped.

"You may be right, Cortez," the sergeant replied. "I've seen you, and these guys were kind of cute in comparison."

"You have eight one deck up, inside the engineering control center. They are scattered around the room, most likely taking positions behind command consoles," Storm informed them, breaking into the banter combat soldiers used to calm nerves.

This time Gregory called four Marines forward. A quick, quiet discussion, and each Marine pulled out two grenades from backpacks. He was not risking more lives taking the relatively compact command center.

They took stairs up one flight, and carefully exited into a short corridor. They found six doors; three, left, and three, right. Another, more substantial door, faced them from the end of the hallway. This was the entrance to the command center and engineering controls combo-bridge.

Aware comm-tac on the 109 would see his view via the live feed, Gregory spoke to Storm: "Storm, open this door in ten-seconds. Keep it open two-seconds, and then close it. Start count **now**."

Exactly ten-seconds later the door opened. The Marines, two on each side, lobbed grenades in high, and low, and then hugged the walls on either side of the doorway. Laser fire erupted through the door, filling the open corridor. None of the other Marines or tag-alongs were hit. Everyone had taken cover in the crew cabins. Two-seconds, and the door closed, followed by eight explosions so close together it sounded like one big blast. The ship shuddered.

"No life-signs," Storm said, as she opened the doors through the hacked operations computer.

The four grenade-throwers went through first, and one called, "It's pretty gory in here, Colonel. We have green and red splatter, and body parts everywhere."

Gregory turned to Sky, who gave him a simple nod. He knew Cooper had seen worse. Twenty-four joined the first four in the command center. Dr. Singh and the two corpsmen were at the LBJ, caring for one Marine, and saving the other.

"There is a lift, and two stairwells which will take you to the top deck," Storm told them. "There is also a lift from the hangar to the hallway outside of the cells, but I have it locked off. One stairwell goes to the cold storage area, and one to a hallway which connects the storage lockers. Beyond the storage are the cells. I read two low-heat lifeforms outside of the cell door. Lifeforms inside show warm."

"We're missing two more," Gregory said.

"Probably in the cold-storage area," Storm replied. "They are cold-blooded, and in that area the scans cannot pick them out."

Gregory sent eight Marines up the stairwell to the cold room, and eight up the stairs to the rear hallway. Any more and they would crowd instead of compliment each other.

The first group hit the door to the cold storage area firing blind. They quick entered, and began covering angles. Two Zenge were crouched behind metal tables, which deflected the laser fire.

The Zenge did not have laser guns. They had knives and meat cutters. They killed two Marines before the six left could put them down.

The second group came out into the rear hallway. They formed a phalanx, facing toward the door which separated the storage rooms from the cells. The two Zenge there had apparently been trying to force the door open. They turned, faced the Marines, and then stuck the barrels of their laser pistols under their extended jaws and fired.

"Colonel Gregory, the last two Zenge committed suicide," the Lt. in charge of the squad informed his commander.

Gregory turned to Cooper, and asked, "You realize what that means?"

Cooper nodded. "I do, and we'll discuss it later. Stay on mission."

"Gregory to Lt. Simpson, when Storm opens that door, sweep the room, but do not fire unless fired upon. Storm, door please."

As the door unlocked, he spoke again. "Dr. Singh, you, and your people can take the lift up to the cells. Storm, release the hangar lift."

The six Marines in the first squad took the bodies of their fallen to the shuttle. The remaining Marines, Coop, and Sky stepped over the headless Zenge. Singh, having stabilized Mitchell, and a corpsmen, joined second squad in the cell block.

The Marines lined the right bulkhead wall, facing a row of cells against the left wall. Inside those cells a dozen species, sentient and not, stared, but did not move. Most sat, or were sprawled on the cell floors, too weak to move.

Cooper directed Sky. "You, Anton, and I have translator rings. Some of these captives will recognize you as Fellen, but will have no idea about Anton or me. Walk along, talk with the ones you can, but do not, I repeat, do not get within arms reach of any cell. You have no idea what these people have experienced, or how they will react."

Sky slowly walked the cell block. She stopped, and held short conversations six times. Gregory, Cooper, and those aboard the 109's command bridge could hear the conversations, but made no comments. For the most part, they were sad to hear. Painful. Hopeful.

Sky returned, and spoke to Cooper and Gregory. "The first cell is for, what you would call, livestock. Eleven animals bred for milk, skins, or meat. The following eight cells hold people from eight separate planets. No Fellen, and no Osperantue. I spoke with six, as you heard. Two species I did not recognize. The last eight cells hold wild animals. Seven are not particularly dangerous. If they have the strength, they might bite or claw you, but none are hunters. The last cell has two Carvide. They are pack hunters from a planet in the Testerray system, where only animals live. Some of the other animals are from the same planet, I think. I've only seen pictures and heard stories."

"Captain Cooper, we have a problem," Kennedy's voice sounded urgent, if not exactly upset. "The Zenge on the second cargo ship initiated a self-destruct sequence. It is not system based. Storm cannot stop it."

"Time?" Cooper asked.

"I do not understand Zenge, but based on what I am reading, and what I can guess from the count thus far, I would estimate more than eight and less than ten minutes. Captain, that cargo vessel has armament stored on board, including torpedoes. When it goes, the combination of the engines, weapons, and the implosion when the hull breaches, will mean a shockwave which could destroy the ship you are on."

"Storm, can you start the engines from there, and get this ship moving?"

"Engines are cycling to come on line. You'll start moving away from the second ship, but not soon enough to get far enough away. The shockwave will go well beyond 40,000 miles, while you will be less than 10,000-miles distant."

Coop said, "Genna, protect my crew. Gregory, your Marines need to find something to hold onto, and hold onto it. Sky, warned the people in the cells to hunker down. Storm, turn on the other ship's engines. Try sending it in the opposite direction. Every extra mile we get could make the difference."

"What about the captives on the other ship?" Sky whispered the question.

"Not a thing anyone can do now," he replied.

Worrying about leaving one life behind to begin another seemed shallow now. In a couple of minutes, everyone aboard both cargo ships might leave everything behind.

# Chapter 46

Kennedy sounded the klaxon, and announced all hands needed to brace for impact.

Genna, at the pilot's console, began moving the ship.

Lt. Adams, at the navigation console, looked down, looked up at Genna, looked down again, and then said, "Excuse me Counselor Bouvier, but it appears we are moving toward the cargo ship, not away."

"Thank you, Lieutenant," Genna said. In order for everyone to hear, Genna said aloud, "Kennedy, I'm going to place the 109 between the cargo ship about to self-destruct, and the one with our people on board. Is there a section of the 109 where the sonic force field is strongest?"

As she maneuvered the ship, and waited for Kennedy's response, Genna noted the Fellen, Storm, left the communications station and literally dove beneath the operations console.

"The sonic forcefield is uniform," Kennedy replied. "But once you position the ship between the two cargo vessels, you can place the engine in neutral and send power levels up to reverberate at RPM's equivalent to 244,000 miles-per-hour. The sonic forcefield attains maximum strength at that speed."

Genna did not have time to confirm with Kennedy, because an angry Captain Cooper came across every channels.

"Kennedy, what the fuck are you doing. Genna, I told you to save my crew, not destroy the 109 in an attempt at a rescue."

"Captain Cooper, you, and the people aboard that ship, are part of this crew. I will do what is necessary to save ALL of the crew. Kennedy, and I have worked out the essentials. I will place the 109 between the two cargo ships, and assist in pushing your ship away. When the other ship explodes, we will have increased shield density to maximum. The concussive wave should pass around the 109, and the break should protect the cargo ship you are aboard."

Cooper spoke again, this time more measured, more in control. "Genna, *should* is not *will*. I, **we** appreciate what you want to do, but the armaments, along with the implosion and explosions which are going to occur, will create too strong a wave. The 109 will get tossed aside, if not totally destroyed, and this ship will be shattered. You need to save as many people as you can by getting the 109 as far away as you can, and you have only a couple of minutes to do it."

"Captain, my plan gives you a chance. Your plan gives you no chance."

"Kennedy?" Cooper spoke directly to the AI.

"Yes, Captain Cooper."

"Remember the discussion about insane decisions. Genna is making one now, and you are going along because she's human, and you hope her decision will turn out justified. But you have to take control, and remove yourself from this situation. It isn't about me, or the crew aboard this ship. It's about the SFPT-109. Right now you are the only ship Space Fleet has with a chance in hell of stopping the Zenge if they return. If you are destroyed, Earth goes with you. Do you understand?"

"Yes, Captain Cooper. I am taking piloting controls."

**"WAIT!"** Storm crawled out form under the operations console. "Coop, I've reformatted the shield coverage patterns like we did aboard the *Star Gazer*. We can pad the shields. If Genna places the ship at the proper angle, I can increase shield density by ten-fold to protect the blast area. The concussive wave will pushed us forward, and if your ship is set properly against the PT-109's, you will ride along."

Then Kennedy broke in. "I have examined the angles, and with Storm's changes, if we are at a twenty-two degree angle against the incoming concussive force, both ships will ride the shockwave until it dissipates."

Storm, at the communications station, reported, "We have three-hundred-twelve seconds. You have to do something now."

"Bouvier to Cargo ship, hold on, we're going surfing." She turned the bigger ship to twenty-two degrees, placed the front tip of the 109 against the front hull of the cargo ship, ceased movement, and while in neutral, revved the primary engine to rpm's equivalent to 244,000mph.

Storm realigned the shield density, as the rpm's rose.

In her head, Genna spoke to her AI: *"Kennedy, I'm turning over the maneuvering thrusters to you. You will have to make a thousand adjustments to keep us on the wave. I'm not fast enough."*

The stolen cargo ship exploded, imploded, and exploded again, sending a particle-dense shockwave at the two ships.

The plan worked, and the two ships rode the force of the concussion like an extreme surfer riding a multi-story wave. With no wipe-out at the end. It lasted 40,000 miles. Those inside both vessels experienced a rough ride, especially those in the under-powered cargo ship. When the wave dissipated, the two ships drifted to a stop less than one-hundred miles apart.

Storm tried first contact, using her personal trans-com. "Sky, you there?"

"Storm, we're alive. Bruised, but everyone is fine. Even the stupid animals in the cells are okay. Sky, out."

Storm retracted the auto-straps on her seat. She grabbed Genna in a bearhug as soon as the avatar released her straps and stood. She held her away, told her "Cool!" and hugged her harder.

Once freed by Storm, Genna gave Kennedy a mental *thank you* before contacting Captain Cooper on the ship-to-ship open channel.

"Captain Cooper, I am prepared to accept any punishment," she told him.

"Stow it, Genna," Cooper replied. "You made a command decision. Even if we ended up scattered bits and pieces, what you did was proper. When you have the chair, you make the decisions you think best. Even if it seems insane at the moment. Right, Kennedy."

"I do not think I will ever fully understand," the ships' AI responded, "but I do believe I enjoy the process."

Cooper took command, and issued orders.

"Listen up, people, we have a lot to accomplish. Counselor Bouvier, you need to get Dr. Trent and his people to the *Star Gazer*. Nathan, you listening?"

"To everything," he replied. "Now that I'm still alive, this has been a fascinating trip."

"As soon as you get to the *Star Gazer*, contact Commander Cornitsch. The two of you figure out how to get you, your team, and your equipment on that ship. The install of the space-fold array is priority number one.

"Genna, you contact Dr. Coptonitsch, he's their head of medical. Sky will send info on how many aliens, races, and possible medical issues we have here. You need to pass them on to Dr. Coptonitsch. Our injured may overwhelm him. His ship is already dealing with massive casualties. God knows how many victims they have aboard. Dropping a hundred more on him is going to seem, well, inhumane, so prepare to offer any assistance. We have the three medics here with Dr. Singh. Offer help by the nurses on the 109 to him if he needs help. Dr. Singh, and his corpsmen will triage here. Hopefully, not every captive will need medical aid.

"Storm, as you get medical reports, data-dump them to MSD and EMS2. They can begin preparations to assist. When we return, they can have facilities and staff ready to go.

"Kennedy, you, and Genna, and the engineers aboard need to figure out how to get Demon either onto the 109 or the Star Gazer. She doesn't have maneuvering, so somehow you will have to push, pull, or drag her into a hangar.

"Casey, I want our sensor arrays on deep scan, full penetration, total coverage, three-hundred sixty degrees. If anything shows up, anywhere, I want everybody to know immediately. We do not need to get blind-sided while we're licking our wounds.

"Is everybody clear?"

A chorus of "yes, sirs!" responded.

In the spirit of a long-ago spaceship Captain, Cooper ended with "Make it so."

# Chapter 47

The PT-109 left Cooper and the others on the cargo ship, while it sped to the damaged *Star Gazer*.

Before departing, Coop asked Genna a personal favor: "Please ask Commander Cornitsch if he can check the survivors from deck 282. I realize the ship is chaotic, but I would appreciate it if he could see if two young Bosine, names Rosz and Chaspi, survived the attack."

Genna repeated the names, confirmed the request, and engaged space-fold.

"Are they the ones you wanted to trade music with?" Sky asked.

Cooper nodded. He headed for the cold-storage area, leaving Sky in the cell block to translate for the Marines and Dr. Singh.

The meat hanging in the locker was a combination of livestock, wild animals, and people. Cooper was not going to order his people to take down anything they thought was once a sentient being, and wrap them for burial, unless he was willing to assist. They were Anton's squad, but they were his crew.

He worked, keeping his stomach intact, and his anger in check. Anything which appeared not from an animal, they wrapped in tarp-like material found aboard. There were probably errors, and they had prepared animals or animal parts for burial, but everyone preferred that mistake.

He considered wrapping everything, but the Carvide, and some of the aliens might need the protein and other nutrients in the meat.

Gregory reached Coop over a private comms channel. "We've vetted the alien captives. The few Sky cannot translate are too weak to cause trouble, even if they were so inclined.

"The cells are filthy. Seems the Zenge would only occasionally hose them down, using the drainage vents in the floors at the rear of each cell. The waste and water shunted to a recycling system in the engine room.

"Singh says the air quality, and nothing in the environment is going to make us sick. He's almost positive we aren't going to catch anything from the captives, or the animals. One-hundred percent sure if we don't make any skin-to-skin contact.

"Coop, it must smell like a zoo's shit-pit in here. I want to move the aliens into the hallway and wash this place down, before I let our people get out of their EVA suits."

"Give us a little time to get the butchered bodies, and the dead Zenge into the weapons' storage unit," Coop replied. "Then do what you need to."

The animals got washed down with their cells.

The aliens, under loose guard, waited in the corridor.

Blankets found in storage were placed in the cells to provide cushions for the people. Cooper hated having to return the aliens to the cells, but it was the only space available. He made sure they knew the doors were left unlocked.

With the area cleaned, Singh gave the okay for the team to remove EVA suits.

A couple of enterprising Marines set up showers in the rear of each cell, providing sheets thrown over strung cable for privacy. The aliens took turns showering, and seemed to appreciate the opportunity to clean up, even if there was no soap. Food had been liberated and set out. Since the humans had no idea who would eat what, they let the people in the cells go through the boxes and bags, taking whatever they wanted. Bowls of water, and cups were also set out.

Dr. Singh and his corpsmen found a desk, chairs, and a table. They triaged one alien after another, with Sky's assistance. Those who could not walk without assistance, were examined in the cells, prior to being carried out and the cells hosed down.

There only issue now was the two Carvide. Gregory did not have their cell washed down, because one appeared so sick it could not move. He did not want to hurt the animal even more.

A rank smell of waste, dirty animal, and sickness waifed from the cell.

"I'm going to put them down," the Colonel said to Cooper, both standing outside the barred room.

"The one in the rear is breathing, but hasn't lifted its head in the last two hours. The other one is just plain mad. Sky says it should probably weight over 300 pounds, but looks under 200. It still has big teeth, claws, and a bad attitude. It's protecting the sick one."

"Tranqs?" Coop asked.

"Singh can create a cocktail from what he has with him, but nothing says it will work. And we have no way to administer it. We don't have dart guns, and no one is getting close enough to use a needle. If I put down the big one, maybe we can do something to save the other."

Gregory unsnapped his laser pistol, but Coop placed a re-straining hand on his arm.

"Get a blanket, and a couple of your guys. I'll keep the big one busy, and you get the other one out. Anton, when you get it out, keep it outside the bars, but near. Make sure you have something for a muzzle, and tell your guys to put extra padding on their arms."

"Can we back up a step on that plan?" the Marine Colonel asked. "About the part where you'll keep the big one busy. I don't think it's gonna play fetch with you, Coop."

"It's undernourished and weak. Having a hard time staying on its feet. Right now it's eighty-percent bluster."

"And eighty-percent bigger teeth than a tiger," Gregory replied. "We have advantages from the Project, but do you think it's enough to take on that beast?"

"Let's find out," Coop looked at his friend. "But no 'we,' Anton. We would get in each others way. Your people may need your strength and speed to get the other one onto the blanket and out."

Gregory called over two of his strongest personnel, explained the plan, explained he was not kidding, and told them to prep. When they returned, and did not throw the blanket over Cooper to restrain him, testament to their oaths to follow orders.

The cells had simple locks, but no one bothered finding keys. Like the others, Gregory shot the lock off with his laser pistol. The blast of hot light agitated the big Carvide. Cooper quickly stepped in and moved to his left, surprising the big wolf-like animal. The beast wasted no time, and attacked; growling, and baring teeth.

Coop stood still, waiting. The Carvide made the same mistake Sky made during their first sparring session . . . it leapt. All four feet off the ground; speed and agility lost in the jump.

Cooper, cat-fast, dropped, then rolled as the Carvide sailed over, trying to twist in the air to get to him, raking claws to tear at him. He missed the man, but hit the cage bars . . . hard.

Cooper, back on his feet, reversed and returned. He straddled the dazed animal, grabbed the scruff and loose skin behind the base of its head, where it joined the long neck. He pushed the Carvide onto the deck, using his impressive strength. Foggy from the blow, underweight, undernourished, and, most likely, dead tired, the Carvide remained powerful. Coop's biggest threat now came from the animal's rear end. Strong hips, buttocks, and thigh muscles attempted to buck the human off. Claw on its rear feet searched for him at the same time. It tried to rise and roll to get him off.

As soon as Gregory saw Coop reverse and straddle the Carvide, he and the two Marines jumped into action. Trusting his friend to control the animal, he muzzled the sick one with a belt. The three of them hoisted it onto the blanket, grabbed the corners, and quickly got out of the cell. It grumbled, but did not resist.

Singh waited outside the cell. As soon as they lay the animal down at his feet, he asked the Colonel, "How does the Captain plan on getting out?"

Gregory looked to where Cooper was struggling to keep the Carvide down, smiled a crooked grin, and replied, "No idea, but entertaining, I am sure."

By now every Marine not involved in a job elsewhere, Sky, and many of the aliens who were ambulatory, stood pressed together watching.

It spoke volumes to the drama unfolding that humans, and aliens stood side-by-side, with no thought of it being odd. The conflict between man and animal playing itself out, touched something inside of each of them.

Singh administered a sedative. He examined the sick Carvide, constantly looking up to watch the action.

When the big Carvide took a moment's break from thrusting and thrashing, Coop used his re-engineered speed to step off, and to the side. He then used his strength to slide the animal across the cell, away from the door. He had not thrown it, because he did not want it hurt landing on the hard floor.

Sky yelled "RUN!" Gregory held the door half open, but Coop was not making a mad dash for safety. He stood his ground.

The Carvide rose, claws raking the deck in the scramble to regain its balance, expecting a chase, but stopped short when it realized the man had not run for the door. The animal growled at Coop, and at the crowd outside. He saw his companion outside, and down, but no one was harming her, so he turned his full attention on the man in the cell with him.

The air was foul, but he could still scent the human. He sensed tension, but not fear. He could smell the fear coming from the crowd of mixed aliens outside the cell, but nothing from the one inside. Prey always stank before being downed. It was a scent that pushed him to finish a hunt.

The Carvide was tired. The short struggle to escape the man's hold taxed it even further. He remembered home. Running for miles, playing, and hunting with his pack. They had never been beaten, until the cold-blooded ones hunted them with flashing light that killed and maimed, and flexible metal cages which dropped down and trapped them. He was tired, but he was not beaten. He was exhausted. This being was not prey. His companion was gone. He was the last of the pack.

He sat. Let this one escape. He sat. Nothing left to fight for.

The cell block went dead quiet. No one, not one being moved. Then Sky whispered "fuck," as Cooper started walking toward the Carvide, instead of to the cell door.

The Carvide, head held forward and down, with ears back, watched him come closer. Not quick, not slow. Measured and assured. No threat. He watched the man's paw, palm turned up, no claws, reach toward his head and sharp teeth. The hand slipped beneath his jaw, and stoked his chin. He whispered words no one else could hear. Soft. Kind. Then he walked away, his back to the Carvide; unprotected. The Carvide watched the man walk through the bars. The big  canine relative laid down. His ears perked up as the Marines began to applaud, soon joined by the aliens.

Today a conflict began and ended with weapons of war. Today, another conflict had been avoided by empathy and kindness. Both hallmarks of humans. The ability to fight. The capacity to care.

# Chapter 48

Using ship-to-ship communication, Genna, Kennedy, Storm, Elie, Mags, and Cornitsch came up with a plan.

Since the LBJ was on the cargo ship, they decided Elie, and Mags needed to fly Angel 7 to shuttle Trent, his engineers, and equipment from the 109 to the Star Gazer.

Only problem was Elie, Mags, and Demon were drifting in space without maneuvering thrusters. They had no way to get aboard Kennedy for the switch.

Storm solved the problem.

She would remotely operate the escape pod she and Sky had been flying when the Star Gazer found them. It was not big enough to act as a shuttle for the people and equipment, but it could provide a push.

Cornitsch cleared the hangar, opened the doors, and Storm flew the pod out. She set it up behind Demon, and pushed the fighter into the 109's hangar, which had been cleared by LCMD Smith. Sounded simple, but it took a lot of bumps and thumps, starts and stops until Demon finally floated into Kennedy's hangar.

Elie let Demon drift to the farthest wall. She dropped the landing pads, using the magnets to pull the ship down, and locked the fighter to the deck. Storm recalled the escape pod to the *Star Gazer,* where Cornitsch had left the doors open and the hangar depressurized to speed up Angel 7's arrival.

The 109's crew, under the directions of Henry, loaded Angel 7 with the crystals, lasers, and equipment brought from Mars. Elie and Mags got comfy in the cockpit while Trent, and his five engineers and technicians got uncomfortable in the cramped cabin.

Elie's displayed her skills as a pilot to jockey Angel around Demon, and fly out the hangar doors. The jaunt to the *Star Gazer* a piece of cake.

Storm provided translator rings for Elie and Mags, giving both women hugs on meeting them. She also gave them to Trent's team — rings, not hugs.

Within an hour of docking, the humans were in the cruise ship's engineering section with a half-dozen Bosine engineers, and an equal number of tech-savvy Woolifer technicians.

It took the combined brain power and experience of everyone involved six hours to agree on the best way to integrate the temporary space-fold array with the cruise ship's operational and flight systems. It was a sad fact, but since the ship was being run from engineering instead of the command bridge, it made the integration process simpler.

It required an additional sixteen hours for installation. Done, they were positive the *Star Gazer* could produce, and then operate as a space-fold capable vessel.

During the time spent installing the array, Elie and Mags wandered around the giant space cruise ship, meeting aliens who were both friendly and appreciative. More than once, the two pilots found themselves tearing up. While the conditions were sad, this was how first contact should take place. Handshakes, hugs, fist-bumps, (yep, fist-bumps from aliens. Who knew?), and kind words between species.

Cornitsch located Rosz and Chaspi. They, and their families, had been in their cabins at the other end of deck 282. There was enough time for them to escape before the emergency systems closed the hallway and shut off those above and below.

Storm gave the good news to Coop, who sat with Sky, leaning against the hull across from the Carvide's cage. Almost everyone else aboard the cargo ship slept.

The smaller, sick Carvide was a female. She had received fluids, antibiotics, vitamins, and already showed improvement. With Cooper on point, she had been replaced to the cage, which had been hosed down. The big male hosed down with the cage.

Singh washed the female by hand, using antibiotic salves on any open soars he found.

The male, still wet, lay beside the female. Coop had feed him cut-up pieces of meat with vitamins hidden inside. He would only feed him a few pieces, but did it every hour, not wanting the animal to overeat and get sick. Sky found a bowl, filled it with fresh water, and slipped it through a slotted section in the bars.

"Busy few days," Coop said. Sky moved close enough to lay her head on his chest.

"Almost over," Sky said. "You go to your ship, Storm, and I go to the *Star Gazer*, and we all go to your Earth . . . or Mars . . . or wherever it is we go."

"Well, if we're all going to Earth, or Mars, or wherever anyway, seems to me you, and Storm could stay on the 109," Coop said to the top of her head.

Sky did not answer, but she did sigh, and snuggled closer. And fell asleep. Coop looked up, into the eyes of the Carvide. Things were far from perfect, but everything sure seemed a whole lot better.

Daniel Cooper lived as a loner by choice, not by nature. Maybe the time had arrived when the natural order of things should return. He had, after all, made first contact.

# Chapter 49

The *Star Gazer* popped out of space-fold into natural space less than one-hundred miles from the cargo ship. Trent decided the short trip could act as the test run. Either they had engineered everything correctly, or they had not.

SFPT-109, the *John F. Kennedy*, entered natural space five minutes later, and five-hundred miles further on. She would stand watch.

Angel 7, with Elie, Mags, and Nathan aboard, exited the *Star Gazer* hold. They flew a couple of hundred miles further out to also stand watch, and so Nathan could experience space at the edge of the solar system.

The rest of the plan changed in the past couple of hours. Instead of trying to shuttle aliens and animals from the cargo ship to the badly damaged cruise ship, Coop decided to fly the entire Parrian box container ship into the *Star Gazer's* massive hangar.

No one questioned his sanity . . . out loud. But they did decide they would launch the LBJ before the attempt.

Commander Cornitsch had his hangar ready, including returning the Fellen pod to its private bay.

Storm released the hauler's computers, and Sky joined him at the flight command console, in the blood-stained engineering section, to help interpret controls. Translator rings did little for written directions.

Captain Cooper, ex-test pilot, practiced shadow maneuvers in open space before warning everyone he was ready. The shuttle LBJ launched, and would stand by.

Coop, with thirty years of experience flying experimental vessels, brought the alien ship onto the *Star Gazer*. He set her on the deck so softly, Col Gregory actually asked, "Are we down?" when Coop walked away from the console.

Communications were opened and busy across all channels, except the civilian-public ones within the *Star Gazer*. Plans created, modified, and confirmed.

Angel 7 with Elie, Mags, and Nathan would leave for MSD immediately. She would arrive in eighty-four hours. They would assist the space station, and Space Fleet, prepare for the arrival of a giant interstellar cruise ship and 240-plus-thousand aliens and animals.

Though data was streaming to the space stations continuously, the reality of extraterrestrials would still come as a shock.

Col. Gregory, and half the Marines would stay aboard the *Star Gazer*. This included Singh, his medics, and two of the four nurses. They would aide and assist Dr. Coptonitsch, and his medical staff. The other Marines and medical staff would join Cooper, Sky, and Storm when the LBJ returned to the 109.

Trent's team remained on the cruise ship. They decided to make five short space-fold jumps, instead of a single extended one. The trip would take more time, but this option allowed opportunities to check the temporary array, make any adjustments, and keep the massive ship and occupants safe.

To prevent space-fold sickness, each panned layover would last a minimum six hours. They estimated six-days four-hours to reach MSD, if the temporary array worked as expected. Supplies on the *Star Gazer* would last the journey. The supplies on the cargo ship would support the captives, who would remain quarantined for the trip.

While Sky and Storm packed, Coop, with Cornitsch's help, found Rosz and Chaspi. He made sure they were well, and promised to find them again when they reached the end of the journey.

He was also happy to discover Assistant Captain Sonoritsch and Ensign Fallenitsch were not on the bridge when it was destroyed. They escaped before the command sphere had been sealed off. Pansoitsch and Pictor perished along with Poonch, and 620 other crew members.

There was a memorial service for the lives lost. There were still bodies trapped in the *Star Gazer's* sealed compartments. After they arrived at Mars, recovery would begin immediately. Hundreds had been lost to the void, so Commander Cornitsch led a memorial service over the PA, followed by a moment of silence.

The LBJ returned to her berth on the 109 and parked adjacent to Demon, which had been moved by Smith and his crew, using a variety of equipment not originally meant for manhandling space fighters in cramped quarters.

Genna and Kennedy coordinated the first space-fold jump with Cornitsch and Manny Hernandez. The 109 would make the same five jumps, assuring the *Star Gazer's* security at each location. Providing assistance if needed.

Coop took Gregory aside for a private meeting. They decided the risk-reward of going after the remaining Zenge Primary did not make the gamble worthwhile. The last deep scans indicated it was still rudderless, heading out to the edge of the solar system. They decided to let it go.

Before he boarded the LBJ for the short trip to the 109, Captain Cooper performed a final inspection of the cargo vessel.

He thanked every Marine personally, including Anton. He paid his respects to the two fallen Marines safely stored in the ships hangar, far away from the Zenge bodies stored in the weapons room. The concussed Marine, Kassar, and Mitchell were in beds in the medical ward of the Star Gazer. Mitchell, awake and stable, would recover from her wounds.

He checked on the aliens, happy to see they had cots, mattresses, chairs, and tables. Fresh linens and toiletries had been provided by the crew and people of the *Star Gazer*. They were made as comfortable as possible under the circumstances. He received smiles, words of thanks, and slaps on the back. Even a handshake from an alien who resembled Big Foot.

Last, he checked in on the Carvide. The female was up, looking healthier thanks to the food, the vitamins, and care provided by Dr. Singh, who had a future as a vet if he decided to switch professional callings. She was shaky on her feet, and stayed to the rear of the cell, but she neither growled nor bared teeth.

The male, looking fitter, trotted up to the bars when he recognized Coop.

Without fear or hesitation, Coop reached in underhanded and scratched the animal under the chin. Slowly, he pulled his hand backward so the animal could follow the motion. He reached up and rubbed its head.

"I haven't made a friend, not a real friend, in nearly twenty years," he told the Carvide, who tilted its head to listen the same way Storm did. He laughed softly at the image. "In less than a week I've doubled my friend count, if I include you."

The Carvide chuffed, then returned to comfort the female. Cooper did not know if his friendship had been accepted, or rejected. Guess he would find out if the over-sized wolf from another world tried to eat him the first chance it got.

After the LBJ settled, and Captain Cooper's feet hit the deck of the 109, the ship's PA announced, "Kennedy is aboard."

Yes, he was.

# Chapter 50

The officer stood at attention before a formal, beautifully carved wood and slate desk. The person seated behind the desk was not military, but he was his superior. He was everyone's superior.

"I understand the wormhole creation engine worked," the one seated said.

"Partially," the officer said. "Data recovered indicates they were able to escape by creating a wormhole, but the dark matter released to maintain the channel walls killed everyone on board. Over 60,000 Zenge, and over one-thousand of our own."

"The Zenge are replaceable. It is a shame about our people, but they died for the cause," the seated one said. "At least we were able to get our ship, and the data."

"Yessir," the officer replied, maintaining eye contact with the painting above his seated superior. "We are having the bodies removed, and making certain dark matter radiation is cleared from the ship."

"I wonder why the captain came here instead of Osperantue, where he launched from, or even to the Zenge system?"

"The recovered data indicates the computer system that guides the wormhole engine selected a path of least resistance," the officer answered. "Between where they were, and here are no intervening systems or dangerous gravity wells. It was the quickest route to a safe haven."

"A remarkable accomplishment, even though, otherwise, their mission was a complete disaster. You don't need to remain at attention, General," the man said. "I'm not angry with you."

"Sir," the general said, and relaxed his posture, but only a little. "We do have the scans, and reports regarding the chase to capture the Osperantue cruise ship, as well as the information on the solar system where the battle occurred. It's a system no one has visited, or at least reported a visit, in over two-hundred years. They appear to have made a great deal of progress in a relatively short amount of time."

"Three ships from this system destroyed six of our battle wagons, two battlecruisers, and forced a Class One Carrier to retreat. Two-hundred years ago they did not have intersystem travel. I find that remarkable," the man said.

"They also appear to use space-fold technology for propulsion," the general added.

"We now have a much more dangerous enemy to deal with," the man behind the desk said. "We will need to augment our forces, and improve out own technology if we are going to face this unexpected threat.

"General, I want you to double the efforts on Fell to find, and take their hidden technology centers. Complete the mission plan for our upcoming invasion. It is more vital to our success than ever before. Begin making plans to confront this neoteric enemy. We know where they are, and we know a lot about what they have. Speed up the refitting of captured space ships with armaments. We may need the additional numbers.

"I will contact the Zenge system, and make sure we have more soldiers, and more of them are capable of staffing the captured ships."

The leader stood to face his military advisor. "I want space-fold," he said. "With such ability, we will halve the time until our ultimate victory. Please go now, General, and send in the gentleman waiting outside, if you will."

The general was quick to leave. The civilian nearly as quick to enter.

"We can send drones through wormholes," he stammered, not waiting on his leader to ask questions. "With the innovative gas conductors, we can build a torpedo-sized drone with enough negative-matter displacement that we, that *you* can send and receive communications through a wormhole in twenty-five-percent of the time it would take a ship to travel the same channel."

"When?"

"The data we recovered from the Class One Carrier that created a wormhole provided the information needed to complete the design. Now we need space-saving crystals powerful enough to provide the power to create the negative matter, and also propel the drone."

"We should have everything we need soon, Doctor. Everything we need . . . soon," the man replied.

THE END

# EPILOGUE

Captain Cooper sat in Fleet Admiral Patterson's office at Central Command, Toronto, Ontario, Canada.

The SFPT-109, and the *Star Gazer* completed the return trip without issues. Three months later, conditions settled enough to begin the process of dealing with short-term concerns, and long-term plans.

Settled did not mean back to normal. Earth had a new normal, along with a quarter-million potential new citizens, currently being introduced to the planet in New Zealand. The island nation's population had been decimated by the pandemic, and thirty years later, only a fraction of the original inhabitants remained. The Kiwi welcomed the newly arrived neighbors with open arms and, more importantly, open hearts. They also recognized the bounty being sent their way. Building the infrastructure necessary to sustain the alien refugees would generate a huge windfall. Paid for by the United Earth Council.

Alien livestock were being studied by experts at Clemson University in South Carolina, trying to determine their value, and potential problems if introduced in the world. Wild animals from a half-dozen alien worlds were being kept in a preserve in Kenya. Again, being studied and kept safe.

The Carvide had been released into a 25,000 acre reserve in the Australian outback where feral sheep, cattle, and other native animals had grown to unhealthy numbers. The Aussie population had been reduced to where they could not maintain the ranches which now made up the electronically controlled space. They were monitored twenty-four seven. Coop's personal computer received those readings and video when available. The Carvide seemed happy and healthy.

Sky and Storm flew through the vetting process aliens endured before allowed open, though monitored, access to the planet. Dr. Trent's assertions they were bringing with them communications and operational technology which would advance human systems by hundreds of years helped a great deal.

Coop tried to introduce Sky and Storm to his favorite places on the planet. Coop's fame, both from his years as the face of space exploration, plus the entire planet having now seen the video of the fantastic battle to save the *Star Gazer*, rescue the refugees, and save the captives aboard the cargo ship, coupled with Sky and Storm's striking looks, unique coloring, and arresting eyes, turned an evening out in Quebec into a near riot.

To prevent further commotions, he used their status to get private late-night tours of museums, art galleries, and exhibit halls. They were being discreetly placed in private boxes for shows and concerts. He used credits deposited over the last thirty years to rent a private island in the Bahamas for a week, where he introduced them to snorkeling.

He kept his promise to Rosz and Chaspi, taking them to a rock and roll concert in Arizona, a few days after they and their families were cleared to locate to New Zealand. They wore street-wise clothes, hoodies, and shades, and fit in with the crowd.

Space Fleet had been active since the return of the PT-109. Its sister ship, PT-99, the *Franklin Delano Roosevelt*, was due to launch in two months; earlier than originally planned. The ship's AI and avatar were in communication with Kennedy and Genna. Genna and Adele (the FDR's avatar) becoming friends. They visited the rental house in the Bahamas.

"We still haven't made a final decision on a Captain," Patterson told him. "Captain Black requested a transfer back to the Navy. Her actions in space will make sure she is precluded from future command. Funny, you did not bring charges for dereliction of duty while engaged with an enemy. Equally funny, she did not try to bring charges against Genna, for assaulting a senior officer." She gave Cooper time to reply. He did not. The private time he had with Black, during the return trip to MSD, had been kept private. They both honored their agreements.

"When the FDR is ready, the 109 needs to investigate what is happening with the Zenge," Cooper said. "We can't wait, and we certainly can't hope they will not return."

"One lone Earth ship against who knows how many enemy ships? The Council will not see that as a positive move."

"We have to convince them it's our best action. I've spoken with the alien captives on the cargo ship. Between what they told me, and what we have from the people of Osperantue, and Fell, there are worlds out there who would welcome our presence. We have dozens of potential allies. We have a common enemy. I'm not talking about taking on the Zenge, Admiral. I'm talking about good, old-fashion military reconnaissance. Find out where they are, what they are planning, and who out there will help us when the time comes to fight.

"You read Anton's after-action report. He and I agree we are dealing with fanatics. The Zenge committed suicide on the first cargo ship instead of allowing themselves taken as prisoners. The second cargo ship was mass suicide and homicide. They martyred themselves, and took the captives with them.

"When we were fighting to unite the planet, Anton, and I faced both religious and political zealots. We cannot let them take the initiative. Track, trap, and destroy are the requirements when fighting extremists . Then you find out what made them obsessive, and go after the causes. But first you eliminate the threat. They've been here, Pam. They will return."

"It still isn't an easy sell, Coop, but I agree with your assessment."

"Then add this to the mix. There were eight Lisza Kaugh from a planet called Rys in those cells. They believe the Zenge are making their way toward Rys. Admiral, mines on Rys produce crystals which power everything from miniature devices to generators. I think the planet is the original source of the crystals found on Mars."

Coop allowed his assumption to settle before continuing. "If we get there first, we can collect more crystals. We would have the capacity to build more space-worthy ships. If the Zenge get there before us, they may have enough information to use crystals to create their own space-fold arrays."

Patterson's background was military intelligence. She recognized the importance of reaching Rys before the Zenge. "Put together a crew list, and write up a mission statement," she told Cooper. "While we wait on the 99 to launch, you train your crew. I will try to convince the Council."

Cooper reached into the inside pocket of his jacket. He handed the Fleet Admiral a folded sheet of paper.Old style.

"My crew list," he said.

Patterson gave it a glance, and looked across to her number one Captain, and friend. "Quite a mix of characters," she said. "Coop, I know you don't care about politics. All of us hoped those types of intrigue gone with the pandemic. But humans are still humans. There is a movement to keep Earth isolated until we are better equipped to deal with aliens. That same movement has members of the military, and in the UEC who think Space Fleet needs to act more professional . . . more structured."

"More like a branch of the military," Coop said, having heard the same reports. "And aliens don't belong on Earth's space ships," Coop added, having heard those rumors, as well. "Politics and policies will not stop the Zenge if they decide to launch an invasion. We need the expertise of these aliens, and we need allies in the galaxy if we're going to survive. Earth is a target, now the Zenge know we're here. The first step in Earth's defense should be getting to Rys, and replenishing our store of crystals."

"If this mission is approved, I see one interesting trip in your future," Patterson said.

"It's not the destination," Coop replied, quoting an old adage, "it's the journey that makes life interesting."

**The End of the Beginning. (3/17/16)**

donfoxe.com

foxeography.com

@don_foxe

facebook.com/donfoxe.spacefleet


**Space Fleet Saga** novels and short story collections are available at Amazon Books - Don Foxe.

Don Foxe lives in the scenic southern town of Bluffton, SC. He and wife, Sarah, own Beach City Health and Fitness on Hilton Head Island, SC.

www.ingramcontent.com/pod-product-compliance
Lightning Source LLC
Chambersburg PA
CBHW031308170626
46807CB00001B/329